KUDOS FOR A BRILLIANT, EXCITING NOVEL

"Handled with expertise . . . The intensely felt metamorphosis of the ordinary into the macabre seems to me a special mark of Mrs. Reed's talent. In AT WAR AS CHILDREN it informs her judgment of her generation"

—*Commonweal*

"Fairly bursts upon the reader . . . absolutely authentic"

—*America*

AT WAR AS CHILDREN

BY KIT REED

POPULAR LIBRARY · NEW YORK

.

Dedication: For both parents

The characters depicted in this novel
are imaginary and no reference to persons
living or dead is intended.

I

In my lifetime I have sustained a number of losses, yet it is hard for me to believe that any of these people whose lives have been bound up with mine are really gone, really lost to me. Some people, for all I may see of them, never take on any more substance than half-remembered chairs in some furnished room, while others, like Pearson, Bunker, Katherine—even Pat Castine—are vivid, solidly present, even now, when I may never see any of them again. As long as memory serves me they will be with me, and I may be halted in my tracks at any given moment by a sudden fullness of vision, a completeness of memory so rich and colorful that it would seem for a moment that I could keep it forever simply by calling out, or by closing my fingers on it. I am surrounded by wraiths—of these four, of all the people whose lives have been bound up with mine—so that none of them will ever be gone completely. I begin to believe that there is a design in this gift of memory, this sense of common past, that lives interlocked remain interlocked for eternity, for a reason.

If I try to get at this now it is because I find myself in a time of change, moving in a hope or plan that began to crystallize one night last summer, when Pearson Swift and I met for the last time at a party on the Sound. Even though nothing has been the same since that night the one moment which comes back to me most strongly is one of almost no movement, intact and inviolable.

I can still sense the mass, the *presence* of Pearson next to me, his dark face at rest for once. Eight of us, the last survivors of the supper hour, sat suspended a few inches above the ground in a child's canvas trampoline, eating chocolate pie. I remember Pat Castine and Glenda Jarboe sitting opposite, and I see four others, faceless now except for Mack Glendauer, who made us laugh with his gentle, rambling commentary on the couples who had gone off into the dark. We must have been cramped sitting there in a tangle of arms and legs—I remember everything was coated with a light dusting of sand—but at the same time we were enthralled by the moment and we rode snugly, with soft darkness around us and the sound of water just beyond. It was a little like being together in a lifeboat, slung by the side of a ship.

Pearson must have been struck as I was by the light, swaying motion, the sound of the water, because he turned to me and said, "Denny. Heave ho and all that."

I said "Yeah," and laughed.

He squinted into the darkness. "Good night for it."

"That it is, skipper."

"This is probably as nautical as we'll ever get."

I remember thinking of his brother Bunker who was on a destroyer that year, removed from both of us, and saying, "You know, you're right."

He yawned. "It's probably just as well."

"Yes," I said after a minute. "It's probably just as well."

Pat picked it up and began singing, under his breath. "Has anybody seen our ship, the H.M.S. Peculiar . . ."

"Well, Glenda," Mack said in a low, pleasant voice. "Your cousin Sally seems to have found romance."

Glenda clapped her hand to her mouth. "Oh lor. Where?"

"See? Out there, at the end of the dock."

"Good for her," Pat said drily. "Nothing like being in love. Builds character."

The breeze was light and it was almost as if the darkness moved past on either side of us, leaving us in stillness, stationary and safe. Pearson sat with his knees up, more relaxed than I had ever seen him, and he seemed to take such pleasure in his surroundings, in the simple business of the cigarette, that I wished the night could stop right then; I must have known somehow that something was ahead for us, because I was afraid for it to go on.

Pat sang "Heave ho, my hearties, sing Glory Alleluia . . ." and for the moment we rocked in safety, suspended in air, in time itself.

This was only last summer—a short time ago—but already all of us are different and everything has changed, as it will go on changing, so that Pat calls me now and then, bewildered, and says, "Where *is* everybody?"

He seems not to know that they're all around. The air is full of wraiths—Glenda, Mack, all the people of all our childhoods, together in one childhood even though they may never have met as children; Bunker laughing, square-faced at nine, foreshadowing only in his unchanging air of privacy Bunker blond and perfect in his uniform at twenty-one; Katherine with her hair down in the amusement park; Pearson in a hundred glimpses, as child or as man; Pearson in the museum with all time coursing past and beyond him. Whether he knows it or not Pat joins them, sometimes gay, sometimes fuming, fixed like the others, each in a separate, living unit of time past, so complete, so inviolable that I have only to try to grasp a moment to find it dispelled, like dust when the fingers begin to close on it.

I've learned with time that the only way to hold these moments is to let them go, delighting in the sudden completeness of memory but knowing at the same time that it can go as quickly, not minding because the memory, the potential for memory is always there and will be there until the brain is destroyed.

If I try, now, to set some of this down it is because my life—as I have known it—ends within a few days, because I become something new and I want to leave some record of the years, the moments that have brought me to it.

II

I met Pat Castine when I was twenty, the day we all went to the amusement park. It was a funny, luminous, uneven sort of day—the day Katherine decided she was going to take up orphans.

Later Katherine married a lawyer and within a few years was totally settled, with more kids than either of us would have believed possible, but at the time she was wild-haired and engaging, completely good and almost belligerently innocent but always a little baggage-y in the way she wore her button-down shirts with the top two buttons undone, and her skirts a little tight over the rump. Sometimes she wore glasses, and even that seemed to add. I can't explain exactly, except to say that she would be standing with her hands tucked up on her hips and one chunk of hair falling, half-abstracted, half-aware, talking about Francis Thompson or the artist and the image with an intent, almost cross-eyed look on her face, in a way which Pat told me later had a maddening sort of appeal.

Pat has always liked to play with talk, leading people into grave little conversations the way another boy might bring out a deck of cards or do a parlor trick, and it is always hard for me to remember that all the intense looks, the questions and any serious talk which may come out of them are only a diversion to Pat, part of one of his games. Later, when he would have to forget one girl and would try to forget with a great many, Pat would advance to more complicated games. At the time his life was simpler, and he was in love with Katherine. If she had one of her ideas and said she wanted to take out one of the children from Our Lady of Good Counsel, Pat would say OK because it was one more chance to be with her, and if she said she wanted me to go along because it was a slow weekend and I didn't have anything to do, Pat would say OK.

So I found myself riding along in the back of Pat's '46 Plymouth, marooned in the car with him, suddenly, when Katherine told us to sit tight while she went into the orphanage.

At first we both had the idea that she would be right back, orphan in tow, and I slumped and Pat whistled through his teeth and drummed on the steering wheel, keeping his eye on the door as if he expected her to appear any minute. Then I pulled myself back from whatever I had been thinking because the silence seemed more than temporary, and Pat's tune had begun to drag.

It had been all right when he was still whistling and I was still thinking, but we were beginning to be uncomfortable now, strangers together, with nothing to say. We both had cigarettes ("Match?" "Mmm." "Got it?" "Almost." "There." "Thanks." Silence.) and then we both watched the front steps and the driveway and trees and people going here and there on paths and then it became apparent that we were stuck for a while and we would be forced to talk.

"Wonder what's keeping her?" Pat said.

"Kat's always late." I thought a while and then said, "What are you majoring in?" That was always good for a few paragraphs. Pat was at Yale.

"History of Arts and Letters," Pat said.

"No kidding?" I expected him to go on.

He yawned. "It's a gut."

We were all in shorts that day, khaki, because it was spring; Pat looked like a colonial in his. He looked then the way I would have expected Bunker to grow up—blond, blunt-faced, with a warm expression that engaged you even before he had begun to smile. (I remember being surprised later that year when I saw Bunker again, because he was still blond but he had lost all of his old solid squareness and his head was lean and military, with that spare, fine-boned look that will always remind me of a greyhound just about to run.) Pat is smoother now, and he has gone in for tab collars and suits tailored for him at J. Press, but he still has that warmth and a way of surprising you into talk, so that you don't realize at first that the talk is coming too easily, that it is only one of his games and he is bringing you on.

9

I had one foot up on the back seat and was poking a pencil through a hole in my sneaker. I had the only red ones that year, and they were beginning to go around the toes. Pat shifted as if he were about to say something and I looked up, expecting him to go on, but instead he was half-out the window, watching a bunch of kids spill out of one of the side doors, bouncing around somebody who must have been a matron but didn't look it in a short, girlish haircut and a flowered dress. The boys were giggling like maniacs in that high, uncontrolled way that I think all boys must pick up at two and perfect before they are six. They were running in tight little circles and making passes at a red patent-leather handbag dangled by one of the girls. The kid with the handbag waved it carelessly, pretending not to notice the boys were after it, and it was only a matter of time before one of the boys grabbed it from her and the whole group broke and ran after him. Pat sighed.

"I wish I were little," he said.

At the time I didn't know Pat very well, and for some reason I was touched. I thought for a minute about being a kid. Then I said, "The hell."

He was surprised. "You wouldn't like to be?"

"Not on your life."

"Look at them." He waved one hand. "Nothing to worry about."

I kept remembering being little and unsure and I said, "You've really forgotten what it was like?"

"Maybe some of it." He was quiet for a minute. "You didn't have to figure out something to do, or something to be."

"I know what I wanted to be." I must have sounded grimmer than I intended, because Pat looked amused. "I wanted to be a grown-up."

"And?"

"Now I am." It was funny to be able to say it. There are still times when I wonder whether it's true. "Do you think I'd go back?"

"What was wrong with being little?"

I didn't know Pat well enough to know he was bringing me on. I hesitated, trying to think of a way to explain. "There's so much to *learn*."

"Seems to me it didn't matter what you learned," Pat said. "You could just be around—you know—not do anything."

I was shaking my head. "If you learned to tie your shoes, then somebody else learned how to whistle and you had to

10

learn to whistle. If you learned to whistle somebody else learned to ride a bike. It was so—incomplete."

"If that's incomplete—" Pat said wistfully. "It was so *soft*. No worries."

"So you'd worry about everything." Some of the threads were pulling loose from my sneaker and the fabric was thin. I shredded at it, trying hard to explain. "It was all about worrying, and about having some faint idea about what you were going to turn into some day, and trying like hell to turn into it."

"A fireman?" Pat said, relaxed enough to want to tease.

"A person. I don't know how to say this, but kids don't—" I stopped for a second, reaching for words.

"I wish," Pat murmured, because he hadn't really heard me.

"—they don't have the—the *backlog* of—I don't know —they don't *know* enough to be able to have fun. Look," I said, wanting badly for him to understand, but he was distracted now, because Katherine had just come up with the little girl, and he didn't even look back to me to see what I had been about to say. I remember trying to get back to it later, after we dropped the kid at the orphanage that night, but Pat had already forgotten and I let it go.

The kid was short, shaped like Nancy in the comic strip, tremendously excited and all done up in a fresh plaid dress.

"This is Janie," Katherine said. "Janie, this is Denny and that's Pat."

She mumbled something and got in the back with me, and Pat and I didn't talk any more. She had some pennies tied up in the corner of a handkerchief, and a box haircut just short enough so you could see where the back of her neck had been shaved.

"Where to?" Pat said.

"Preston Park."

And we were off.

At a light, Pat looked back, trying to make conversation. "Hey, Janie, what's your name?"

"Janie," Janie said.

"No kidding?" Pat said, with such surprise that even Janie laughed.

Katherine turned to her. "Have you ever been to Preston Park?"

Janie shook her head. She was sitting back on the seat with her feet stuck out, braced, with her arms straight and her fists pushing down on the upholstery.

I tried to get her to look at me. "It's rides. Ferris wheels and things. Even a merry-go-round."

She was still rigid, delighted but at the same time scared, as if she were out doing something she knew she shouldn't be doing.

Katherine turned. "What would you like to ride first?"

Janie looked helpless.

"What rides do you like?" Kat said, trying to get her talking.

Janie looked at me and I said, "She likes the low rides."

"The slow rides?"

"Not slow rides. The round rides."

Kat grinned. "The ground rides?"

Pat offered, "Merry-go-*round* rides."

We were getting silly now. "Faster-than-sound rides."

Pat, Cockney. "Arf-pound rides."

Katherine. "Underground rides."

"Lost and found rides."

"Renowned rides."

Me again, out of a rhyme. "You know—the true rides."

"The through rides?"

"The red-white-and-blue rides." Pat let the car jump.

"Shiny and new rides."

"Toothpaste and glue rides?"

"Hail to the crew rides." We all loved words.

Pat did Vachel Lindsay doing The Congo. "Half-a-buck half-a-buck half-a-buck DOWN."

Katherine picked up the beat. "Two for a dollar or half-a-buck DOWN."

I went into falsetto. "Chute-the-chute or slide."

Then Katherine, over our accompaniment, began naming the different kinds of rides and we fell into a fugue, faster and faster, and began to improvise ("Joe McCarthy likes the rides." "O ferris wheel . . ." "Gary Cooper likes the rides . . ." "I sing of love tun*nels* . . ." "No matter how she runs and hides, Greta Garbo likes the rides") with Kat interrupting herself for an occasional recitatif ("O ye huddled masses at roller-coaster's feet . . . O American fun . . ."), all of it tangled together and syncopated so that even Janie had relaxed and was giggling, beating time, not caring that we'd all but forgotten her. It was very grand. It got a little like Bach at the end.

We subsided just as Pat pulled into Preston Park.

I took Janie's hand because Pat was engrossed in Katherine, and we set out across the parking lot. Right at the fringes of the park were a couple of kiddie rides, the Fairy Whip, for one, and when Janie was afraid to go on it alone Pat swallowed a grin and went with her, knees doubled in one of the little cars. They swooped along not four feet from the ground with Janie squealing as they went around each curve, waving the frozen custard we had bought her until it dribbled in the wind. Katherine and I were mucking around the ticket box, waiting for Pat, when she looked up and saw the top of the Tarantula, just as one of the cars was hurtling past with a sound that made you wonder when the whole thing was going to collapse. She looked great, with her hands in her pockets and her sleeves rolled up. She had her Oxford-cloth shirts starched, no matter what it said inside the collar, and they didn't pull out and bag around the waist the way mine did, even when she pointed up, to the peak of the roller-coaster, as if she were trying to reach it. "Hey," she said, and poked me in the ribs.

And I followed her finger and gulped. People were screaming—it seemed to be part of it—and whipping by so fast we could hardly follow them, even though perspective slowed the whole thing up. "Hey," I said. It looked great.

"Pat," Katherine went to meet Pat and Janie, who was looking flushed and pleased and jumping at the end of his arm. She pointed. Another car was rattling past, far above the trees.

He swept Janie up on his shoulders. "Let's quit messing around."

We went through the midway in a rush, sensing that it was bright with palmists' signs and different kinds of food, but not paying much attention because we could hardly wait to get to the Tarantula, to be in one of the cars notching itself up the grade to the first peak. Then we were in its shadow, and we knew at once that it was a fine roller-coaster because the struts and stays underneath shook magnificently each time a car went past. They had a decaying, dangerous look, as if the whole thing were just about to go.

"Hey, Pat," I said. "Let's go."

He set Janie down at the base of the ride and went to get tickets for four. Just as he let go her hand a car came down a slope not far from us and racketed into a dip. The whole rickety frame trembled as it came and then I fell back a step because Janie had pushed against me suddenly, pressing her face against my side. I looked up then, and saw what she must have seen—a network of wood looming, advancing, just about to grab her and swallow her up. Probably the worst thing for her was that she was our guest, or our prisoner, bound to do anything we wanted her to do, even to trusting herself to one of those open, precarious cars.

I gave her my hand.

Just then Pat came back with the tickets and Katherine said, "I don't think Janie wants to go."

"That's OK," he said, and stooped beside her. "We're going on the ride, Janie. You wait right here. OK?"

Her face looked unsettled, almost ready to crumple, but she nodded. Then her hand closed on my fingers like a little vise and I looked down and saw how desperate she was.

"Hey," I said, "I don't have to go." I was dying to go. "I'll stay down here with the kid. I can go when you get back."

"That wouldn't be fair," Katherine said. She looked down at Janie. "You'll be all right, won't you, sweetie? You can just sit on that bench. We'll keep an eye on you."

Janie just crammed herself against me.

"It really wouldn't be fair," Kat said. "Tell you what. I'll stay."

"I don't mind."

She looked at me closely. "You really don't? No, I'll stay," she said again, but all her weight had shifted toward the Tarantula, and I could tell that all she needed was for me to say it was OK.

"It's OK," I said. Then I took Janie and we backed off to a bench in the shadow of the Tarantula and waved to Pat and Katherine the first time they came by.

I wasn't being noble. It was partly because Janie was scared and needed somebody to stay with her, partly because Pat wanted to go with Katherine and I couldn't ask either of them to stay behind. But that wasn't the important thing. By the time it came right down to it, I was too depressed to go. I think I was awash in Janie's feelings: scared of the ride but something more than that; lost, maybe, or somehow unexpectedly aware of how deep the shadows, and how helpless we can be. I don't think it was a sense of kinship so much as a glimpse into the darkness we forget when we are grown because we have shored up so many thoughts, skills, belongings to keep it at bay. I only know I was depressed as hell, and for the moment the midway and the rides seemed so garish, so dirty and so ominous that I wanted to pick up the little girl and run out of the park.

I got her a hot dog and some soda to cheer us both up. The Tarantula went full circle and then Katherine and Pat went around again, because Pat had bought tickets for four. When the car coasted to a stop by the ticket-taker for the second time the two of them looked over at us with that apologetic grin you see in cartoons, the one that shows all the teeth, and Pat paid the ticket-taker for another ride.

In between I took Janie once on the merry-go-round. We rode in the swan boat and she clung to the edge, laughing excitely in short, ragged little breaths. She had cotton candy after that and wasn't able to finish it before Pat and Katherine came down from the Tarantula. In all, they had been five times. When they came down, finally, laughing, Pat was holding her hand because he couldn't *not* hold it, with a pleased, unsteady look that I have never seen in him since. He offered to go on the ride with me but it was getting late and by this time I was in no mood to go, with him or alone.

He won a plaster pig for Janie at one of the lottery booths, and when he couldn't win her a panda he went to another booth and bought her one. She carried them both back to the car in her arms, still dragging the remainder of the cotton candy wand in one hand. I remember being cheered because she seemed to be feeling better, giggling a lot, but I think now she was too excited to have any real fun that day.

In the car she sat with those feet straight out again, flushed and a little grubby around the hands and mouth, cuddling the pig and the panda on her lap. She'd gotten some bubble gum on the bottom of one of her Mary Janes. She seemed to want to be quiet and I was glad, because I didn't particularly want to talk.

We drove back by the water and I slouched with my head just level with the window, looking out over it and thinking about nothing in particular. The sound of Pat and Katherine talking in front reminded me of drives cross-continent with my parents, with me put to bed in the back, half-listening to the comforting drone of their talk. Their voices had that same gentle, intimate sound.

Then Janie squirmed next to me and said, "I think I'm going to be sick."

Katherine and I used to talk about this, and if there was one thing both of us hated, it was throwing up. We could count the times we'd done it and name the places and just exactly what we had been eating that had brought it on.

The very idea that somebody else might be about to threw us into a sympathetic panic that didn't lift until the danger was past. Now all three of us were focussed on Janie, trying to talk reassuringly, to take her mind off it or jolly her out of it, giving each other what-now looks over her head. We made it back to Our Lady of Good Counsel in double time and we handed her out delicately, fixed on getting her into the building before she could be sick. She stopped a minute to thank us and we rushed her, saying a sketchy goodbye because we had the idea we were handling a time bomb that still might go off, a little ashamed at ourselves for doing it but hurrying her just the same. It was like juggling an egg on a spoon.

"Too bad," Pat said as Katherine took her inside.

I was hunched in a corner, still a little nervous about the place where Janie had sat. "Maybe we were too much for her."

"She's all right," Pat said reassuringly. "She just ate too much."

Katherine got into the car. "I think she was kind of glad to get back. They were all piling around to pick her up."

"Watch your skirt, Stir."

"Wup wup *wup* wup." Pat started the car.

Then we started laughing, exploding with relief.

We bounced, we sang, going along with all the windows open and no particular aim in mind.

On impulse, Pat stopped at a bakery. It was a Saturday, and the stores were open until nine. He came out with a box full of gooies—éclairs, cream horns, Napoleons—a sort of tribute, and a contrast, too, to Janie, and we parked outside the college grounds and ate them, yapping at each other and smearing ourselves with chocolate and cream. It was then, I think, that I wanted to pick up my argument, to explain to Pat. Being a kid is too serious, too much for keeps. I think you have better times—you're younger, in a way, when you've begun to grow up because you have developed some assurance and some sense of time, some awareness of the moment and of moments missed, a backlog of all the moments of memory; you have found a place to stand and look at life, and can see everything more clearly. You realize that the moment is good and that it is fleeting and you grab it with joy, knowing how important it is. You are not children but act as children, and being some distance from childhood gives you some self-knowl-

16

edge, awareness of what you are doing and some degree of control, so that you live with joy because you know how soon it will be done.

After a while Pat pulled up in front of the building where Katherine and I lived. I took the left-over Napoleons for our third roommate and went inside, leaving the two of them alone. If things had been a little different I think he would have married her. As it was she put him out of her mind after that summer and I was her maid of honor when she married a Fordham Law graduate the week after our commencement the following June.

I didn't realize until some years later, after I had lit in a job near the city, after Pat had gone into television and Katherine had died of some two-bit children's disease, that I hadn't needed to explain to Pat that night, that he had begun to understand what I was getting at not long after we left the little girl off at the orphanage.

I was in the city for the day and Pat had invited me to meet him at the Yale Club for a drink. He was a new enough member still to be a little tickled about the whole idea and wanted to show it off to me. I wasn't used to seeing the workaday Pat and I didn't pick him out at first because he came in with a group that went on to the elevators, and he looked as tall, as businesslike as all the rest. He had an attaché case and a Wall Street Journal tucked under one arm and since I was sitting, looking at chest level and not expecting to know any of the faces above, I didn't look up and see him until he had stood for a minute or two beside my chair.

"Denny," he said.

"Oh, Pat. Hi. *Hi*."

The business about Katherine was fairly new and we stood soberly for a minute, talking about her.

Pat grimaced. "It just doesn't make any sense." Then he shook himself. "Hey," he said, and took my arm. "Come see the smart ladies' dining room."

At dinner we talked about everything we could think of, feeling better, and when it was time for dessert I ordered a Napoleon.

Pat grinned when it came and made me give him half. "It was the funniest damn thing about that day," he said, not needing to explain. "After you left I kept thinking about that thing Scott Fitzgerald wrote, about the two of them being on top of the taxicab, bawling because nothing would ever be as good again."

"At least we *knew*—"

But he broke in, as if he still hadn't comprehended. "If we could just be *kids* again."

III

My full name is Denise Rogers McLeod, and Bunker Swift and I were born in the same hospital in Norfolk, in the same month in 1932. Our fathers were classmates at the Academy, and that year both of them were serving as junior officers on the same ship. My mother took care of Pearson while his mother was in the hospital with Bunker, because his father was away at sea. Nobody had any money and there were times at the end of the month when they had to debate between something for the house and cod-liver oil for me, but both my parents and the Swifts had live-in girls and they used to entertain each other at Poverty Hall dinner parties, and they still claim they never had more fun.

When Bunker and I were six months old his father was transferred to a destroyer based in Pearl Harbor and a month later we packed up and moved to Washington. Our parents said goodbye lightly as Navy people do, because they know they're likely to be together in just a year or two, stationed in the same place again. Before the war the service was a small town where lives crossed and recrossed and people in Panama and Manila seemed no more remote than those who had gone to Bremerton or Newport for a couple of years. For some, it is still that way. When they meet they may not have written or talked for years, but after the first few minutes they find little has changed.

I've been away from the Navy for a long time now, but my being a Navy junior is still one of the important things about me. It has a lot to do with the way I am, with the way I value friends. If you know any service children at all you can recognize them, perhaps because the first impression is a little too smooth and bright, perhaps because of the attentive look, which never wavers, or the apparent ease with which they say hello. This comes from years of getting started with a group of strangers not five minutes after the movers have left and the excelsior has been cleared away. ("What's your name?" "Denny McLeod. What's yours?" There was always a long pause while they—and they always advanced in twos or threes—made up their minds about you.) If you know people who have grown up in the service you may think they make friends easily, and envy them for it.

It isn't so. I was in three fourth grades and I have lived in at least a dozen cities, and I count about four close friends. I can be fairly easy talking to new people, but anyone who watched closely could see that there is a certain reserve between us, and only at a certain point which may come after a few meetings, or may never come, will I begin to use the particular person's name. I make friends slowly, and I value them because I make them hard. At twenty-seven I am fortunate in having four.

Bunker was the first. Our families were together again in New London when Bunker and I were seven and in the second grade. We lived a block away from the water. In all we were in New London three different times, and each time my father found us a place within the range of the foghorn, and I seem to remember a whole series of walks along breakwaters, or to narrow, blasted beaches where Daddy and I, usually chilly after a large Sunday dinner, would sit on the rocks and watch the grey surface of the waves.

The house we rented was outsized, rambling and shingled in brown. It had been left furnished by the owner, so that our own things were in storage and there were certain rooms closed off, dim and too spooky for me to explore alone.

Bunker and I hit New London about the same time, and because we were new together, we were friends, even though I was a girl and we would be going to different schools. Our fathers had the duty almost every night for the first three weeks, and our mothers wanted the rest of us to be together while our fathers were at the base. Each duty night the rest of us would have dinner together, sandwiches and cocoa on Jack Benny night at the Swifts' or creamed chipped beef on toast at my house. We'd all make desultory passes at helping our mothers with the dishes, and then Bunker and I would play and Pearson would go off to read. Once or twice the Swifts spent the night at our house (I think at first my mother was frightened by the size of the place and the variety of its noises) because we had plenty of room, and there was a family feeling about Bunker and me being around in our pajamas that I will never forget.

Pearson was two, nearly three, years older and seemed almost like a man to me, a little sulky and remote. If someone had told me then that there would come a time when I hated him, I would have accepted it without surprise. He kept to himself and had little to do with either of us, choosing instead to talk to the adults in the room. Even when Bunker, with the easy generosity that has always characterized him, sensed that he was lonely and would ask his advice about a school project or a checkers game, Pearson would stand over the table with a weary look and give his advice in a tone of condescension edged with scorn. At times he terrified me because he was quick to anger when we disturbed him, and his face would darken and contract until his eyebrows almost met.

Once, after he lectured me for putting one of his books down on its face, so that it might have cracked the spine, I went into his room and took all his rock samples out of their labelled boxes. I stood with the rocks heavy in my skirt, and after a moment of uncertainty I knelt on the rug and spilled them out, arranging them so that they spelled a word—FOOEY. I was just putting the tail on the Y when Pearson came in and stood over me, so mad he couldn't speak. I ducked around him without even getting up, and hid in a closet under the stairs. The walls of the converted summer place where the Swifts were living were no more than painted cardboard, and through them I could hear Pearson still in his room, throwing his rocks at the walls with systematic fury.

By the time the duty schedule had settled down Bunker and I had gotten so used to spending most of our time together that it seemed natural for me to go around and yell for him every day after school. He didn't seem to care that I was odd man out in the neighborhood because I was the only kid who went to parochial school.

I wasn't exactly sure of the difference between schools at the time. Public school kids seemed to get out earlier than I did, and they took their lunches and didn't wear uniforms.

I learned of another difference when Bunker and his mother came to school early to pick me up for a birthday party, and Bunker was enthralled by the nuns. I understood why when I visited Bunker's school. The teachers put me off at once. I'm sure now that some of them were young, and they may even have been pretty, but they all seemed like old women to me, with lined faces and wiry permanents or hair pulled straight back like the old maids' hair in cartoons. They seemed a jumble of colorless dresses and glasses and orthopedic shoes and their faces, stern and unsoftened by the white frame of a habit, seemed extraordinarily grown up to me and, in their own way, formidable, so that it was a relief to me when the afternoon was over and I could go home. In that dim building school seemed like a serious business, and not all the cut-outs in the windows and construction paper flowers on the bulletin boards could change my mind.

There was serious business at my school too, but at first it all seemed so abstract that I could not be concerned. We were preparing for our First Communion, poring over the catechism, reciting the Commandments, experimenting with the concept of sin. I understood parts of it very well; Sister explained about confession, and one day she brought Necco wafers in and we practiced what we would do when we went up to the altar rail. We would all have veils and white dresses and it meant new shoes for most of us, First Communion presents—new prayer books, or rosaries in white leatherette cases fastened with a snap. But false witness and taking the name of the Lord in vain—to say nothing of adultery—were only words, no more than abstractions, and I learned dutifully, only memorizing what was taught. Then Bunker and I, who had simply been friends as kids are friends, took part in an adventure that bonded us, and I began to understand.

We had learned about money earlier that year, when our fathers gave us each a grave little talk about money and an allowance of a dime a week. We always spent it at Ginsenger's, a dingy neighborhood store, not even bothering to look into the chain drug store across the street, where everything was cellophane-wrapped and cost a nickel at least. We would string the pennies out, getting at least three trips to the store out of each dime, and we would come into Ginsenger's like the huns or the vandals and decide all at once, swooping down on sour balls, Guess-Whats or little paraffin bottles with sweet syrup inside, or wax buck teeth

22

with a sweet taste that came out when you tired of wearing them and began to chew them up.

One week the money seemed to go all at once. It was a Wednesday, a half-day for some reason, and Bunker and I were sitting around my room, listless and stuffy with the steam heat.

Finally, when we were almost sick with boredom, Bunker said, "Let's go to the store."

"We can't," I said. "I don't have any money left."

"How about your First Communion money? You had fifty cents last week."

I looked up crossly. "Well, it's gone."

"That's OK." He was already getting up. He fished in his pockets, considered for a minute and then stuck his hand out with a ready generosity and said, "Here's two cents. You can have half."

We raced to the store and pulled up inside, already revived by the cold air. We got Guess-Whats because there was always a surprise—some toy made in Japan—tucked in the paper wrapper along with the taffy kiss. Then, because the air had been like a cold bath and we were ravenous, we opened them without looking at the prizes and gobbled them all at once.

Bunker crumpled his paper and threw it away. "Now what?"

"I'm hungry," I said.

"Me too."

"Maybe if Mr. Ginsenger thought—" I began.

"If he *really* thought we were hungry—"

Not even embarrassed by our naked bad manners, we hung around the counters, hoping Mr. Ginsenger would notice us looking at the candy and give us some. Instead he came out of the back of his shop with a harried air and when he saw that we weren't buying he began to rattle things impatiently, so that we finally understood what he was getting at and left, complaining before we ever hit the street.

"We could get cookies at home," Bunker said, but his mouth went down at the corners.

"That's no good."

We were in front of the big drug store now, wandering up and down in front of the plate glass windows, and before we'd had a chance to discuss it, we found ourselves inside.

"Look," Bunker said. "He's making milkshakes."

I groaned as the counterman dropped a blob of ice cream in the aluminum glass. Then I jerked at Bunker's elbow and turned him toward the checkout counter. "*Look*."

There, untended, were Life Savers and Hershey Bars, all tumbled in an open carton in a display that rose to a pyramid peak. Without looking to see whether he followed me I went over to the display and stood in front of it, with a sharp feeling that rose in me until I was so restless that I could hardly contain it, and I went out into the street.

Bunker seemed to feel it too, because he ranged back and forth in front of the plate glass show window, hunching his shoulders and grinding his knuckles across his nose. Finally he turned to me, fishing in his pockets. "I got a whistle," he said, looking at his Guess-What prize for the first time. "What did you get?"

I brought out a pink celluloid baby-doll, no more than half an inch high.

"Huh," Bunker said, looking at it with disgust. "But if we put them together—"

"Maybe Mr. Ginsenger would like them," I said, forming a plan.

He finished it up. "Maybe we could swap."

All we wanted in exchange were a couple of coconut bits, tricolored and no more than an inch from end to end, but Mr. Ginsenger screamed and turned us out of the store.

It probably would have gone differently if it had been one of us alone. But we were hungry, or thought we were, and we fed on each other, naming all the candies we could think of and going over and over the scene with Mr. Ginsenger, feeding on our hunger and our impotence until we had to do something or die. Without actually planning it, almost before we realized it, we were back in the drug store again, hovering over the untended counter, and I found myself reaching out like a practiced shoplifter and whipping a candy bar out of the display and into my skirt. Then Bunker, with a look that sealed us, slipped a package of Life Savers into his pants. We turned, tremulous with the unreality of it, and left the store.

On the sidewalk I was slowed by a sudden sinking feeling as if the whole street had gone dark, and when I looked at Bunker, he had turned white. He looked at me and we began to run.

Bunker helped me eat my candy bar when we got home. We huddled under the front porch and bolted it without tasting it. Then he took his Life Savers home and buried them in the back yard.

If I go into this now it is not so much for the theft as for the feeling that came on me as soon as it happened, a sense of disharmony, or of loss, as if my whole world were suddenly out of joint. I can't explain it exactly, except perhaps in terms of what I am. With most of us, Catholic is not so much a thing we believe as a thing we *are*, an awareness of who we are and what God is, a longing to be at one with Him, and whether we accept or fight or deny it everything we do is colored by it. For me this seems to involve a sense of order, or rightness, and once I have gone against this I am uneasy, and will not feel right or whole again until I have set the thing, whatever it is, and myself right. For me this feeling of disharmony is a force, almost tangible, and more than once when I have been on the verge of doing something doubtful, a whiff or foretaste of it has made me consider, and the simple desire to keep right with God, not to have to carry the feeling around, has kept me from going on. I have never gone against it without being sorry. For want of a better word I'll call it conscience, and if I describe it here it is because I could not go on about myself and the lives that are bound up in mine without acknowledging it. At the time it frightened me because it was so strong, and because it was new.

I never talked about it with Bunker because I knew, without knowing how I knew, that for all he gave to me he held some of his thoughts private, and that we were friends because I knew this, and would not intrude. I would never ask him how he felt about taking the candy, or suggest that he do something about it, and he would never discuss it with me. We could go on being friends because this was understood.

I think now that it was over for him as soon as he took a dime to the drug store and dropped it down, into the candy display. He didn't tell anyone what he was going to do; he never said anything to me and so far as I know he never confessed to his father, not because he was afraid of punishment but because he was fiercely independent; it wasn't in him to take any problem to another person and he would resist the idea of being moved by someone outside himself. He never told me anything but I know, somehow, that this is what he did. I also remember that he was so happy, so relieved after it was over that at the time I almost wished I could be a Protestant too, and forget about confession, get rid of the trouble in some easier way.

For a couple of days I was almost able to tell myself that everything was all right, that I hadn't really done anything, but on Sunday when Daddy went up to the rail to Communion I wanted more than anything to go with him, to be a part of what was going on. I almost told Daddy about the whole business that day, I think because I wanted him to help me make it right, but I knew even then that it was up to me alone. In our catechism were two pictures of milk bottles. One was white and unsullied, and it was supposed to be your soul as God saw it, full of grace. The second was empty, marked with dirt, and it signified the soul after you had committed a sin. Only going to confession and putting things right would make it white again.

Until then, confession had been nothing. We marched over in a double line every other Friday and went in turn, reciting the formula that Sister Marcella had taught us, thinking up one or two things—forgetting our morning prayers or being disobedient—to say. Then Father Collins (it was usually Father Collins) would give us our penance and we'd say an Act of Contrition and that would be all.

But now I had something to tell. I didn't know what Father Collins would do or say and the possibilities didn't frighten me half as much as the prospect of kneeling down in that dark booth and blurting out my secret, the idea of putting it into words. But I couldn't shake my discomfort, and I could never pass the drug store or the church without being uneasy, and when I took my pennies to Ginsenger's I spent them without any particular joy.

For a while I didn't know which was worse, the idea of confession or the feeling that troubled me until finally I decided nothing could be worse and nerved myself one Saturday afternoon and went into church all by myself.

The church was dingy Gothic and to me it seemed to have no ceiling, rising instead into a shadowy arch. The rows of pews stretched empty, except for a few people here and there, saying their penance, and others lined up outside the booths. I wondered how they could be so calm. Just beyond the vista of seats I could see the altar, and I remember yearning toward the pure, distant statues which rose in circles of candlelight at either side. I closed my eyes to them and attached myself to one of the lines outside a confessional, standing without thinking because it seemed easiest that way, so that when my turn came I managed to get going without hesitation, and ducked into the booth.

I collected myself, rehearsing the formula, "Bless me Father for I have sinned, it has been two weeks since my last confession . . ." and then the little door slid open and Father Collins was listening. I began the formula aloud, gathering momentum, whisking through the neglected prayers and the disobedience, and then I told him about it, talking all in a rush without even stopping for breath, waiting at the end for the world to collapse. He may not have heard or understood, or he may have heard perfectly. I only know that the moment I finished and my head began to thunder he said, without letting a silence begin, "For your penance say three Hail Mary's," and then he coached me through an Act of Contrition and it was over.

It was a lifting of heaviness, a feeling of joy or relief or both compounded, and I remember wanting to sing out some kind of thanks without being sure then how, or why. I have always hated going to confession beforehand, and I have always felt that joy or relief to some degree, that gratitude for something lifted, most of all for the simple fact that it *can* be lifted, when I have received absolution and it is over.

I ran. I wanted to sing. I followed the bus line from church to our house, because it would take me to a corner where I could see the whole street stretching ahead, and beyond it the water. There was a quicker way but I followed the bus line that day because I wanted to see our house rising up at the end of the street, tall and brown-shingled against the water. Daddy was in front, polishing the car. I must have charged him from the corner, bounding at him in my sneakers, because he watched me come with a surprised look and then put down his rag and lifted me high with an expression that made me want to cry for reasons I couldn't have understood. The air was clear and the sky was like silver, and the intensity of the moment, some new, glimmering awareness of its impermanance might have made it unbearable if Bunker hadn't come along just then, trailing some deposit bottles in his wagon, and said, "Let's go to the store."

Daddy gave me my allowance without asking why I hadn't come to him for it that morning, and I took it and followed Bunker to the store. We parked the wagon outside Ginsenger's and I helped carry the bottles in. Bunker had already discarded the idea of a funnybook or a mask and was ranging up and down in front of the showcase of candy, waiting for me, when I poked him and said, "See you in a minute."

He gave me a sort of rabbit-look of surprise (he was missing some teeth that year) but he didn't say anything because he would never intrude, and would expect the same diffidence from me.

I said, "I've got to go across the street," wanting him to know.

He said, "Yeah," and I can't describe the look, except to say that it was the second time I had seen it that day.

In the drug store I waited until the man wasn't looking, not really caring this time whether he was looking or not, and then dropped my dime in the candy display, watching until I was sure it had lost itself between the Life Savers and the root beer rolls.

On the way home Bunker handed me a pair of wax candy lips without saying anything, and wouldn't even listen when I promised to pay him for them when I got my allowance the next week. He stayed for supper that night and came along with my mother and me when we drove Daddy out to the base.

We must have eaten early, because Daddy had to be at the base by six on duty nights. He had on khakis, and despite all the times I saw him in civilian clothes, in suits on weekends, or in slacks around the house, I always picture him in his uniform. Bunker and I sat in back and saluted the guard as we went through the main gate, Bunker in a pair of the wax buck teeth, I in the wax candy lips, softened at the edges now but still brave and red. Daddy stopped at Ships' Service and bought Necco wafers for each of us, and then he made my mother promise to take us to the early movie on the base. He kissed me goodbye and stopped outside the car window to talk to my mother as she slid into the driver's seat, lowering his voice so that Bunker and I stopped listening and played. The next evening she would drive out to get him and he would take over the wheel again, but a little silence fell after he said goodbye and lost himself around the corner of a grey building because for the time being we would be alone together, as we often were, waiting until he came back.

The movie was a Shirley Temple and Bunker and I couldn't have been happier. The sailors probably hated it. We must have fallen asleep on the way home, because the next

28

thing I remember is being alone in the back seat, probably after we dropped Bunker off at his place, and then I got up because we were home and shambled into the house.

As I look back, I think this must have been one of the last times Bunker and I played together in New London, because he and his parents went to Panama right after school was out, and we didn't see any of them again until the war.

IV

I saw Bunker and his family again when we were nine, on a day that seemed too warm for midwinter, in a ramshackle house in Florida. Our fathers' subs were in the Pacific, in the war. When they found the house, my mother and father explained that this would be our duration home. I wasn't clear what it meant, but I remember believing that my mother and I were stationed there, as surely as my father had been stationed in New London or at Bremerton, before I was born. The move may simply have had to do with the reasons my father gave: fuel shortages wouldn't matter in the warm, short winters, and Florida would be one of the last places they would bomb. But I suspect that my father made the decision before he made up the reasons, prompted by a quick but full vision—like a glimpse into a lighted room at night—of the cities where we had been at home, changed with sudden money and the awful, urgent wartime pace.

At the time, I think our fathers thought being together would make it easier for the two women, and at the time, I suppose they were right, but my mother never speaks of that time without a certain pain and much as I loved Bunker and much as I loved Pearson at first, I think we would have been better off alone.

We met in a welter of barrels, crates, the debris of more than a dozen moves. Bunker and I were a little in awe of the house, which still echoed because there were no drapes or rugs to absorb the sound. We were edgy, circling stiffly as strange dogs do when they meet, uncertain because we hadn't seen each other for nearly two years.

My mother and I got there first. We found the place, with Daddy's help, deciding on it finally because this house or that house had a space heater or poor wiring, or a Northern family already backed up to it with too many children and not enough yard. It was big enough for two families, and it had an upstairs screen porch.

We had taken Daddy to the train that morning. He would go to Washington and transfer to a flight cross-continent, to meet his boat. Now, back in the house without him, my mother and I fell silent, at loose ends suddenly because there was nothing to do until the moving men came back to un-crate our things. We picked our way among the crates and barrels, walking quietly, as if we had no right to be in the house. My mother pried at the top of a china barrel, gave it up and pretended to be preoccupied with the inventory. I went through the kitchen to the back door and looked out without enthusiasm. Under the spread of a big tree, the yard was bare, except for a few patches of grass and a blasted stump. The kitchen was furnished with chairs and a table painted apple-green, and on one of the shelves the last ten-ant had left a pile of dime-store plates. I looked around, hat-ing the place. Neither my mother nor I would be at ease un-til we had our things unpacked and marshalled against the strangeness. We moped, waiting for the Swifts to come.

My mother followed me into the kitchen, trying to make conversation. I may have acted the way I did because I re-jected the idea that she might be lonely too.

She said, "Well, which room do you want?"

I wanted the front bedroom, the one that opened on the upstairs screen porch, but I didn't say so. I looked at the chipped apple-green paint with loathing and whined some-thing to the effect that I didn't care.

"Sure you care."

I looked up at her just then and she seemed so tired, so fal-lible in her drooping Palm Beach dress—skirts were still down—that something in me had to protest and I said "I don't," and slammed myself into a kitchen chair.

"Since we found the house you have first choice." She was trying hard to sound bright but her mouth had begun to go soft. It would have been all right except that she bent down to me, as if she wanted reassurance, and said, "All right?"

I have never felt smaller or unhappier, and I wanted des-perately for her to take command and buck me up. Instead, she was looking at me as if there were something I could do

31

for her. I must have sounded like a puppy, yapping. "I don't know. I don't *know*," kicking away at the legs of the chair as if I hated it.

Then, probably because she needed to protest too, she snapped, "Stop that!" and pulled me out of the chair. In the same motion she remembered herself, at least partially, and tried to sit down, cuddling me on her lap.

I almost let myself go against her, but I remember drawing back, so frightened by the new suspicion that she—my *mother*—was doing this for comfort that I yanked away, almost snarling. I don't know what I would have said to her if we hadn't heard a car door slam just then.

She got up with dignity, pulling down her skirts, and we went into the living room just as Mrs. Swift came in. My mother looked at her in a mixture of exhaustion and relief and said, "Margaret, you found us."

"It was a ghastly drive," Mrs. Swift said. She had on a printed voile, pouching just a little over the stomach, and her skirt drooped just as my mother's did.

I was straining past her, trying to see Bunker and Pearson coming up the walk.

The two mothers stood there for a moment, Mrs. Swift taking in the layout and the crates and barrels, trying to place herself in the house, my mother relieved to have her there but uncertain because she had found the house, and it was her responsibility.

Finally she said, "What do you think of the place?"

I remember being uneasy, wild to get outdoors, impatient because Bunker was hanging around the door and Pearson was still skulking outside. I wanted our mothers to stop talking so they could come in and it could begin.

Mrs. Swift threw herself on my mother's neck. "Jen, it's wonderful."

Then Bunker stepped from behind his mother and said, "Hi."

Pearson muttered something and went on past, already clumping upstairs to pick out his room. He was not yet thirteen, but his brows had already begun to grow across his forehead and there was the first hint that his voice was going to change. I think he felt as badly as Bunker and I about his father's being gone. It had never bothered us before, but even though everybody had tried to hide the uncertainty, Bunker and I realized without having to be told that this time, for the first time, really, unless you counted the sinking of the *Squalus*, when some of Daddy's best friends were entombed beneath the surface for thirty hours, there was a real possibility that they would not be back. Pearson was too lordly to admit his uncertainty, but I know now he must have realized more fully than we did just how heavy the chances were. Once we were settled he kept a status map in his room, pretending to chart the submarines' courses with bright, red-headed pins. He gleaned what information he could from our fathers' letters (they were all right the day the letters were written. Fine. Perhaps they had gone in near this island or that one, shaded in on the newspaper maps. Eventually, toward the end of the war, there would be rumors of Bunker's father watching the horseraces through his periscope in the bay at Yokohama), filling the details from the news.

Our mothers were still standing, murmuring little hellos. I looked up just in time to see their outlines blur for a second in the strangeness, the finality (the furniture has come. Well here we *are*), and I realize now that they were very close to tears. Instead of letting us see them crying they began resettling chairs, moving barrels that didn't need to be moved and then my mother said, "Maybe we should have some lemonade," and I forgave her for whatever had almost been in the kitchen because she was busy again, and things were beginning to be as they should have been.

"I've got a Captain Midnight bombsight," I said. "I sent in for it and it's got all ships that you knock over."

"Oh, yeah. I almost had one of those." Bunker looked around the room for outlets, already mentally placing the radio. "What time does he come on down here?"

I shook my head. "He doesn't. I tried every station." Then, to prove I had the bombsight, "It's got yellow bombs."

He said, "Let's see."

And then I remembered that it was packed. "I can't." It was in one of those cartons, where the movers had thrown it and some other toys I had been playing with, along with several pictures and lampshades and even (we would discover with unpacking) some trash and the coconut candy I had been eating the day we moved, swept up when we weren't looking, and it would be several days before we would get to it and I could take it out and set it up. For the first time since we had been plucked up and put down in this out-of-the-way place where there wasn't a base or even a Ships' Service, I realized how far away we were from the Navy, and I could feel my face beginning to go red and funny, in my helplessness.

Bunker must have seen it because he said "Hey," and bolted for the door. "Let's get a look at this place."

I let out my breath and went tearing after him.

Moving as we had in New London, like the huns or the vandals, we went out on the block, looking for bikes or dogs, any sign that there was somebody our age nearby. We ducked behind sparse shrubs and cut through yards, bounding across lumpy red brick streets to look into the screen porches of low-slung Florida houses, treading lightly at first because we were newcomers, getting louder and braver when we found nobody in our way, bouncing a little because there were two of us and we could hardly wait for our first clash with the neighborhood kids. Perhaps it was the palm trees—it was the time of year when the fronds go brown and begin to droop—but there was something fusty about the street, a dry silence that made us know, when we stopped at a corner and let ourselves listen, that as children we were alone in the neighborhood. We kept looking anyway, ranging the blocks around until we came to a vacant lot when it was almost dark and Bunker looked at me and saw that I was about to cry.

"There are Japs in that building," he said, pretending not to see.

"Hit the dirt!" I yelled, and did a belly-whopper in the tall weeds, keeping down until I was sure I wouldn't cry. Bunker wormed along beside me, solid and reassuring, not bothering me with talk. We squirmed on our bellies for a few inches and then he stood up and threw a grenade.

"Got 'em." Then he turned to me with a fierce, military look that gave me my cue and turned the war into something that both of us would think we could handle, and said, "Better get back to headquarters. We've got a lot to do."

We marched home in step, ducking now and then and keeping an eye out for snipers, and when we came in it was with a new bearing that gave us a feeling of significance.

My mother was upstairs, unpacking her things in one of the front rooms. She said, "I put your things in the back room next to Bunker's. Pearson spoke for the room off the porch."

I started to make a face and then drew myself up, the officer accepting an assignment, and said, "Yes Ma'am," trying to sound stern.

"I know you wanted it."

"No Ma'am." I was thinking about putting down a bed-roll, conditioning myself. She looked up. "Your face is a mess."

I rubbed my hand across it. It came away with sweat and dirt. I turned it over matter-of-factly. "Camouflage."

Her head came up. "I see."

She nodded, standing now. "Tell you what," she said. "Save it for when you're out fighting." Then she put her hand on my shoulder.

I pulled back for a minute, still not sure of her. Then the firmness of her hand and some strength I had gained when Bunker hit on the new bearing made me want to comfort her. Even though she didn't seem to be looking to me for reassurance I wanted to give her something and I pressed against her, putting my arms around her halfway down and said, "It's OK. You know what? We'll kick Pearson out when Daddy comes. He'd like to be in that room."

She pulled me closer, saying, "That's a fine idea."

Then I sat with her, letting my head go against her shoulder until somebody called that it was suppertime. She may have cried that night, after we were all in bed. I know I did, for the first time since Daddy left.

Downstairs, Bunker was waiting for me.

The movers had come back that afternoon while Bunker and I were out and everything was uncrated: the Swifts' couch opposite ours in front of the fireplace, teak tables and scrolls here and there, our camphorwood chest with the Swifts' table in the dining room (it was better than ours) and even some of the bric-a-brac placed around, already beginning to make the house belong to us. Our radio was on the mantel, above the Swifts' fire tongs, overlooking the room. Pearson was up on a chair beside it, tuning in the news. My mother and Mrs. Swift fooled around the table, putting napkins in rings and straightening the silver Pearson had put on, waiting for the newscast to be over. Then Mrs. Swift called us to the table. Pearson moved to turn off the radio but she said, "Leave it. There'll be more news," and we ate with the radio going, eating dessert as staticky voices came in from London and Hong Kong and listening after dinner to Lowell Thomas, as we would almost every night, no matter where we were, for the rest of the war.

Our mothers had put on fresh dresses for dinner, trying to make something special of it, and they had decided it would be nice for us to eat by candlelight. They talked of our fathers matter-of-factly, as if mentioning their names would, somehow, bring them into the room. I think we must have been separate when dinner started, feeling a little solitary as families without fathers always do (the feeling is something like being without credentials) but I remember expanding in the candlelight, the five of us growing closer in that tight, dim circle, beginning to meet in a kind of solidarity that would warm us and help us through those first few months.

After dinner Pearson brought out his map for the first time, going over it with model ships and bright-colored pins, involving himself in what he was doing so that he hardly heard when Bunker or I asked him about this ship or that plane. He did everything with a concentration that turned him red up to the ears, and if Bunker or I had interrupted him that night, moving in and trying to place a pin or a ship, I don't know what he would have done. As it was we followed his pins and his little ships with wonder, forgetting that our fathers were still waiting to go out on patrol (my father on the train for Washington, Bunker's already on the West Coast), seeing them already under way in the flat blue surfaces of the map. Later we would abandon Pearson and his map to bounce on the bed in the big front room, not noticing when he tried to keep us at his elbow with a word and a daring sweep of his ships. But just then we were rigid with attention and behind us our mothers watched intently, feeling, perhaps, as we did, that the order of map and pins, of models neatly placed, and a close, businesslike approach would help the war.

V

I visited Pearson at Brown in my senior year at college, after we had become friends again, after a lapse of many years in which I hated him. He had fooled around for a year before college and he had lost two years in the Marines, because of Korea, so that he was three years behind himself and would graduate in the same June as Bunker and me. As I remember it, both Swifts went to Bunker's June Week at the Academy, and in another June I might have gone. I know how it must have been: Captain Swift military and almost embarrassingly proud, Mrs. Swift in a garden-party hat, a tribute to every Navy wife, ushering Bunker's girl of the moment, a little redhead named Julie, whom he almost married later that month. Pearson would have been there but he was finishing his exams. The way he was that year, I think he would have seemed out of place in that bright, flowery June. I know that even in his absence his parents were aware of him. I think they thought about him even more than they did Bunker, perhaps more than they would have cared to admit.

Margaret Swift went to Providence for Pearson's commencement, but Jake was on the West Coast that weekend and couldn't get back, and Bunker—Ben by then, to everybody but me—was visiting Julie's family in Williamsburg My commencement was that same weekend, or I might have tried to go. As it was I sent a telegram in verse, and while he never said anything beyond the usual thanks, I think Pearson was grateful, because it had been a rather drab little ceremony for him.

Pearson had three years on almost everybody else in his graduating class, but if he was set apart from the others it was not so much by his age as by the sense of isolation that troubled him even then. He always made it hard for people to do things for him. Talking to him, I might see how lonely he was and want to make up for all the years when I had cut him off, but there seemed to be no way. He was so diffident, so gaunt and funny-looking, his look so penetrating that he put people off even when reason told them that this word or that action would help. I don't mean to make him out as the Melancholy Dane. He had a sense of humor, his own kind of humor on his own terms, oblique and very quick, and it may have been some glint of this humor or of acute, almost tangible awareness in his look that made him formidable, because you saw him and knew, without even thinking it out, how quick he would be to notice anything half-hearted or false.

I remember once finding him in the living room in Florida, bunched in a corner of the couch after a fight with Bunker, stiff with fury because he had chosen a nickname and nothing he could say or do would make Bunker call him by that name. Bunker had gone off crying, the reason already forgotten, but Pearson would smoulder for days.

For some reason I hadn't sided with Bunker that day so I said, when he noticed me, "Hi, Perry." Then I shrank because he greeted me with a sardonic, gulping grin that mocked me, the nickname, that particular hope, even as his eyes brightened because he couldn't help hoping I would persist. At the time I saw only the teeth, the look, and when I tried to use the name again I choked and couldn't get it out. I knew how badly he wanted the nickname but I called him "Pearson" more pointedly after that, even when I wanted not to, making a point of using both syllables, not letting the second one slur as Bunker sometimes did. There are times when you have to admit to yourself that knowing something isn't enough to make it possible for you to act.

When I first accepted the weekend at Brown I wasn't even planning to see Pearson. I had gotten a cocky letter from my date, so full of plans that there wouldn't be any free time, unless I wanted to ask Pearson to come to the fraternity house that Sunday afternoon to see me before I left, to meet him in an aura of hangover and Sunday papers while Artie and his buddies watched. My date was Arthur Jones Morrison, a teddy-bear with almost no forehead, who wanted to be called Artie and claimed to be descended from John Paul Jones. Artie liked to play the big deal, falling on people's necks and shying away from anybody out of the ordinary, as if he might be classed with them by association. So far it had paid off, in his terms at least. He was his fraternity's social chairman that year, and in charge of buying furniture for the house. The quadrangle was fairly new, and that weekend Artie talked constantly about the price of the drapes and the couch, and described every stick of furniture that was still on order, managing to work in most of the catchwords of the season as he went. I knew Pearson well enough to want to spare him that.

In a way the weekend was fun, even though I knew I had disappointed Artie a little because I wasn't as tweedy as he had thought. He got drunk on Saturday night, getting me back to my room only because that night's dance was in the same hotel, trying to bring the elevator to our floor of the Taft by yanking at the little arrow above the door, and almost passing out just as he told me good night. I knew he wouldn't be around to pick me up until well after noon the next day, so after church I left a message at the desk and slipped away to see Pearson Swift.

Pearson's room was off campus in a high, brown-shingled boarding house. His landlady let me in, apparently pleased to find a girl calling on him, and left me sitting in a tall, dark paneled hallway while she called him down from his room. I was depressed but comforted by the quiet darkness, the single bright panel of sunlight refracted through the stained-glass window on the landing.

When the landlady came down she bustled into the kitchen without speaking to me and began working over the stove. I heard the pots and thought rather lonesomely of breakfast, because I wouldn't eat again until Artie pulled himself together and picked me up for lunch. A few minutes later I heard Pearson on the stairs and turned to see him, hurried and distracted, even more disjointed-looking than he had been the preceding summer, perhaps because he had lost his tan. His landlady appeared in the kitchen door, intercepting him before he could speak to me.

"I made you some eggs," she said. I think she had the idea that if she could catch him while he wasn't thinking, she could make him eat.

"Not now," he said stiffly, adding, "Thanks."

"You look peaked," she said, ignoring me. "You'll get run down if you don't eat."

He hesitated, embarrassed. "I don't—"

She appealed to me. "He doesn't care what he eats." Then she patted him on the arm. "You come."

You don't just touch Pearson like that. He pulled away,

suddenly cold and formal. "No thank you, Mrs. Consiglio."
I don't think he was even aware that she backed away from
him, hurt. He had already turned to tell me hello.

After a first stilted greeting he motioned and I followed
him upstairs. I thought I could hear Mrs. Consiglio scraping
the eggs into the trash as we went. It may have been this, or
the idea of being in a strange house in a strange city, but for
some reason I felt as adult as Pearson had always seemed, and
for the moment Pearson seemed almost approachable. He
was still tall, but he didn't loom the way he had when we
were children, and there was a kind of boyish self-con-
sciousness in the way he showed me into his room.

The room was dark, shadowed and spare, that stock, depressing combination of dark woodwork and Bronx cream.
If Pearson had ever learned to make his bunk in the service
he had given it up; he had spread an old Army blanket over
the disorder in deference to me and now he gestured to me
to sit down. There was a film on the bare window, and I
could make out a heap of dirty shirts and trousers under a
chair. One or two prints, good ones, were tacked to the
door and under them a calendar. Books spilled everywhere,
but for all the clutter the impression was of bleakness, of a
room occupied by someone who cared nothing for color,
for objects, for the junk that even the most indifferent at-
tract, like filings to a magnet, after a given time in a given
room.

For the first time, neither of us had anything to say.

He tossed a book at me—Rilke—and said, "You ought to
read this."

"I will," I said. (I never have.)

Remembering himself, he dug in his desk and came up
with a bottle of Harvey's. "Would you like a drink?"

I grinned, because this was the first time I had met Pearson the host, and said yes. He brought the sherry in heavy
crystal glasses which I remembered as being his grandmoth-
er's, clear, perfect and out of place in the tumble of his
room. "Mother left these," he said, as if I had asked, and
then grimaced. "I think she wanted to make drapes."

I eyed the window, tall, bare and cold-looking and said,
"It wouldn't be such a bad idea."

He turned abruptly, taking the offensive. "Where are you
staying?"

I tossed it off. "The Taft."

"Your mother would have a fit."

My chin went up and I think my voice was cold. "I'm the same at the Taft as anywhere else."

He looked at me sharply. "You are, aren't you?" Then he let his breath out, almost exasperatedly, as if he didn't see why I cared.

I was busy with a pile of papers at the end of his bed, confused by the chicken-tracks that separated themselves, only after I squinted, into letters and diagrams. They looked unbelievably complex. "Math?"

He shook his head. "It's a sort of take-off from the square of opposition. You know, in logic—"

"Doesn't look much like it."

"I'm taking it a little bit farther." He bent over it, the host, wanting to explain. "See, if you—" He started on one of the long, abstruse explanations that delighted him, not realizing he had lost me until he looked up at an important point and then let his voice trail off, disappointed, because he could see that my eyes had glazed. "Oh."

"You lost me," I said, wanting to apologize.

"It's just—" He did a wide circle with his hands, wanting to make me see. "If you could just—" Then he saw that he couldn't possibly explain it to me and had to laugh, even though there was a helplessness in the way he dropped his hands. "It's fun," he said.

I remember being surprised that he had never learned that there would be a point, in almost every discussion, when he'd leave his listener behind. I think now that he may have known but didn't want to let himself admit it. I may have wanted to tell him that, to tell him something. Instead I said, "How does it tie in with pre-med?"

He sighed. "It doesn't."

I riffled some of the papers. "You said you were planning on medical school."

"I am."

"I thought you were interested in it. Really interested." For some reason I needed for him to be interested, to be working with something in mind.

"I guess my parents still think so." His voice went flat. "I'm not."

I dropped the papers. "Maybe you'd better tell them."

He was already shaking his head. "It's too late. They're all geared up to it. They've been *telling* everybody." He began collecting the papers and stuffing them into his desk. "What the hell? Doctors are useful, in their way."

41

I knew it as well as he did, but the way Pearson said it, it was somehow beside the point. He was talking with a detachment, a matter-of-fact resignation that made my blood go cold.

"But if it's not what you want—"

"What if it's not?" His eyes were a clear, metallic grey. "If I have to be something, I might as well be something useful."

"Look, if you really care about this other thing, symbolic logic, or whatever it is, your parents are going to understand . . ."

He looked at me in a way that made me know he didn't care. "They're happy with the idea of me being a doctor, so why not? One thing's as good as another."

I banged my fist on my knee, fighting him. "It's *not*."

"It's the least I can do," he said without feeling. "Since I didn't try for the Academy—"

(I remembered Jake Swift talking of it a little bewilderedly. "He's *too* bright in a lot of ways. I think he wanted to do it for me, but he knew even before I did that it wouldn't work out. If he'd entered right after high school he'd be an ensign now, and not just—" and not being able to finish because even he didn't know exactly what he meant.)

"I guess he liked the idea of his son being in the family business," I said, thinking how proud Jake would have been.

Pearson went sullen. "I never wanted that." He straightened the rack of his shoulders with a jerk. "I'd look swell in uniform."

"This medical business," I said. "There's more to it than just *fixing* people. Maybe if you went into research—" I wanted more than anything to catch his fancy, to offer him something that would engage him. I wanted him to be *set*.

"Dad said I might want to go into Navy medicine," he said, pretending not to hear. He was trying it out on me. "What do you think?"

"Well—" I didn't know what he wanted to hear.

"The pay is pretty good." He seemed to be trying to convince himself. "Maybe I wouldn't look so bad in uniform. What do you think?"

I was working on the Army blanket, smoothing down the edges. I thought of Pearson in uniform and then his brother rose up in his place, lean and perfect in khakis, and I found myself forgetting to answer, saying instead, "How's Bunker doing?" because I had to know.

Pearson looked at me closely and then, with great tact,

pretended to go through the confusion of papers on his desk.

"I mean," I went on carefully, "I mean, I just wondered if you'd heard from him."

He shrugged. "We don't write. Mom says he's putting in for subs." He pulled out the desk chair and sat down. "The family business."

I nodded, satisfied because there was nothing in the answer to give me extra worry, to add to the feeling of responsibility for Bunker that I had carried since one day the summer before. Subs seemed appropriate. Our father's were both in submarines, and if I had been a boy it would have been right for me to be groomed for the Academy, to follow Daddy as Bunker was following Jake. I had more feeling for it than Pearson, for a number of reasons. I loved it and I always would, but by that time I had grown enough to realize that even if I had been a boy, I would never have belonged at the Academy. "It's kind of nice to have one of us carrying on." I rushed on, wanting to catch Pearson off guard, to surprise him into an answer that would mean something. "How about you?"

He straightened defensively. "I told you. Navy medicine."

"You don't give a damn about Navy medicine." I was on my feet now, riffling through the papers on his desk. "The stuff you're really interested in—it's so—abstract."

"It's a game," he said, dismissing it. "If I went into it, it wouldn't be long before I was finished with it."

I was furious with him. "How do you *know*?"

His look chilled me. "There's nothing you don't come to the end of in time."

"I suppose doctoring is different," I said, trying to bait him into some kind of stand. "You aren't even interested in it to start with, so that makes it better."

He must have seen that I was appalled, and he smiled, perhaps determined to show me a different face. "You're finished in that one too," he said, grinning as if we'd been having a pointless argument and he had me now. "That's its charm. You're finished before you start."

"Oh, sure." I sat down, disgusted with him. "With diseases taking over whole continents and people being splattered all over the highways and typhoid and encephalitis and bubonic plague—" I ran down finally, a little shaken by my own excitement and the encroaching shadows of the miseries I had conjured up.

"That's just the point," he said, still looking amused, dismissing the horrors without even examining them. Then

43

the smile, or shadow of a smile began to fade and his face went dead. "Anything I did would make an infinitesimal dent. Nothing I do will touch even a particle of a fraction of all your poor damn tortured billions. It's kind of appropriate, in a way." He looked so hopeless that I wanted to protest. "It shows you just exactly where you are."

"Pearson!" There didn't seem to be anything I could say. I wanted to give him a trees, rocks, clouds speech, to say something that would crack this profound, intolerable detachment, to say something that would make him *care,* but Pearson had rejected the one reason I knew for caring a long time ago, with arguments too elaborate for me to refute, and if he ever came to any sort of belief it would have to be on a long, tortuous road too devious for me to conceive of, too complex for me to chart.

"You're never an ensign in Navy Med," he said, more to himself than to me. "You intern as a lieutenant. Quarters, commissary—the works."

I forced a "Swell." He sounded so indifferent.

"Promotion guaranteed."

I was collecting my pocketbook, beginning to wonder when Artie would come. "That's nice to know."

Then, abandoning it with a sweep of the hand, he said, "You know what I think I'd like to do?" I think now that he hadn't thought of it before, that it had just come into his head and he was trying it out. "I'd like to go into intelligence." He looked at me, to see how I was taking it. He may have been offering it, just to please me.

"No kidding?" I was so relieved to see him looking interested that I think I overdid it. I said, "No kidding" again, and waited for him to go on.

"It would be different, maybe dangerous." He leaned forward. "There might be something I could do, some point to it."

"You'd have to pass a heap of tests."

He looked down his nose. "I'd do all right. I can fake a personality as normal as Shirley Temple on those psychological tests."

I laughed.

"No kidding," he said. "I've had enough psychology to be able to pull it off."

"You'd need a language."

"Russian. I've been teaching myself to read it anyway. They have intensive language schools. Two months and I'd be *zound*-ing lige a *nay*-dive." He managed a wild, Cossack look.

"But what would you do? I can't see you throwing bombs."

He thought about throwing bombs for a minute, and I could tell he rather liked the idea. "Reconaissance. Remember those maps? I'd be great in reconaissance." He leaned forward again, begging me to egg him on.

"Reports and stuff?"

"I'd hole up in some border town and go across for information. Send it back on a radio—" He was animated now.

"—concealed in your cigarette pack."

"I'd end up with a citation. Service to my country. No kidding, I think I could do some good." He waited, wanting me to encourage him.

"Twice as much good as some ensign," I said. By now I was only half kidding.

He snorted. "Ensigns are machines. This would be real work, take real thought."

I wanted to keep him going. "You'd make a swell spy."

"Yeah." He was up and pacing now. He ended by the window, looking through the filmy glass. It was bleak midwinter outside. "Yeah, sure," he said dully, back in his chair in a tangle of joints before I could prod him on to a new idea, subsiding. "Screw it."

I hesitated just long enough so he would know that I was serious, if not about spying, then about wanting him to care about *something*, and then I said, "I don't know what you'd be doing, but you could have one hell of a career in CIA."

"Not me."

"I mean it," I said, trying to draw him back to it. It had been so good to see him going along, following an idea, even a crazy one, as if he might really be interested in something after all. "I've only heard rumors, but it sounds great. You'd have to figure out a lot of things for yourself, be on your own doing Lord knows what. Something important."

"Not for me, Denny. I'd come to the end of it, like everything else." He made a downward gesture, as if to stop me but I think that, as he had once before, he wanted me to persist.

"How could you?" I said, keeping on because I needed to spark his interest. "You can't come to the end of *people*. There are too damn many of them, and they're too involved."

He was hunched over in his chair, considering, when there was a tap on the door.

"C'min."

It was Artie, pouched-looking and puffing.

"Artie," I said. "Hi."

He pretended to crumple with exhaustion, hanging on the frame of the door. "You watching for forest-fires up here? I had to climb all the way up from hell."

I went to the door and motioned him in. Pearson was still slouched in his chair. "Pearson, this is my date, Artie Morrison."

Pearson grunted.

Artie made a face at me over his head.

"Artie, this is Pearson Swift."

"How the hell are you," Artie said and dropped on the bed, just beginning to look around Pearson's room.

Artie was done up in a rep tie and his grey flannel suit and his cordovans (the cordovans were new enough so that he still talked about "my cordovans"), and that particular day he'd put on his pink shirt (very much in that year). He gave me a onceover with approval—modest wool dress for Sunday dating—and without bothering to say anything further to Pearson, he looked around with distaste.

I can only explain what I did by saying that no matter who you are, there is a time when you need to ally yourself with the ordinary, when you are no more courageous than most. I followed Artie's eyes around the room, and without being able to help it I was suddenly embarrassed for Pearson, angular and uneasy in gabardines and a wide-collared shirt with a fine grey plaid in it, for his diffidence and his oddness, for the jumbled, cheerless air of his room, and when he said, "Even with people, you get to a certain point and then what?" trying to pull us back together in the old conversation, perhaps at a more important level, I let it go by, even though it was the last thing I wanted to do.

"That was some dance," Artie said.

Pearson had his head up, challenging, and I could see Artie shifting on the bed, shoe-looking, uncomfortable and almost bored, and even though I knew full well where my sympathies were, I waved Pearson's comment aside, and rattled because I knew Pearson sensed my embarrassment and was watching me acutely, I said, "You should have seen Artie at the dance," playing to my date, trying to win him back. I went on, in a burst of disloyalty, "He was smashed," associating myself for once and all with Artie and the pink shirt, even as Pearson withdrew.

"Smashed out of my mind," Artie said. Then he turned on Pearson. "You in a fraternity?"

Pearson had a dark, hawk glare. He drew in his feet. "No."

"About CIA—" I said, feeling terrible.

"Spy stuff," Artie broke in. "My Government prof thinks I ought to try for CIA."

I turned away from him, appealing to Pearson. "No, really, Pearson, if you just—"

Pearson didn't say anything.

"If I don't go into politics, of course," Artie said.

"Shut up, Artie." I wanted to make it all right with Pearson again. "Look, if you ever want a reference—"

"You said you had to get some lunch," Pearson said, shutting me out.

I sighed, already getting up. I knew Pearson well enough to know we were finished talking for the day. "Hey, thanks for the sherry."

He led the way to the door. "Thanks for coming, Denny." His eyes were bright, still friendly, as if nothing had happened that he wouldn't have expected if he had sat down ahead of time to think the morning out.

I stood back and let Artie go out, watching until he started down the stairs. Then I took Pearson's hand. "Thanks for having me." He tightened his fingers around mine in a quick, spastic grip that mended several things between us, and then turned and went back into his room.

I started downstairs then, feeling better. No matter what we did to each other, Pearson and I would never be completely at outs again. We had been alienated for too many years (until the summer before, when I came to the Swift's house for some word about Bunker and we talked for the first time in more than ten years) to cut each other off completely. But I counted that day as a loss, and wonder that I did not see that it foreshadowed more serious failures, more serious losses to come.

I caught up with Artie at the bottom of the stairs. He was jollying Mrs. Consiglio, and I had to wait while she fixed him a plate of eggs.

VI

We had barely gotten settled in Florida before the three of us—Bunker, Pearson and I—were thrust into three separate schools. I was to go to the parochial school several blocks from our house. My mother wasn't a Catholic but she was close enough to Daddy in understanding to want what he would want, and she arranged it and drove me to school that first day. Bunker would go off in the other direction, on foot, to the neighborhood public school, with his mother because it was the first day. He would make her tell him goodbye at the principal's office and go into the new class-room alone. Pearson, always inscrutably adult, had already boarded a bus for the junior high school halfway across town, not noticing as he counted his tokens that Bunker and I watched with envy.

Bunker and I stood awkwardly on the front walk in the cool morning, shuffling, not saying much, waiting for our mothers to finish their coffee and come along. Neither of us had wanted much breakfast.

"I wish it was at least the same school," I said.

Bunker was setting his feet one in front of the other, care-fully, because he had on new basketball shoes.

I kicked at the bole of a palm tree. My wool plaid skirt felt scratchy on my legs. "Or in the same block at least," I said.

Bunker was still putting heel to toe, heel to toe, follow-ing the border of the grass. "Why can't you come to my school?"

"I have to go to St. Anne's."

"That's dumb." Bunker turned and started back in my

direction, heel to toe, heel to toe. "Just tell 'em that you've changed your mind."

I began smoothing the dirt around the palm tree with my foot. I wasn't sure why, but I knew I wouldn't. I looked up. "Why don't you? You could come to my school. We could—"

"Not Catholic school," he said, not even letting me finish.

"Why not?"

He lifted his head with a flash of pride. "And get turned into one? I wouldn't."

"But—" I didn't want to go on, but I did. "But why?"

He looked puzzled, but his answer was quick and firm. "I just wouldn't."

In all the time we lived together I never saw Bunker's mother make any indication that she even noticed where I went to church or school, but I caught in Bunker's tone that day some edge of feeling that made me uneasy, that hinted at a backlog of difference, of a half-formed idea that I had never before had reason to suspect. It came to me then that I was usually the only Navy kid in my class, that Daddy and I seldom met anybody we knew at church and none of our friends ever went with us, and at the same time I remembered the few Protestant churches I had ever seen with a new fondness, as places where there was a lot of singing and no place to kneel down, where big-hatted ladies clustered on the front steps and chattered like kids at a party and life seemed much taken up with Bible pictures and church suppers. I found myself thinking that if that was all there was to it, it must be fun to be a Protestant; life seemed easier somehow, with less to worry about and nothing you really *had* to do. Bunker's reaction, unreasoned but as quick as if he understood, made the whole business seem unfair in a way. I wanted to press him on it, to try to find out more, but I knew better than to pursue it.

Just then our mothers came out and it was time to go.

"See you." Bunker waved his lunch-box bravely and started down the walk.

"See you," I said, and got into the car.

Everybody else in Sister Marcella's fourth grade had on a uniform—navy with a big collar and a battery of white buttons for the girls—and I would have given my soul and all my belongings to be wearing a uniform just then. Sister Marcella had on a habit which looked pinched and black after the generous white veils and gamps the nuns at my

49

old school had worn. I don't remember much about her, except that I think now she must have been very young. Her face was plump and her voice high, and it was easy to tell from the temper of the class that she was excitable.

One of the boys in the back said something about me and four of them began to giggle. The girls stared frankly and two boys in the front row began an argument in stage whispers, taking advantage of the fact that Sister Marcella was occupied with my mother at the door. She turned and told one of them to move to a back seat, talking without assurance, as if she wasn't positive she could make him go, and then waved me into the empty seat.

The kids around me stared over books and from behind hands and then began whispering to each other, boisterous and extra-loud because I was new and it made them feel so secure. This was my first indication, a sign which at the time I could not read, of how insulated, how isolated they were, growing up miles away from war and change in a quiet, dry Florida city where a new face in the classroom was such an uncommon thing that it would take them days to settle down. Kids in Navy towns are used to seeing new people come and go, quicker to make friends, but a school like St. Anne's in that time might get one, maybe two, new kids a year, and would take its time with them.

The boy behind me had just poked me in the back with his ruler to introduce himself when Sister Marcella whipped around.

"Children," she said, and her voice hit four notes, all of them uncertain.

The noise faded a little.

She turned back to my mother and the noise began again. The boy behind me, who had huge front teeth and hair like a black bird's nest, poked me and said, "What's your name?"

Behind him everybody else was whispering and poking and trying to get a better look at me.

"Denny," I said, just as Sister Marcella turned again.

"All right, class," she said. "Half an hour after school."

It worked. They were quiet until she had told my mother goodbye and turned back to us. At the door, my mother turned once before she closed it behind her and looked at me just long enough so that I knew she wished me well. I dipped my head, acknowledging her and then the door closed and I was alone.

Sister Marcella asked me to stand and introduced me to the class.

I could hear the hiss—"Denise-se-ise-denis-s-s-s-s-s-e"—as all of them tried it out. Then she made a signal and they mumbled a ragged hello in unison.

"All right," she said, and opened her book. It was catechism time.

The girl next to me had lank hair and a fever blister that reached almost to her nose. She kept dabbing at it with a Kleenex and I was so preoccupied with it, so oppressed, that I didn't pay much attention to anything else that day.

At noon Sister asked her to show me the way to the lunch room, checking to be sure I had a quarter for the hot meal, and then I found myself cast adrift with the girl, shuffling across the dusty grey sand and tufts of grass to the school cafeteria. We went through the line without saying much and then sat down on benches next to a window. The lunch was spaghetti, and in time it would be my favorite, but that day it seemed pallid and thin, no more than noodles chased through orange coloring and laid across a plate. I was so distracted by the fever blister sitting across from me that I didn't have much appetite. I got out one of the bombs from my Captain Midnight bombsight and began fooling with it, hoping we might begin to talk about the war.

In time the war would catch up with her through the movies, the maps in the paper, the shows on the radio, but that day she didn't even ask me what I was playing with. And when I said something about air raid drills in my old school, and the day they thought they spotted enemy planes a few miles off the coast and sent us all home, she looked bewildered and I got all tangled up in my hands, trying to explain, and finally said, "You know, the Japs."

"Oh, the Japs," she said, completely uninterested.

I excused myself as soon as I could and went outside, pretending to inspect the playground while everybody else ran and bounced and pretended not to stare. When we got home Bunker and I would look over Pearson's maps again, and from about five o'clock on the afternoon would go downhill as we rustled restlessly and hung around, waiting for the news. I spent most of the afternoon drawing flaming Zeroes in the margins of my new notebook, and I ran for the car after school without looking back, tremendously relieved to see my mother, the Navy sticker on the windshield and the base tags which we hadn't bothered to remove.

Bunker was brusque and businesslike when he came home. He had a little swagger because he'd been in touch with boys his own age again, and I think that for the moment he had forgotten the war. We sat on the curb without saying much, throwing rocks into the street. He asked me once what my new school was like and I shrugged and scaled another rock. The classroom full of new faces put me off—it always did—but that wasn't what troubled me. I don't know that I could have put it into words, or that I could explain it now, and instead of trying I said, "My bombsight's unpacked," and Bunker and I spent the rest of the afternoon setting up and bombing cardboard ships, using matchsticks to make extra loads of bombs.

After the news that night I helped my mother clear the table. I think all my questions were beginning to come to a boil, but the worries and the duties, the war and my being a Catholic were so tangled in my mind that there was nothing I could say, and when she turned unexpectedly and said "Denny, is something the matter?" I only said, "How long before I get my uniforms?"

"Mrs. Breen down the street is making them," she said, relieved, I think, that that was all I had asked. "They'll be ready Monday. Why?"

"I just wondered." I put the napkins in their rings in the buffet drawer: Bunker's, a round with the alphabet on it; Pearson's steel, initialled USN; mine, left over from babyhood, oval, with a standing duck. "Do I have to get oxfords?"

"They're part of the uniform," she said, and then sat down in the chair at the head of the table, the one with the arms, and pulled me onto her lap. "We'll take your picture in it and send it to Daddy."

I pressed my head against her for a minute before I got down. "Okay." Then I went outside looking for Bunker.

He had set up the ships in the side yard, and was messing with a rock and a board, trying to make a catapult.

"Hey, that's great," I said, and helped him set up an arrangement of boards and rocks, collecting ammo for him to fire at the ships.

Neither of us minded that it wasn't really a catapult, or that all our rocks fell short.

Then Pearson found us, and when he saw what we were doing he bent over the toy, examining first the board and then the rocks we were using.

"If you're going to hit anything, you've got to figure out a trajectory."

"Leave me alone," Bunker said.

"No, really," Pearson said, dropping in the dirt beside him. "You really ought to know about this."

Bunker dropped the rocks he was holding and sat back on his heels.

"Look." Pearson brought out a piece of paper. "Just pace it off and figure the angle of the board for the right trajectory. If you figure it right you can smash every ship." He paced the distance to the ship and then measured the board, disarranging Bunker's rocks to do it. He was already too interested in his figures to notice that Bunker was sitting on his heels with the stubborn look he got whenever anyone pushed too far into his business.

Pearson kept rearranging rocks and calculating, talking on and on. "If you don't get it on the first hit, work it out by bracketing—one short and one over." He turned to Bunker with a blind grin.

But Bunker's face was closed. I looked at him, wanting to offer something, but I knew he wouldn't want to be bothered and I fell back, letting Pearson talk on.

"The angle of the board is wrong for the distance. You have to multiply—" Pearson didn't even notice that Bunker squatted grimly, not listening. "Get it?"

Bunker stuck out his jaw.

"Okay," Pearson said, really wanting him to understand. "I'll give it to you again." He went through the whole business, explaining patiently, but talking too far beyond us to make any sense. When he finished he said, "Now do you get it?"

Bunker got up. "Go away."

"But this is so much easier—"

Bunker's ears were red. "I don't *care.*"

"You don't understand." Pearson got up, disturbed. "If you just understood—"

Bunker looked at him coldly. "Go to hell." Then he turned on his heel.

I remember shrinking a little, expecting one of Pearson's rages, but he seemed more puzzled than angry, a little hurt and confused, and when he spoke all he said was, "If he'd just try—"

Because I was troubled too I said, "Maybe he'd rather do it his way."

He turned on me. "There's a *better* way."

"He doesn't care," I said. "He'd rather be left alone."

He looked at me bleakly. "I know."

It would be a while before they would make it up but they would make it up, in a sort of tacit generosity that no child without brothers or sisters will ever fully understand. I knew better than to say anything more. Instead I went out front to find Bunker.

He was on the curb, tossing pebbles into the street, and he greeted me with a glare that warned me not to say anything, not to intrude.

I acknowledged the look and sat down and began tossing stones.

"Thanks," he said finally, after several minutes of silence.

I said, " 'S'okay."

We sat tossing pebbles into the street until it got dark.

The girl with the fever blister turned out to be named Betty Jean Howland, and once she decided I was all right and began to talk to me, I was able to see past the fever blister and we got to be pretty good friends. When it finally went away (in a matter of days) I didn't notice that it was gone, or remember that it had been there at all. The boy with the bird's nest hair was Richard Gallaher, who distracted Sister Marcella to tears and took all his punishment —extra writing, staying after school and, once, a crack on the head with his own arithmetic book—with huge good humor, giggling and making the rest of us laugh. By the end of the month I had my uniforms and found that even though I still regretted the isolation and missed Bunker, I was beginning to be at home at St. Anne's.

Bunker and I went our different ways on bicycles each morning, coming back to the half-deserted neighborhood after school each day, poking around for something or somebody new to take us out of ourselves, finally falling back on the talk that sustained us every afternoon. We would bring up everything we could remember about the sub base at New London, talking as if it were close and we could get on our bikes if we wanted to and pedal up to the main gate. And we talked about the war, about Zeroes and Messerschmitts, dwelling on the maps in the paper and plotting the Japs' progress across the Pacific, not ready even then to name the reason for our close involvement in the war. I was still troubled by the memory of our exchange that first day of school, by Bunker's blithe carelessness about certain things, his apparent freedom on Sunday mornings, but if there had been a time when I could talk about it, it had passed that same first day, with his instinctive rejection, with the pact of privacy we had sealed that night on the curbstone. If I was bewildered about the differences between us I was still sure in one idea: that I had to do everything I did as well, as completely, as I could because every hope, every certainty might hinge on it.

That spring all my preoccupatons fused and I found myself with the beginnings of an answer. It happened simply enough: we were having catechism, droning memorized answers to set questions as we had every school morning since the first grade.

"What is Baptism, Denise?" Sister Marcella said.

I stood up, tugging at my uniform, and said, "Baptism is the sacrament that gives our souls the new life of sanctifying grace by which we become children of God and heirs of heaven." Satisfied because I had gotten it off perfectly, I sat down.

Then she turned to Albert Hoffman, across the aisle, and said, as matter-of-factly, "Why are Baptism and Penance called the sacraments of the dead?"

He scraped to his feet, stalling, and in the itchy silence I found myself going over the last words of the question, hearing them, echoing and spooky, as they might be on some program on the radio.

"Of the dead." I let them echo, "of the dead, of the dead," and I found myself uneasy, not sure yet why.

"Well, Albert?"

He scratched. "Baptism and—P-penance—are—called— sacraments of the—"

"Dead," Sister Marcella prompted.

"Dead, because—uh—because—"

Sister finally gave up on Albert, putting a dark mark in her book, and turned to a bright, pinched little girl in the front row. "Roxanne?"

"Baptism and Penance are called sacraments of the dead because their chief purpose is to give the supernatural life of sanctifying grace to souls spiritually dead through sin." Roxanne finished her singsong and sat down.

If I remember the words so well now it's because we were drilled in catechism from the beginning. At first it's a matter of learning by heart to get through, and sometimes the meanings don't come in until years later, but almost every Catholic who has gone through this remembers it, at least vestigially, and whether he likes it or not he knows who he is and what he has to do.

"Why is Baptism necessary for the salvation of all men?" Sister Marcella paused, looking for somebody vulnerable, and then struck. "Richard."

I looked back. He was drawing on the cover of his catechism, but she should have known she couldn't catch him like that. He was bad, but he was bright. "Baptism is necessary for the salvation of all men because Christ has said: 'Unless a man be born again of water and the Spirit, he cannot enter into the kingdom of God.'" He made a prissy mouth, reeling off his answer in a fresh way that she wouldn't be able to pinpoint or punish, and then dropped his gaze to his book.

Ordinarily I would have giggled with the others, maybe a little louder than some to prove that I was OK, but I hesitated over the words, trying for the first time to sort them out. It seemed so relentless, so unequivocal. I thought of my mother and went cold.

"Protestants," I said finally, waving like a spastic until Sister turned and acknowledged me. "Does that mean Protestants are going to hell?"

She explained then, carefully and pointedly, that most Protestants baptized, still using the proper form, and I remember relaxing because my mother was an Episcopalian. All right. Then I thought of the Swifts, who weren't anything, and I remember my face tightening, straining with a question, but Sister Marcella had already turned to Betty Jean, and was going on.

"The priest is the usual minister of Baptism, but, if there is—" Betty Jean hesitated. She gave an even, uncomprehending inflection to every word.

"—danger," Sister Marcella said, to get her going again.

"—danger of somebody dying without Baptism, anyone else may and should baptize," Betty Jean finished, sitting down heavily.

The idea of tending the dying seemed so improbable that I didn't pay much attention when Sister Marcella described the form. I had my book open now because I had already had my turn and I was hurrying on to the next question, hanging on the answer when Sister pointed to another girl and it came.

"Those who through no fault of their own have not received the sacrament of Baptism can be saved through what is called baptism of blood or baptism of desire."

I knew about baptism of blood—martyrdom. And then, it seemed, came an answer that could let me relax a little: "An unbaptized person receives the baptism of desire when he loves God above all things and desires to do what is necessary for his salvation."

I sighed unevenly. Good enough. Bunker and Pearson could come to it on their own. They had plenty of time. Something still troubled me but I couldn't pursue it, or pin it down just then because we were putting our catechisms into our desks. It was time for arithmetic.

Then the day was over and I was on my bike, pedalling home alone. I used to ride looking down at the pavement as it went under my wheels, telling by dips or breaks in the concrete when I was coming to a corner and it was time to look up. I don't think I looked up at all that day, because my mind was going faster than the pavement, taken up with a new pride, a certain worry, whirring with possibilities. I was glad for once for any discomfort, for my differences, because all unprepared and unwittingly I had been born into the way—the Way, as it's written—and if I wanted Bunker to come into it, it wasn't because I wanted him to be like me but because the whole business was so consuming, so important that it could not be set aside. Even then I knew he wouldn't buy it from me, that it would never be my place to approach him on it; it was understood. But he had time. He had years. And I thought then of Jake Swift, halfway around the world with time running out, and me with no way to get word to him.

Perhaps I had a first dim understanding that our fathers, all the fathers, were vulnerable, but my mind turned on one father—not Daddy, who went to sea with silver-framed pictures of me and my mother, and a St. Christopher's medal tucked in his cap, whose vulnerability I would never be able to admit—but Bunker's father, the unbaptized one, cutting through dark waters without the water and the spirit, and in the fear which I would not name or entertain I fixed on him, adding his name to my prayers even as my bicycle jumped over the curb and I came up our front walk.

Bunker stalked down the steps just as I parked my bike. "They've taken Corregidor."

"Yellow rats," I said. "Damn yellow rats."

Bunker gnawed his lip. He seemed unsure. "Come look at the map."

We bent over it, jaws set, and in my concern I gave myself to maps and plane models and ship movements, renewing my close, consuming preoccupation with the war.

VII

All that summer we telephoned strangers. Bunker would open the book on the bedside table and read out a number while I dialed. Then we would yell into the telephone together. I made up the verse:

> Hotsy totsy, you're a Nazi.
> Fliggle flap, you're a Jap.

We always hung up before the person at the other end could say anything. It seemed to us that we were doing something for the war.

The war was everything to us. Our lives were so bound up in it that we went through the last weeks of school paying the barest attention to whether we got promoted or not, suspended in unreality from the time we got on our bicycles each morning until we came home in the afternoon, bumping over the curb and coasting the last few feet up the walk, hurrying inside so it could begin again. We followed the maps and arrows in the newspapers with fierce incomprehension and whispered the names of obscure islands like a litany, losing ourselves in them completely when school ended and we were alone in our half-deserted neighborhood. We kept war stamps and went to war movies and stayed up for radio shows about soldiers spurred on by the voices of valor and memory, trying out each new military phrase, using it until it passed into the language. We pressed tin cans and assembled the plane models that came in our cereal, taking in our feeling for our enemy and our country whole, so naturally that neither Bunker nor I could hear the Marine Hymn played without wanting to cry. (Sometimes I have trouble still.) There were late summer afternoons when Bunker and I were alone in the house and we crouched in the curve of the stairway with shoes or alarm clocks in tight fingers, ready to die killing the first Jap to come in the front door. To us, invasion seemed almost imminent.

Our mothers seemed to face the prospect with serenity. With their things gathered around them they tried to make life seem as it had always been, shopping, gardening, writing letters, apparently swept up in the order of the household, and there were times when it was a relief to go out on the screen porch and let them talk about how we were doing in school or when were we going to straighten our rooms, to rid ourselves of the terrible immediacy of the war.

Bunker is taller than Pearson now, and still blond, the perfect picture of the young Naval officer, but when I think of Bunker I always see him as he was in Florida, chunky, square-faced, with a short crew cut that we both thought made him look like a marine. He was much more even-tempered than I, and I think he must have been much more generous. In all the time we were in Florida I only saw him give way to anger twice, and both times he went more than half-way to make it up. I have never had a better friend.

If Bunker had been a little less open, a little harder to get along with, Pearson might not have seemed so unapproachable. As it was he never let down. If he lost his temper, some grownup would be sure to say "But Pearson, Bunker and Denny don't seem to mind. Why don't you—" and then his face would go red-and-black, clotted, and he'd turn without saying anything and go out of the room. Even then, I think he expected too much of us, of everything, and much of his anger came out of his disappointment, his refusal to settle for anything less. He towered over us like a grownup and he clumped through the house like Heathcliff, so adult that we spent every free moment teasing him.

There were times when I sensed some kinship with him and tried to draw him into something I was doing, but he had lumped me with Bunker in his mind, as a little kid, beneath contempt.

He came into the living room one day to find me reading the Beowulf. Don't ask me how I happened to be reading the Beowulf. It was in the back of a book on Robin Hood that I'd brought home, and I don't know now whether it was a cut version or the real thing. It had plenty of gore, great for kids. I was in the corner of the sofa, with my feet up and one of the seat cushions behind my back, when Pearson came in.

He riffled a stack of newspapers on his mother's morocco hassock, brooding, and then went to the submarine model on the mantel, a present to Daddy from his last crew. Bunker and I had agreed tacitly that nothing would happen to either of our fathers (though I might worry about his secretly, and he mine) but I could see that Pearson had no such protective discipline of mind, that he was thinking about his father, and because secretly I thought he had good reason I wished there was something I could say to him.

He had pressed his forehead against the mantel.

I rattled and he jumped. He turned quickly, with such a look of resentment at being caught that I had to say something, to make it better. I pretended I hadn't noticed and said, "Hey, have you read this book?"

His face began to cloud. "No."

"It's about this monster named Grendel." I saw him brighten a little. "They tear off his arm and beat him over the head with it."

I could tell from his expression that he had read it, and I think he was so lonely that for the minute he wanted to give in and talk to me, just to be talking to someone else about something, anything, I think. He hesitated, turning to straighten the submarine so I wouldn't see his face, and then he heard Bunker outside. He drew back then and said instead, "You shouldn't be reading stuff like that."

"They go down into this mere for Grendel's mother," I said, still trying to reach him. "Terrible fights under water."

He set his jaw. "You shouldn't read that."

I sat up. "Why not?"

He had to recover himself. "That isn't for little kids."

"I'm not a—"

But by then he had turned and gone out of the room.

"All right for you," I said, and at dinner that night I swiped his piece of cake. He wrestled me for it in the driveway, but by that time it was too late.

By the time the Swifts left Florida I hated him. If things had happened a little differently, I might hate him still. I can understand why he hit us that day in the bedroom, but even now I can never forget.

We were on the telephone again. Letters had come for Bunker and me that morning and we felt good, smug because we had answered right away, including pictures of flaming Zeroes with insignia colored in with crayon on the

61

V-Mail forms, relieved because today at least we knew our fathers were all right. There had been nothing for Pearson except a note included in the letter to his mother, and she had read the paragraph to all of us, stopping at the end because, she said, the rest of it was secret. Remembering the posters about spies who might be listening, we said we understood. A second sense kept us from twitting Pearson about not getting a letter, but the same instinct that told us he was vulnerable demanded that we do something about it, so we hid his maps and stuck all his pins in the underside of his pillow, where he would find them when he got into bed. Then, before he could come upstairs to his room and find the maps were missing, we went into our mothers' room and got on the telephone. We were on the floor, between the twin beds, yelling the challenge in unison, when the door opened and Pearson came in.

"What in hell are you doing?" His hair was ruffled, and I could tell he was worried about the maps.

We said "Nothing," and hung up.

I got up first, and faced up to him. "Besides, you shouldn't say 'hell.'"

"You were calling the neighbors again, weren't you?" He let his voice drop a register, sounding so adult that it irritated me.

Bunker was on one of the beds now, playing with the tufts of white chenille. "We wouldn't call the neighbors," he said, and he was so beautifully innocent that I had to cover a laugh.

"You were calling absolute strangers?"

Bunker came around the end of the bed and we stood together, uncomfortable because we had to look up such a long way to talk to him. "Spies," we said. "We're getting rid of spies."

He was turning red. "The hell. Cut it out or I'm going to tell."

I was still feeling good about the letter, and because I liked the sound of it I said, "I'm going to tell you said the hell," and said it again.

Bunker picked it up, and without having to look at each other or at Pearson, we lunged forward and tackled him.

We were all on the floor when Bunker's mother poked her head in and we sorted ourselves out and got up, thinking the noise had brought her, trying for some semblance of respect.

"Denny," she said, ignoring the tangle, and when I got up, she motioned me out of the room.

I could feel rather than see Bunker and Pearson coming to their feet behind me, bumping together anxiously, crowding to the door.

It was dark and chilly in the hall, but that was a time when a sudden summons made any room chilly, when, no matter how well you kept your fears unformed, you thought "Telegram" defensively every time a grown-up called you, believing that things you worried about never came true.

Mrs. Swift was standing under the stained-glass window, white and somehow thinner, with colored sunlight in her hair.

I said, "Where's Mom?" and swallowed, wanting to put off knowing, at the same time wanting to get it over, if there was something to get over, before I died of holding my breath.

"She's lying down," Mrs. Swift said, trying to do something with her hands. Then she said "Missing," convulsively, because that's all she needed to say, nodding when I said "Daddy?" and reached out to comfort me.

I pulled away from her, thinking of my father missing, not fully realizing it but trembling and furious, suspended and almost exploding with the need for action, because there had to be something I could do.

Pearson was standing in the doorway when I turned; he and Bunker had been listening. I don't know what he expected, or what he wanted to say. I pushed past him, punching at him, and Bunker seemed to know what I wanted because he was at the telephone before me, dialling blindly, and the two of us, not thinking of anything but what we were doing, screamed our war verse into the telephone. We dialled again and again, not caring whether we got numbers or not, yelling until we reached someone at last and a voice yelled back. Then without being able to help it we dropped the receiver and laughed at the tinny, angry little voice.

"What in *hell* do you think you're doing?" Pearson was standing over us, eyes tight in his red face, black brows meshing, and we turned as one and screamed the verse at him, until I thought our insides would come up with the words.

"You little bastards." He grabbed at us, shaking us by the shoulders, and said, "Don't you know what's happened?"

and when we kept screaming let us go and hit each of us as hard as he could on the side of the head, flailing, still hitting, even after we had ducked away from him, bawling with rage. He was loud, incoherent, and I think he was crying too.

I don't remember what I said or did—but I think Pearson knew how much I hated him.

I'm not clear what happened after that, but I know when you're that age you go to bed for the day and pretend it never happened, and someone brings you supper on a tray. My mother and I ate together that night, on a little table Bunker's mother set up in my room. It was a tremulous time. I was in bed the next day too, I think; my mother and I seem to have been insulated, like convalescents, gathering strength in separate rooms, and it was while we were still in bed that Sister Marcella and the Mother Superior came.

I was in bed reading, almost managing to forget everything, when they appeared at the door, bobbing their heads, and came into the room.

Sister Marcella did most of the talking, the usual stuff about Daddy being with the angels, making me think about something I didn't want to think about, about God and losing Daddy and how it could all happen, picking at it until I sat upright and said,

"He can't be missing," loud and furious, sure now that he was missing because God or I had failed somehow, because none of my prayers had done Daddy any good.

Mother Superior leaned forward then, elbowing Sister Marcella aside. She was short and heavy-set, almost square, and she had a firm, plain face with a light fringe of whiskers in one place on her chin. She was tremendously calm.

"Nobody promised you he wouldn't, Denny."

I gnawed my mouth, furious. "But I did everything I could—I prayed—" I was trembling, outraged, trying to make it easier for myself by placing some blame and wanting badly for her to tell me how sorely I had been wronged.

Instead she straightened, as if I were an adult, and said, "Nobody said it was supposed to be easy."

Then I bent my head and said, "I know."

We sat in silence for a few minutes and then the sisters got up to leave. Mother turned in the door and said one more thing. "He will never really be gone."

I watched her, straining with my whole body, trying to catch her meaning, and as she left I began to realize that she was right. It was true in one way, because my mind was filled with a thousand pictures and memories, snatches of Daddy that would revisit me for the rest of my life and give him a particular kind of existence that will endure as long as I have an atom of memory, and it was true in another way that had little to do with Sister Marcella's platitudes about the angels, in a deeper way which I was not then ready to understand. Since then, even though Daddy has been declared officially dead and there has been a requiem, I have never thought of him as really dead.

As I remember it, it was easy for me to cry after the sisters left, and once I had cried it was easier for me to get myself together.

Bunker brought a pint of ice cream up to my room after supper and we ate it all by ourselves, without saying anything. We pretended we weren't talking because we were so busy eating, and when there was nothing left to eat and nothing to say Bunker scratched nervously, letting out breath he must have been holding for some time and said, "I got to go," and I said, "Okay," settling under the covers again, not caring how long I had to stay in bed.

The next morning my mother was downstairs again in a jersey print dress and leg makeup instead of stockings, doing things as she always had, and I knew it was time to get up. Bunker and I talked about finding my father on one of those islands, and then understood that it was better not to talk about it, even that way, and went out to play.

There was a tree stump embedded in the side yard, waist-high and splintered where Bunker and I had chipped at it with screwdrivers driven by rocks. We had the idea that if we kept at it, we could demolish the whole stump some day. That day we went at it directly, with a gardening fork and a trowel, chopping murderously because it made us feel better somehow, and because today at least, war games were not appropriate. It was a while before we noticed that Pearson was behind us, watching with his shoulders hunched and his face locked, and when I turned for a fraction of a second and saw him, I hit the stump so hard that Bunker jerked his head up, knowing Pearson must be there.

He grimaced, face clotting with the terrible effort, and said, "Hi."

Bunker managed a half-salute and turned to the stump again. We hacked grimly, ignoring Pearson, and Bunker must have felt some of the same need for solidarity that I did, because our strokes slowed and we were hacking in unison, engrossed in the feeling of working side by side.

Pearson approached once, backing away again when Bunker paused and said curtly, "Watch out for chips." He waited at a distance and kept on waiting, until I wondered whether our arms were going to give out while he was still watching, and we would have to quit.

When our strokes had slowed to almost nothing, Pearson moved in and tried to say something. Bunker motioned me to stop, pretending that we did it just so we could hear what he had to say. We had to rest our arms.

". . . thinking about going to the movies," he was saying. "It's Pinocchio. You guys want to come?"

I wouldn't even look at him, but Bunker shook his head and then, switching hands, went back to the stump.

Pearson drifted until he was right next to us. "You know. Walt Disney." And then, when Bunker kept on chopping he said, loud, "My treat. OK?"

Bunker paused for a minute. He seemed to be waiting for me.

"That's that," I said, and pretended to be dusting the stump. Then we put down our trowels without answering and walked away.

We didn't see him again until late afternoon, when Bunker and I were sitting on the second-floor screen porch, tilted back in chairs with our feet up on the rail.

Pearson came out and messed with his boat collection. He was making models of the fleet out of cardboard and balsa wood. He bent over them in a corner behind us, while Bunker and I stared out through the dusty screen, squinting until the mesh merged with the trees beyond, and I had almost managed to stop thinking about anything when I realized that Bunker was looking at Pearson through the wicker back of his chair.

Pearson seemed to know it and he straightened, looking big and red and awkward. I had never seen him hang around so much before. Then he made a terrible face and said, "Hey you guys, the phone—"

Bunker looked at me quickly. Pearson was watching me too, through the frame of wicker, and because it was important to keep hating him, because there had to be *something* to hate for what had happened I tried to make my face go hard. He may not have seen it, through the wicker, because he seemed to bloat a little, miserable, and said "I mean I'm sorry," and then just kept standing, not knowing what to do next.

Because it had been my father, Bunker deferred to me, and when I leaned back there was a long pause while Bunker and I put our feet back on the rail.

Behind us Pearson was still standing. It might have been different if he had gone away mad then, as he would have any other day. But he just stood there, not giving up, and when he thought we were looking he scrubbed his fist across his mouth and said, "Who's for a Popsicle?"

And Bunker must have been drawn by his look of misery because in his essential kindness he leaned out, betraying me, and poked his head around the fan back of his chair. "OK."

"See you in a minute," Pearson mumbled, turning in a rush so Bunker couldn't see his face. "I've got to get some dough." He pushed the boats away not caring how they landed and banged into the house.

Then Bunker looked at me and said, "You coming?"

My face was so stiff that I couldn't answer, so I just shook my head.

He was on his feet, almost as red as Pearson, and his scalp shone pinkly through the blond crew cut. "You sure?"

Everything piled up and I flashed at him. "How could you, after what he did?"

Bunker shrugged, begging me to forgive him because he couldn't explain, and followed Pearson into the house.

He was on my bed with a new model Howitzer the next morning, and because I loved him and I couldn't really blame him for the betrayal, because I could not sustain any more losses, I accepted him and war games resumed. They were consuming, more intense than ever because of the brief respite—better, vacuum—but no matter how engrossed Bunker and I became there was between us an almost imperceptible curtain of difference, of reserve. I remember half-wishing, without wanting to, that there would be a telegram for Bunker too, not to hurt him, but so we would be alike again, and closer together. I knew more than he did now, and could comfort him.

I must have said a few words to Pearson—to ask for my turn in the bathroom, or to ask him to pass the butter—but I don't remember ever speaking to him again. Later, when we were in our twenties, he was able to forgive almost anything I might say or do, consciously or unconsciously, to hurt him, because he understood better than I did what had happened in the bedroom that day to make me hate him for so many years.

It had to happen that our mothers drifted apart, his under the strain of living with mine and pretending that things hadn't changed, mine because it is so hard to live with the living, and Bunker and his family moved away at the end of that year.

We spent that last day as we'd spent a hundred others, poring over funnybooks and atrocity pictures in LIFE and books of plane silhouettes, studying them so we could spot the enemy when he came into our skies. I think Pearson may have wanted to make one last stab at regaining me, and it is to his credit that he did not intrude that day. Bunker and I played fast because we had to get everything in, but without conviction, because the movers had already come for the Swifts' furniture and Bunker's mind was fixed on Norfolk where he would rejoin his father, so that for us, that particular phase of the war had come to an end. When the car pulled away the next morning Bunker leaned out of the back window with the same awful grin I knew I must be wearing, and despite his betrayal, despite the fact that he was riding in the backseat with Pearson by choice we looked at each other with a love that had nothing to do with romance and survives still, even though the time of rupture and change had begun for us long before that day.

The car turned the corner. Mrs. Swift blew the horn once and then the street was still. My mother, in a printed voile dress, was behind me, face still turned to the corner, looking almost disjointed in her last wave of goodbye. She turned, letting her arm drop, and said, "Well, Denny," in a breathless voice.

I worked my face, unable to speak.

"It's Charlie McCarthy night. Would you rather stay up and listen or would you rather go to the show."

"The show," I said and then, because she seemed to need it, I said, "Maybe we could have waffles?"

"Waffles." She managed a smile. "What a good idea. Then we'll get all dressed up and go down to the Florida."

"Great," I said, wanting to run and cling to her legs.

She held out one hand casually, waiting until I caught up and took her fingers. "We'd better hurry if we're going to get everything done."

We went into the house together, glad to have something to hurry for. Inside, I folded the map Pearson had left behind and put the pins away, sticking them in my mother's tomato pincushion, red cotton and filled with sand. My mother and I moved around the house uneasily at first, re-arranging furniture so that it wouldn't look so bare without the Swifts' things, so our stuff would look more as if it filled the place. I think now that we must have seen the place with a new, proprietary air. We would get some new pieces and make new drapes, because this wasn't for the duration any more. For us, the war was over, and from now on this would be home.

VIII

"I don't know what she thinks she's doing," Pat said. He pulled his mouth down and let his eyes go long in his face, like a basset hound's. "She probably wants me to see what I missed."

"Oh, Pat, come *on*." I looked through the window behind him, at the statuary in the court. We were in the cafeteria at the Museum of Modern Art. I go there every time I'm in New York and sit for a few minutes in front of The Moon, watching the network of silver wires and then the shadows on the ceiling above it, and I'm still not absolutely sure it's the moon that's moving, and not the shadows alone. It had seemed like a good place to meet Pat.

He ran his hand through his hair, trying to ruff it up, but by that time he was going to a good barber and it fell back smoothly, close to his head. He hadn't realized that he would always be a little too well-groomed, too civilized to be a tragic figure. "She wants me to see how close they are," he said bitterly. "Maybe it isn't even that. I'm an escort service."

"If I wanted an escort I'd hire a St. Bernard," I said, losing patience. "It would have been easier for me to stay on the train." I had come up from Washington, where I was trying out a museum job—my first job after graduation —and not liking it, and Katherine had asked me to get off in New York, meet Pat and ride the rest of the way to Stamford with him. No matter how simply you wanted to do things, when you tried to do them with Katherine they got baroque.

("I want to see him, but if he comes alone he'll go into

70

his act—you know." It was typical of Katherine, newly married, to invite Pat whom she had almost married to visit her, to try to domesticate him, to fit him to her image of the faithful family friend, perhaps not totally aware of the situation she was creating, but aware enough to find some excitement in it. And it was typical of her to invite me at the same time, in a burst of careless generosity, wanting some of the same kind of happiness she had for me, but competing in all innocence even as she tried to match me up with Pat, because she would expect his attention for her to be as flattering as it had always been.)

Pat was saying, "Maybe I won't go."

I slapped my fork on the table. "Oh, fine. Fine." I knew as well as Pat did that he was going, but he had something on his mind, a scene we would have to get through before he would be ready to leave for the train. Pat loved scenes. "Okay," I said. "Why don't you want to go?"

"I'm not up to it."

"Oh?" I was trying to sound cold. I think I expected him to make a little speech about losing Katherine, to have me console him and then be on our way.

"I've *had* newlyweds. Up to here."

It stopped me. Katherine was the first of my good friends to marry, and I hadn't seen her since. Perhaps because she was the first and I hadn't given it much thought, I still put marriage in a class with lived-happily-ever-after, a conclusion to a set piece, not necessarily happy, not necessarily sad but finished, something you said "There" to, with a sense of something accomplished, expecting the people involved to stay where they were put.

Pat said, "They cloy."

I thought of Katherine engaged, greeting Jim with a look so brilliant that I had to look away. "They don't think so."

"They will."

"Huh?" I still wasn't sure what he was getting at.

"I saw Bro Richards and his wife right after their honeymoon. It was like being in a kennel—all those close bodies, all that close air."

"You're being pretty hard on them."

Pat turned down the corners of his mouth in a reverse grin. "I think things were getting a little too close for *Bro*."

I picked up my fork and ran it around the edge of my chocolate pie, separating the filling from the crust. "That's what marriage is supposed to be about. Being close." I didn't particularly like what he was trying to say but I was egg-ing him on. If he was going to be ugly it was better for him to get it out of his system before we got to Kat's.

"But it's so *constant*. Making love and then making the bed. Always being with the person and never being able to get away."

If I was embarrassed I must not have showed it, because Pat went on. "It's so constant that even they get sick of it." There are times when Pat's eyes seem to catch and refract all the light in a room. He had turned his face to the plate glass, with a bright, burning look. "Love shouldn't be that way."

"It changes," I said, trying to think it out. It's usually hard to pin Pat down in one of his dialogues, and it's hard to remember that your words are probably wasted because he's only toying with an idea, doing a bit. "It accommodates. By the time people are married for a while it's probably a different sort of thing."

"Love ought to be quick. It shouldn't have to end in boredom." He clinked the salt and pepper together and separated them. "You ought to be able to hit and run."

I couldn't help it. I started laughing.

"What's the matter?"

I pushed my pie over to him to make amends. "You're such a damn romantic."

That pleased him, and he slid the chocolate pie between the salt and pepper and began to eat.

We were finishing our cigarettes when Pat half-stood to wave to somebody at the door. I turned quickly to see.

"Here's Norty," he said. "He's going to take us to the train."

Norty came over to the table, looking rushed. He was tall, well put-together, a little petulant in a tab collar and a dacron herringbone suit. He moved like a personage, someone who is confident of being remembered, who never has to reintroduce himself, and although he had been introduced to me three times in New Haven, it was obvious that he didn't know who I was.

"Denny, you know Norton Jarboe," Pat said. "Norty, you remember Denny McLeod."

"Of course," Norty said, still not remembering me. "Glad to see you again." He stood behind my chair gallantly, pulling it out. "Let's get with it," he said to Pat. "Glenda's double-parked out front."

Glenda was leaning out of the Hillman as we got to the curb. We had talked several times in New Haven, on the two spring weekends when Katherine and I went up to see Pat and Mack Glendauer. It was usually at parties while Norty was off buddying it up with one classmate or another. There were times when he didn't seem to remember Glenda, perhaps forgetting to get back to her when a party broke up because he didn't want to admit it was over and go home. He seemed to like to pretend he was as free as the others, drinking coffee in some greasy spoon and then curling up on somebody's couch in Saybrook for the rest of the night. He and Glenda had been married in his freshman year. It wasn't a Quonset-hut sort of thing; their parents were financing them in a garden apartment done up to look like a picture in a woman's magazine. Glenda was tall and dark-haired, better-looking and better-dressed than most of the college girls who came to New Haven, but sad somehow because she'd been pushed into an adult world without time for transition, for being sloppy or irresponsible. One night Mack Glendauer and I took her home from a party, paying the baby-sitter for her because she didn't have any change, and Glenda must have been thinking about that night because she said "Denny," with a particular warmth, as Pat opened the door and I got into the back of the car.

I said "Hi," a little shy with her.

"We haven't *seen* you." She seemed sorry.

"How's Sarah?"

"Oh, she's fine." Glenda was obviously pleased that I remembered. "We're having a huge birthday party for her next week. Eight kids."

"No kidding."

She looked superb, tawny despite the dark hair, perhaps because of her tan, maybe because of the way her hair curved around her face. I bunched up my raincoat, feeling travel-stained, and wadded it in a corner of the car.

"If it isn't one damn thing it's another," Norty said, getting in.

Pat closed the door. "Some kid'll go home mad. Every birthday party, one kid cries and goes home mad."

"We made you a bon voyage basket," Glenda said, and started the car.

"Oh, yeah." Norty reached down between his feet and came up with a battered purple-and-yellow Easter basket, handing it to Pat. "Bon Voyage."

"You shouldn't have." Pat took it on his lap. "For Denny too?"

Glenda giggled nervously. "More or less."

Pat started pawing through it. There were peaches and bananas, something he wouldn't show me, whiskey in a plastic baby bottle and a little stack of paper cups. "It's too beautiful."

Glenda began, "We couldn't let you go all that way without—"

"It's just till Monday." Pat laughed.

"But here you are going—"

"Watch that cab," Norty said.

"—off to foreign places. We thought you needed a little something for the road."

"It was Glenda's idea." Norty yawned.

Pat leaned over the seat and pecked her on the cheek. "My dear, it's beautiful."

"Pat, you made me run that light!"

Pat ran a hand over her hair. "Stop a minute, and I'll tell that officer."

"Pat, shut up!" She ducked her head, hiding a smile.

Norty turned to Pat. "You'll never guess who I saw yesterday." He went into a story about one of his beloved classmates, embroidering—with gestures—until we had to laugh. ". . . engaged to a redhead," he said, building to a climax. "With great gelatinous eyes."

Glenda cut in, bringing him down. "Norty, here's the station. Where shall I park?"

He broke off, glowering. "Leave it anywhere."

She seemed to be sitting up a little straighter. "But where?"

"Why the hell should I care? Just find a good spot."

She poked her head out the window. "Maybe I should drive through the cab tunnel and just let everybody off. Or do you think I should park?"

Norty shifted impatiently. "Suit yourself."

"If you think I should, I'll park."

"So park."

"Hardcastle is living in Stamford," Pat said, trying to change the subject. "I thought I might look him up."

"Norty, you're on the right side. See if you see a place."

"Not a thing," Norty said without looking.

I don't know why, but she kept at it. She seemed to want to make him responsible, if not for the way her life had gone, at least for this small thing. "Look, just pick me out a place and I'll park."

"You're driving. You find a place."

"Or a lot. I could go into a lot. What do you think?"

Norty barked. "I don't *care*."

"I've brought you all the way down from 53rd Street. The *least* you can do is poke your head out and find a place." She pretended she was kidding, but there was a vindictive note that made me uncomfortable.

"You poke *your* head out."

"I'm on the wrong side of the car," Glenda said. "It's easier for you."

Pat and I finally got out at a corner and walked the rest of the way to the station, leaving them still wrangling about the car. Norty stopped long enough to offer to drive us to Stamford but Pat shook his head. We were both glad to get away. I half-expected Pat to say "See," or "I told you so," when we hit the sidewalk, but he had already forgotten and was hurrying for the train.

We were both nerved up about the visit, Pat because he may have wanted to tell himself he still loved Katherine and was afraid seeing her might change his mind, I because I had been sure marriage would make her different no matter what she promised, and I made friends so hard and slowly that it was difficult for me to deal with any change. Now we clumped around in the little metal cage at the end of the railroad car, stalling, trying to get a look at Katherine before she saw us, trying to compose ourselves before the train stopped for good and we clattered down the steps. The car made its final jerk. Pat let out his breath, craning over my head to see Katherine, and said,

"Here we are."

She was on the station platform in sneakers and a raincoat she'd had for as long as I could remember, chewing her knuckles, looking unchanged, no older or more organized than she'd been the night before her wedding, when she and I had put on shorts with our pajama tops and had talked on the screen porch until three. Her hair was a little different —maybe she'd tried to do something with it and failed—but underneath the raincoat she had on a button-down shirt and a pair of khaki shorts I'd seen her in a hundred times.

Pat was on my heels as I hit the platform, first hesitant, perhaps still trying for a pose, then assured, and I remember being surprised that he seemed bigger somehow, businesslike and self-possessed. He'd confessed on the train that his attaché case was for his toothbrush and extra underwear but now he handled it smartly, as if it were packed with contracts or stock certificates. Then he set it down in front of Kat, seeming to get taller as I watched and said, "I was going to get you a bottle in the city but there wasn't time."

Her face was a mixture, changing as I watched from eager to expressionless to tentative as she tried for a soignée, suburban housewife look and then gave it up because she had never been able to make herself look any way she didn't feel. She spraddled her feet in the sneakers and confessed, "I've been nervous as a goat." She was looking at me.

I got red and then said "Hey," as I always had, elbowing her. She pretended to be off balance and bounced a step, taking Pat's arm to catch herself.

"We never had houseguests before."

"We needed a trip to the country," he said grandly.

She drew back, pleading with him. "You were great to come."

He softened. "Hey, I'm glad I did." Then he picked up his attaché case and my suitcase, looking smaller, more vulnerable, Pat again, and we followed Katherine to the car.

It was a Ford, about four years old, with Jim's fishing equipment in the back and crumbs and old sandwich papers on the seat. It wouldn't start until we cursed it, and by the time we'd trotted out our favorite combinations we were all feeling more normal, so that we talked without stopping until Katherine turned into a side street and pulled up in front of a house.

The place was small and hideous—on one of those terraced little hills that looks best planted with ivy and is usually given over to weeds—stucco, with a wrought-iron house number on a Scottie in silhouette, a peaked shingled roof and an overlay of dark boards that was supposed to make it look Tudor. The stucco was dirty in spots where somebody had thinned the ivy on the front. There was a screen porch on one side; the rusty screen sagged and in one or two places it had rotted away. A big tree in the side yard overhung the roof, dropping yellow flowers in limp, heavy sprays that covered the dawn and cluttered the walk.

"This is it," Kat said, and I'd never seen her so proud. "Isn't it great?"

"It's swell," I said, glad she was leading the way because she had always been able to read my face.

"Nice neighborhood," Pat said, turning his head and sniffing the air.

There was a confusion at the door while Katherine found her keys and let us in.

Katherine had been in the house a month, since the honeymoon, and things still had a cluttered, disorganized look, with one or two unopened wedding presents stacked in a corner of the dining room and crates put here and there as tables, covered with swatches of some bright-colored cloth.

If Pat is troubled by the kennel atmosphere as he says, it is the disorganized, unformed air that makes me uncomfortable in a married friend's first home. You may go into a hundred homes where things are settled, put where they are put with assurance, and not realize what it is that makes them comfortable until you come into a home which wasn't even *there* a few weeks before and suddenly find that it is missing. It's as if the husband and wife are sure of themselves as individuals but don't yet know what they are as a couple, what their joint personality will be, and for as long as they are still finding out everything is on the brink. There are his things and her things and things they have bought together, all still individual *things* waiting for time or love or some indefinable alchemy to snap them into place.

"We're doing the Morris chair in that," Katherine said, pointing to a swatch.

Then Pat and I sat in the living room while she went into the kitchen to make us all a drink.

"Gin and tonic," Pat called after her, and then looked at me.

The room was small, almost the same color as the outside of the house, and the ceiling was low. Pat and I sat at opposite ends of it, he on a radiator in front of the leaded windows, I on the only new piece in the room, the studio couch. It was hot, unpleasant, even though the door to the screen porch was open and we could see the green outside moving in some breeze that did not reach us, and I knew without looking at him that Pat and I were feeling pretty much the same, diminished in some way because we couldn't see the place as Katherine did, and lost.

"Some weather," Pat said, and his voice trailed off.

I looked down at my hands.

He touched his tie. For a minute I thought he was going to take it off. Then Jim was at the door and instead he straightened it, tapping the knot, and stood up.

"Hi." Jim stood uncertainly in the arch that led from the front hall to the living room. He knew us both—barely—from the wedding.

"Kat's in the kitchen," I said, because he looked so ill at ease without her.

He smiled gratefully. "Glad you could come." He was pale

(he looked cold for some reason even though it was midsummer), slender, almost insubstantial in a rumpled cord suit.

"Hi," Katherine said, coming up behind him with the drinks.

"Oh, Kat." He bent over her in an inept, fumbling kiss.

She whispered, "Glad to *see* you," looking up—that blazing look again.

Pat pretended not to see.

"How's your head?"

"OK," he said, but he looked drawn.

"Better get an aspirin, honey." She touched his shoulder as he turned to go and then came into the room. "There isn't much ice," she said to Pat. "Maybe you and Jim can get some at that vend-o place before we eat."

"Be glad to," Pat said, and took his drink. It was in a peanut-butter glass stencilled with yellow and green flowers and a little too heavy for anything in it to taste cool or good. For no particular reason he bent down and pecked her on the brow and she grinned at him, flattered, pleased.

"Tell me what you've been doing," she said, making him move over so they could both sit on the radiator.

"This and that." He put one foot up on a crate. He was done up for the country in an oatmeal linen jacket—he had his almost before anybody else—a madras tie and dark summer. pants. He looked graceful and at ease and seemed to know it because he was particularly charming, weaving a story about his morning and the trip up, winning Katherine. He told her about Glenda and Norty, whom she knew slightly, turning the car squabble into a full-scale story with gestures and embellishments, and he was in the midst of an imitation of Norty saying "Oh, Christ" in a perfect rich-boy accent when she turned from him without apology, because Jim had come back into the room.

"Did you take something?" she asked, all concern.

He nodded, sniffling, "An APC. I'll be fine." Then, looking exhausted, he fell into a chair.

I saw Pat falter for a split second and then draw himself up, and I could swear I saw him solidify before my eyes, locking himself in an entertaining, urbane manner that would drop or falter only once or twice in all the years that we would be friends.

"We had lunch at the MMA," Pat said. "You should have *seen* Denny stuff herself."

("Museum of Modern Art," Katherine explained to Jim.)

"I *didn't*," I said, playing to him because it seemed important to help him settle himself.

"You did." He grinned. "You ought to be fat as a rhino. You were a disgrace."

I pulled a face. "*Who* ate two pieces of chocolate pie?"

"And getting a candy bar in the station. You almost disgraced yourself."

"Sublimation," I said. "I eat the way you buy ties."

He looked wounded. "This is only my third new one this week."

"See what I mean?"

"That's not so many, is it, Kat?"

"It's more expensive than food."

"And less fattening." He wanted to pull Katherine into it. "Isn't it, Kat."

She nodded, laughing. "She'd look silly in rep, though."

"I don't know." He looked grave. "She could make belts out of them. Or use them for snoods."

Jim seemed bewildered and Katherine, on the chair arm beside him, looked down at him protectively. "Pat said he'd go with you for ice, honey. Are you up to it?"

"Sure." He got up, glad to be in motion. "Is there anything else you need?"

"Some lemons from the market."

"I never did get that bottle," Pat reminded her.

"And Pat wants to stop at a package store."

"Sure." Jim looked at him shyly. "OK?"

Pat got up. "All set. Which would you rather have, Katherine? Gilbey's or some burbs?"

"Anything you see, Pat," she said, and then, remembering, "Let Jim decide."

Jim, in the doorway, was protesting that they didn't need anything.

"Yes you do," Pat said with a lordly flourish, ushering Jim out of his own front door. We could hear him as they went down the walk. "My treat."

Then Katherine and I were alone in the house.

There seemed to be nothing to say.

Kat was fussing around with the drink glasses.

Finally I said, "When do you start work?" I knew she'd been offered a job with a university press.

She shook her head. "I'm not."

I can't explain now why hearing it disappointed me. "How come?"

79

"It's too much of a commute."

"You can write at least," I said. She won an Atlantic poetry prize in her sophomore year and again when she was a senior, and for as long as I'd known her she'd talked about a novel, about having time to write.

"I'll do some." She seemed embarrassed. "I guess I'll just —be around."

"Oh." I meant to sound bright, but I couldn't conceive of anything like Katherine without some job or some purpose, just being around, and my voice must have dropped. She bit her lip and then, wanting to please, offered, "I have a new poem. I just finished it."

"Let's see."

She rummaged in some papers in a box and came up with it.

It wasn't as careful or as sharp as most of her stuff, but it had something new in it that I liked. Like most of the things she would write for the next couple of years, until she gave it up entirely, it was about Adam and Eve.

"It's good," I said.

Then she landed on the couch beside me, sprawling her feet in their sneakers, and said, "How's the Bitch?" to prove she hadn't changed.

"Schrader? The same. She's done something new and awful with her hair."

"Did I tell you what she said to me before the wedding?"

She told me, laughing, and I went on from there about Schrader and her job, and my job, and for a minute or two we were on the old wave length and it was almost as if she hadn't changed. Then the phone rang and she went to answer it.

"That was Mrs. Dyer," she said, coming back. "She wants me to collect for the United Fund."

When I am away from them I have a way of thinking of my friends as constant, unchanging, doing only the things I have done with them or can picture them doing, but as she spoke I thought suddenly of Katherine living in a place where there were neighbors, not her mother's neighbors but hers, and I had an unexpected, full vision of Kat at the market, Kat involved in some neighborhood project, Kat the young matron, and I knew then that for the first time since I had known her Katherine had a life which was completely apart from anything I knew or would imagine for her and that from then on, our lives would be separate.

She seemed to be as aware of it as I because she said, "Hey, can you come for Labor Day?"

And because it would help bind us together, I said "Yes."

"We'll have a picnic on the Sound."

"Great. I'll bring my picnic hat." Then, because we both knew we were on a new basis, I added, "I'll see if I can dig one up for Jim."

She nodded, confirming it. "He'd look great in straw."

We were in the kitchen, mulling over dinner, when Pat and Jim came back.

Dinner was as unsure as the house just then, beginning to be good, but still unrealized. Pat was so urbane that there were times when I wanted to kick him, and I could see Katherine wishing she had unpacked and used the crystal, pushing more chicken on Pat and begging him to like it, waiting for the look he finally gave, which meant he thought it was good. Pat must have felt the strain because when the rest of us went out to do the dishes he retreated to the living room.

I found that I was at ease now with Jim and Katherine, if not yet comfortable among the things they had picked to surround them, and we took our time in the kitchen, kidding a little but getting along. The talk was good-natured but low-keyed. When we rejoined Pat in the living room we sat for a few minutes, making talk. Then Jim stretched and Katherine looked over at him.

"You feeling all right, honey?"

He seemed all nerve-endings, younger and less strong than we even though he was twenty-six at the time, to our twenty-one. He ran a hand across his face. "I'm a little tired. Is it OK if I go on to bed?"

Katherine stood up. "It's been something of a day—"

She got out linens for Pat and me, and helped him make up the hide-a-bed they'd set up for him on the porch. I was letting down the couch, which jack-knifed, and spreading it up for myself.

Jim and I talked about law schools as I worked. I was interested in what he thought of Yale and Columbia because Pearson had mentioned the law as a possibility at the beginning of the summer, and then he'd let it slide.

"He couldn't do much better than Yale," Jim said. "Some pretty important people dip into every graduating class for their clerks."

"Maybe he'll try it. He just—" I found myself tiring, and instead of finishing I waved one hand.

Katherine was back in the room. She and Jim stood for a minute in the archway, his arm around her shoulder. They were just there—duo—together—in a closeness that almost dazzled even as it cloyed, as Pat had said it would. Pat murmured something and as he did Jim said "It's late," turning, "and we're pretty tired."

Pat and I exchanged looks as they went. People will always look knowingly when a new couple excuses itself early, and it's the fact of the look, finally, the denial of privacy, that's troubling, not whether they're really tired or just want to be alone.

We smoked for a few minutes, not talking much, while they got through in the bathroom and then Pat took his toothbrush and went in. As he came back through the living room he told me good night, shyly, and let himself out on the porch.

I was awake for a long time. On the porch Pat must have fallen asleep reading, because some light came through the window shade that covered the glassed-in frame of the door. I lay on my back, looking at the play of the light on the ceiling, trying to assimilate everything that had happened that day and trying to forget it, so I could sleep. I suppose I should have thought of Pat out there on the porch—as Katherine had intended—and imagined the same thing, the house, the rest of it, for us, but for some reason I knew then that it would never be that way for me and I had a lightning idea, too quick to catch or examine (nor can I explain it), that for me at least it would never be enough. I was stiff, squirming on the humps in the upholstery, and as I turned, shifting and trying to make the lumps of cotton stuffing dip and change to fit my body, I thought again of Katherine and Jim together, of Pat sleeping on the porch in a nest of light and security and I felt completely alone, alien in this country, and I fell asleep troubled by the half-remembered fragment of a quotation, ". . . the fox in the field has his hole, but the Son of Man has no place to lay his head."

For all his complaints and sophistication, something about seeing Katherine must have put Pat in a marrying mood, because he stayed on the train past New York, riding as far as Philadelphia to keep me company, and when he got off at the 30th Street Station he turned sharply and said something light which could be taken up or, if I didn't want to hear it, could seem as if it had not been said at all, and then he waited, as if for something between us to begin. I let it pass, saying, "Give my love to your friend Norty," and made a face. When I saw him again the mood, the susceptible time, had passed. I think he was in the middle of an affair, and whether he was or not didn't matter, because by that time he had begun playing the game.

IX

The lifeline goes down my left hand like a line on a palmist's map, clear and plain and promising a hundred years, but there are two lines in my right hand where the single lifeline should be. This is not a single line, broken, but two lines, one beginning about a quarter of the way down, overlapping the span of the other slightly but unconnected in a way that made Pat's classmate Mack Glendauer, practicing amateur palmistry at Glenda's party last summer, spread the palm thoughtfully and say, "You must have had one hell of a trauma somewhere in there."

"No kidding?" I bent over it, thinking of Daddy.

"Not so long ago."

I thought, *Bunker*, and rejected the idea.

Mack seemed not to notice. "Or you were sick and nearly died."

"Not sick," I said, trying to see when, to read some time scheme into the thing.

"No?" Mack looked up from my hand. "No pneumonia? Measles, maybe."

"Sorry." I shook my head.

"No traumae?"

"Not since I was nine."

"Too early," he said. "But I'm not sure when it was. It's hard to figure out years, because we don't know how many years this lifeline means."

"Five hundred and two."

He touched the spot. "You were probably around fifteen."

I tried to dig up something for him and couldn't. "Sorry, nothing at fifteen."

"You've forgotten." He was mock-ominous. "Or maybe I'm wrong. Maybe it's in your future."

"Help," I said.

"Cheer up." He handed me back into the trampoline. "This is all a bunch of crap."

Like Mack I have never held with predictions, believed in plotting the future in tea leaves or reading it in the stars, but there *is* something in my hand. It's not an augur or an omen or even a record, in the sense that Mack indicated, but the break in my hand signifies something to me. I see the two pieces of lifeline, disconnected and floating, never touching or meant to touch and I am reminded of a rootless, bootless, footless, disoriented period I put in the summer Katherine was married and I was living at home in Washington, trying out the first of many jobs. I had just gotten my degree and that particular short-term program was finished, leaving me with no plans, no aims, no ambitions to hold hostage to the future, in a time when the next thing, whatever it was going to be, had not yet begun. I wasn't drifting in the sense that Pearson drifted that year, because there seemed to be nothing worth doing. The failure was not in the possibilities, but in me. I didn't fit. In my first job, I could project myself into a dozen other jobs and see that none of them would be quite right. I was simply at large, unsettled, not sure yet which of the myriad possibilities I would fix on, where and how I would choose a specific concern from the many concerns worth caring about and begin to care.

The office where I worked was in a hall of anachronisms, part of a complex of museums where great whales swung from the ceilings, dinosaur skeletons rose bone by bone, and simulated cave men huddled over synthetic fires. Each morning the elevator opened on each floor just long enough to show me the disorganized shapes and dusty vistas, artifacts dimmed by grime and fluorescents glowing under ultra-violet light. And each morning some uneasiness made me resist the urge to leave the elevator and go among them, to try to see everything that sat or hulked or loomed, waiting in those silent rooms.

I remember thinking, "I wish Katherine were here," or "I wish I could show this to Pat," but I couldn't, and this, I told myself, was the difficulty. Katherine was married and Pat was busy in New York; Pearson was out of town and even the people I counted not as friends but as acquaintances had fallen away with graduation, trying themselves in new places, so that essentially I was in Washington alone, living with my mother but sealed off from her as surely as I sealed myself off from the people in that musty government office. I let Kat and Pearson and Pat be my excuse for staying in the elevator, telling myself that I didn't have the heart to go through the building without them, drawing into a corner of the elevator, encased in solitude. At my floor I would turn out of the elevator mechanically, going past busts of anthropoids, low-browed and almost chinless, serious or warlike or maternal, which lowered at me from the unreachable tops of file cabinets, hurrying me faster and faster until finally I fled them around the last corner and into the office where I worked.

Inside, I might have been in the Navy Department or at the Pentagon. The office was fluorescent-lit and painted green, clattering with office machines, an island of order insulated from the shadows of the past which gathered around the exhumed bones of prehistoric men filed like so many back letters (CLAVICLES, MESOZOIC; JAWBONES, PLEISTOCENE; FIBULAE) in tall cabinets just outside, and massed like a dark cloud and rolled on over cases of rocks and gems and artifacts, the beasts of dead species, the men of lost races which swam in the mists below.

Still put off balance by the shadows, I would go to my desk. No matter what time I got there, Mr. Rankin was already bent over his work in the corner, and Netta Freeward was already uncovering her typewriter at the desk next to mine. The others would straggle in, apparently untouched by the shadows, unaware of what they were doing or what they had escaped, ready to begin the day as if the work in front of them was the only thing that mattered, their own concerns the only reality. I had been for so long among people my own age—people who were in transition, who hadn't *decided*—that these office people, set in their chosen patterns, made me uneasy in a way I couldn't define. I found I could not talk to them, perhaps because I had not learned to adjust to people with whom not everything is understood, and I used silence to protect myself, gagging on a welter of unsaid words.

"When a new instruction comes through, you look for the old one and write CANCELLED on it," Mr. Rankin would say in a burst of friendliness. "But you don't throw it out."

I would nod quietly, about to explode.

"We're getting together a bowling league," Mary Wharton would say, touching her greying hair. "Turkeys for the winners, and a party twice a year."

I would shake my head and then withdraw into a silence which by then had compounded itself, waiting for her to leave me alone.

Finally Netta, drawn to me because we were both young, would say, "Have you seen the new guard?"

And out of loneliness, I would answer her.

"He's blond," she would say. "I haven't seen him, but he's supposed to be a doll."

"No kidding?" I would pretend interest and she would go on, pleased.

She couldn't have been thirty yet but she had started working right after high school to support her mother, and commonplace pressures had solidified and aged her, setting the shape of her mouth and pulling down the lines of her face in a way that made it seem pathetic that she was still unmarried, and doubtful that she would ever have a chance. She had a long, pinched nose and a smile so tentative that it was appealing, in a way that a man would need a lot of patience to see. She went in for transparent blouses which displayed a network of straps—bra, slip, skin left white by her bathing suit—but she was so thin that the effect was relentlessly chaste. She seemed not to be aware that any substantial past, any future she had was in this office, and I rebelled for her, offering any hope I could that she might leave it some day.

There were things I would rather have talked about— almost anything—but there wasn't much I could say to Netta that wouldn't involve a wealth of explanation. She seemed to be interested in men in a sort of wistful way, and I remember talking about men to her because it cheered her and made her seem young. I had the idea that if I encouraged her, she might do something about it; she might even happen onto someone and marry out of the office for good.

"There's a new geologist," she said one morning. "He came in today." Mr. Rankin hissed over his shoulder at us, even though the work day hadn't begun.

"No kidding?" I uncovered my typewriter. I'd been reading *Joseph and His Brothers* on the bus, and it was hard for me to pull out of it.

"Mary saw him. She says he's a doll."

87

Mary Wharton was at least fifty, and younger in her way than Netta was. I made a face and then, because I saw Netta begin to withdraw, I said, "Hey, I'm doing some letters for Mr. Starr in P&S. Maybe you could take them down and get a look at him."

Netta put her hand to her mouth. "Oh, I couldn't. I have all these reports to get out." (She worked doggedly, brooding over the perfection of each page. So far as I could tell she never saw beyond the particular page in front of her, or saw any long-range scheme in what she was doing, and I remember hating her narrow concentration, the short-sightedness that would let her work overtime on something she would never understand, that probably didn't matter, when she ought to be out seeing about her life.)

I said, "You could take them on your coffee break," and then, sounding more girlish than I liked to sound, "What if you do lose a minute or two? This is important."

She looked up, grateful to me for saying that it was. "I wish I'd known. I would have worn my navy shantung." She had on a green skirt with the nylon blouse that morning, and she patted it over her hips and rearranged her straps, apparently depressed by the way she looked.

I jammed the tail of my button-down shirt tighter into my waistband, hating the conversation. "How about those earrings I saw in your desk?"

"The white ones?" Her eyes brightened.

"They'd look nice with your blouse."

She perked up, propping a compact mirror on her typewriter while she tried them on. "What do you think?"

It was worth it to see that blurry, tentative smile when I said, "You look fine." I handed her the letters and grinned. "See you."

She ducked her head and went out the door.

I retreated into my work. I bent to the anthropologists' project statements, reading first without paying attention, then with an increasing sense of unreality that Mr. Weigand from the inner office would be doing his particular book until 1958, that Mrs. Warnke expected to finish her project in 1962, that the others had books or projects which would not be finished in that decade. They wrote with such matter-of-factness, with such calm confidence about these far, unreachable dates that I boggled, unable to believe that anybody could be so sure about what he would be doing five or ten years from that day. They wrote as if everything were settled for them and they weren't still on their way to something as I felt I was, as I began to hope Netta was, but as if they had chosen an alternative and settled in it, and hoped to move on, along a clear, unchanging track, for long, untroubled years. A part of me envied them their certainty but I hated the finality of it, resisting the fact of their choice as much as the thing they had chosen.

Netta's hair was disarranged when she came back and her nose was pink, as if she'd just been backed into a file cabinet in some exciting encounter, but I think this was just something that happened with her, a sympathetic vibration that turned her nose pink against her will and shook strands of hair out of place whenever she was excited. I looked up, expecting a report, but she just said, "Where are you eating lunch?"

I usually took sandwiches outside, under the trees. I opened my drawer wide enough to show the brown bag.

"Come across the street with me," she said grandly. "I'll treat you to some lemon pie."

"Okay," I said, wondering why I found it hard to smile.

Then Mr. Rankin came around collecting quarters for the paycheck pool. It was based on serial numbers, and the nearest perfect poker hand won the pot.

I ate my sandwiches in the cafeteria, watching Netta worry a 50-cent goulash, listening to her. Her nose was pink again, and between bites she worked her shoulder straps, rearranging them.

"—He's blond—well, his hair is kind of thin, but blond, and he keeps the top long so you don't notice it, and he has a nice face, and glasses—" She hadn't stopped talking about him.

I was pleased to see her so interested in something, but her insistence made me uncomfortable and I said, "Hey, who won the pot today?"

"When Mrs. Graybar introduced us he said—" She trailed her fork, dreaming.

"Yeah?"

"He said '*Well*,' like *that*, and when I left he held the door for me." She pushed the goulash plate aside and handed me one of the two pieces of lemon pie.

I took the pie. "What did you say his name was?"

"Goddard. His first name is Stanley, I think." She looked for the twentieth time at the line. "Mrs. Graybar said he might have lunch over here."

The pie was poison yellow. I pushed it around my plate. "Maybe we'll get a look at him."

"I wanted you to see him," she said.

"Swell." Then I noticed she had moved her tray to one side, leaving a vacant place, and I began to wish I had never mentioned the new geologist because she didn't seem to be able to handle even so small a thing.

"Don't," she said when I put my bag on the empty chair. "He might want to sit there."

We sat without talking while Netta watched the line and then her watch, squirming as the lunch hour ebbed away.

Then Mary Wharton slipped into the empty seat. "One number and I would have won. You know who won the pot? Mr. Starr. He needs it about like Eisenhower." She looked at my pie, almost untouched. "That stuff was horrible today, wasn't it? There's something about Government pie—"

Netta looked so distressed that for a minute I wanted to tell Mary to move, as if the new geologist might really be coming to sit in the extra seat.

"I met the new geologist," Netta said timidly, trying to get around to the matter of the place she had saved.

"Oh, him," Mary said. "He looks so young. Would you believe he's got four kids?"

I think I expected a dramatic slow take, something from a story, and for a minute I wouldn't look at Netta. When I did look up she was much the same, except that her shoulders were drooping so that the straps slipped a little, and she had forgotten about the loose strands of hair. She picked up her pocketbook and tucked in the unopened cigarettes which she had bought in case she needed something to get her over the awkward first few minutes with the geologist.

"I have to go," she said.

"Time was when there were plenty of unmarried people in P&S," Mary was saying, "or maybe it just seemed that way—"

"No kidding," I murmured, staying to listen because I knew Netta wouldn't want me to join her just then.

Mary put one hand on the table, studying the heavy veins. "People from outside don't always understand."

I bit my lip, already wishing there were some way I could make it up to Netta, and I looked at Mary squarely for the first time. "I see."

Nothing had been said, and I was frankly surprised when, the next day, Netta produced a brown bag at noon and asked shyly where I was having lunch. I think now that in some blind way she had planned what happened next, wanting to justify herself in some way, to explain something to me, but that she was not quite sure how to do it, or, once we had taken our lunch hour and had come back into the office, what she had done.

We ate outside under the trees without saying much, and when we had balled up our waxed paper and bags and Dixie cups and tossed them in the trash she turned to me, pale with uncertainty.

"There's some time left. Would you like to see inside?"

"The museum? We don't have much time." We had thirty minutes for lunch, but it wasn't the time-limit that made me resist.

"Our section," she said, with a new pride.

I was puzzled until she led me into the elevator, to a hall on the second floor, where cave men, Indians, plaster figures with carefully modelled faces, crouched or knelt in fierce little groups, suspended in separate display cases as if each of them had been plucked, full-feathered and still fighting, from his own spot in time.

In one case, a glassy-eyed Pueblo squaw ministered to a child. "Mr. Weigand's," Netta said, stopping in front of it. "Mr. Bard's," she said, leading me on to the next. Then she went on down the row of cases to a space at the end of the hall, assuming I would follow her.

There were a few rocks in the case recessed in the back wall, and on the wall itself someone had begun a painting of a dim, prehistoric dawn. "Mrs. Warnke's project," Netta said. "She just has a jawbone and a couple of fragments to go on. Some people from Geological Survey are helping her get the background right." She looked at me then, seeming larger because this exhibit gave her something to cling to, to retreat into because she had tried the game I had wanted her to play and failed, and at the same time she seemed diminished, overshadowed by the hall and the exhibits and the weight of the project that would take the next eight years. "I'm going to be her special clerical assistant," she said, offering it, wanting me to see that this was the way things were, to acknowledge it as a good future for her.

All I had to do was say something that showed I accepted it, but I had already backed off, thinking, 1962, so overwhelmed by the drab weight of the years that I could only swallow hard and say "Swell," unable to hide the disappointment in my face. I opened my mouth to begin again, seeing in her eyes that I had failed her even as I rushed in with enthusiastic little comments to cover myself.

If I saw Netta a year from today I might not even recognize her, and I know we would have nothing to say, but I will always love her for what she did next. She pulled herself away from the display case, managing a smile in the face of my betrayal, making herself forget the future she had accepted, for the moment, and she said, thinking to please me:

"You'll never guess who's moved in across the way from me and Mom. Somebody from the FBI."

And we turned, making conversation about the FBI man, and left the hall.

If I remember Netta for that brave little effort, I remember her too for showing me that I didn't need Pat or Pearson or Katherine or any other understanding company of friends to go with me into those dusty halls. While Netta and I seldom ate together after that, I spent most of my lunch hours in the museum, brooding over models of pterodactyls, cases of rocks and uncut gems, figures of craggy forefathers and Ming vases, put on deposit in our building because no one else seemed to have a place for them.

I wish I could say that I prayed over what happened next, and then it came to me, but it didn't happen that way. It just seemed to come out of the variety of the museum, out of being alone among the specimens, the models, the anomalies, out of being in the company of so many undusted reminders of time present and time past all massed, in some way, to give an almost comforting sense of continuity. It was that summer, as I wandered from one exhibit to the next, avoiding the guards I knew so I wouldn't have to talk and dodging little clots of tourists, that I hit on the idea of preparation. It seemed to me that even though my particular job didn't interest me as a job and I could think of no other work that would grip me and take me along, catapulting me into some choice or ambition, there was one way I could give what I did some purpose. I could work with some joy, learning as I worked, gathering things in to myself, if I took it all as preparation for some future which, for me, had not yet been decided.

X

Because she wanted to be strong about such things, and didn't want either of us to be too dependent, my mother sent me to a boarding school in Washington when I was sixteen and a high-school junior. And because neither of us was all that strong, she took an apartment nearby so we could be together on weekends. We packed our things in an aura of uncertainty, moving around the Florida house with a premature nostalgia for the sere quiet of the street, the dry rustling of palms outside and then, when the movers had come and gone we closed the door behind us and set out in the car, almost of an age in our excitement over going to a new place for the first time in seven years, knowing in our explosion of talk that it was more than time.

It was still the end of summer in Florida, with heat broken by afternoon thunder-showers, but the air quickened as we drove north, into fall, and when we reached Washington three days later it was mid-September and I had only a week to get ready for school. Because everyone in my class of boarders already had a roommate I was put into a single room, a cubicle not much bigger than the wooden wardrobe at one end of it. At the time I was glad of the freedom from intrusion, for this one place of privacy and relative safety where, if I needed to, I could shut out the life of the school.

I had never lived with girls before, and the experience was intense. Perhaps because we were at such close quarters, and perhaps because it is in the nature of women when too many of us are put together in any single place, everything seemed magnified. Friendships and even quarrels seemed twice as complicated as they should have; people took things dramatically and they took them hard. Given my choice I would never have a woman as an employer because this same element, whatever it is, makes something as simple as a boss-to-employee relationship too personal to be fair, or even businesslike. I find now that I don't have my choice, but I'm not ready to go into that here.

There were only twelve boarders in my class (the rest were dayhops, who came each morning from home and left after the last class, skimming us in our best moments and then deserting us for home) and they came around in a body to have a look at me, looking battle-scarred and hard-bitten in their tired uniforms.

The uniform was a black jumper, V-necked and given to pouching over stomach and rear, worn over a long-sleeved white blouse which was finished off at the throat with a red enamel bar-pin with the school's initials in gold (someone's idea of chic). I was to learn that the whole business—jumper, blouse and pin and sometimes the slip underneath —could be shucked off all of a piece and hung on the back of the bedroom door, already assembled, so that the wearer could put it on whole in the morning between the time that the last bell for prayers rang and Sister began taking names. Everyone wore oxfords, prescribed by the school and run over at the heels almost as a matter of fashion, and thin white cotton socks that refused to stand up the way crew socks did.

The jumper—gabardine in fall and spring, if you bothered to change off, and some kind of iron wool tweed the rest of the time—took on a high shine after only a couple of wearings. The V at the front soon frayed under fountain pen clips, and it could accommodate anything from apples to knitting to turnovers stolen at lunch without seeming to change in shape. It fit like armor, strong and unyielding, imposing a kind of unwilling sexlessness that made even the most indifferent girls, hockey legs and all, become militantly feminine in an attempt to overcome it. I think now that this may have been part of the rationale because most of the girls I have known who wore the jumper have emerged from it as pretty complete and admirable women.

At the time, they wrote boys from home or pretended that they wrote boys from home, and had male "cousins" visit them in the dark and forbidding parlor and hung out of upstairs windows, watching the dayhops leave with boys. They walked and walked the perimeter of the grounds, especially in a particular area which backed up against a classroom building used by a men's college next door, willing somebody to come to one of the windows and see them as girls, not just blobs in black uniforms.

I learned this gradually, not aware of it when they came in to greet me on that first day. They had already changed from their Peck and Peck suits and high heels and had packed them away. They wouldn't bring them out again until the first long weekend, or the first holiday, when they would reappear in lipstick and clanking earrings and high heels, in such splendor that I would hardly recognize them. At the time, they looked like a pretty motley lot. They came in various shapes and sizes, all of them overwhelming, and because term had begun and there was no use in setting it, they had let their hair go limp. One or two had bad skin from an end-of-summer chocolate binge.

They crowded into that carton of a room, seeming big and friendly and curious, muttering about this and that, coming so fast that I didn't know what to say.

Then the girl in the lead, long-haired and scrawny, with battle-scarred legs that hadn't yet filled out, threw back her hair and said, "What's your name?" and I was on familiar ground. She turned out to be Katherine.

As I remember it, Voka Maris showed me around the grounds that first day, pointing out the bell tower and the nuns' graveyard and the hockey field, passing without comment the break in the wall where one or two legendary boarders went to meet boys from a Washington prep school one night.

Voka was tall and gentle, big-footed and heroically ugly, and as I found out from Katherine later, when we had become friends, almost deaf. She hid her handicap that day, turning to watch my face as I talked, never asking me to repeat. She went on about the dietician and the infirmarian in that big, soft voice, pointing out first this building and then that in almost endless enthusiasm, and introduced me to one of the nuns and a couple of lay teachers who were already at work in the classrooms, saying after we left each one, "You'll love her," in a way that made me wary because at sixteen, almost everyone has some complaints. She told me about the Mass schedule and our occasional kitchen duties, talking about school restrictions so cheerfully that I remember squirming under the impact of so much good will. When she left me off at my room she offered to pick me up for dinner, to show me down to the dining hall and introduce me around and then she waited, mouth working,

95

for me to reply. Without hesitation I thanked her and said I thought I'd make it down all right by myself, and that I'd see her there. Then I closed the door, relieved to be free of her.

If I sound callous it's because I was acutely conscious of the crowd, as kids that age are, of being new and not wanting to jump in too fast. I knew without having to be told that Voka wasn't one of the crowd, never had been and never would be, and I had the idea that I'd better put off any alliances until I found out who was who.

I may have known even then—intellectually, as I would know a fact of numbers—how admirable she was, but knowing it wasn't enough. Even if I had been a better person Voka and I could never have been friends. She was usually in pain, I found out later, because of some trick her muscles played her, and she suffered from a bone disease, but she was the sort who never complained. She took everything that came to her with great good will, offering up any suffering, as the nuns had told us to do, and as we all secretly doubted we'd be able to do if we were faced with actual pain. She was stolid, kind, relentlessly pleasant. She was so good that she embarrassed us, and there came a time when everything that was fallible in us rebelled, when we had to act against her, reaffirming our knowledge of the good in her even as we fought it. This came when I had been at school no more than two months, about the time Katherine and I became close friends.

I remember learning my way around those first few weeks, talking to some of the other boarders, getting to know a few, and watching Katherine. Her room was always the worst on the corridor and there was always something about her uniform that was not quite right, either plaid shoelaces in the regulation oxfords, or cuffs rolled, or the bar pin on wrong. She would sit on her spine in the back of every class, scribbling or fixing the nun with a cataleptic stare of indifference until suddenly an idea or new piece of information would catch in her somewhere and she'd forget herself and make a passionate speech. I admired her for that fine show of indifference.

We got talking one weekend when almost everybody was gone. She was restricted until Thanksgiving because somebody had found her smoking behind the gymnasium, and I was there for the weekend because my mother had gone South to a wedding and she'd asked the headmistress's permission for me to stay at school. It was sunny out, brilliant autumn, but I kept to the inside corridors that first day, skulking along the dark woodwork, because it fitted my mood. Except for a few underclassmen Kat and I were the only people at table that night at dinner, with Kat playing grown-up for the freshmen, laughing a little too loud and making conversation with me over the codfish cakes. After dinner she asked, diffidently, if I wanted to sleep in her room that night. It was something you did when you saw that someone was alone on the corridor, and I could see that she was relieved when I refused. We slouched in the lounge for a while after dinner, pretending that our silence was a companionable silence, and then one of the freshmen came in and asked Katherine to help her with a bulletin board, and that was the last I saw of her that night. Voka had been out to dinner that evening, at a tearoom none of us would have chosen. Her parents lived too far away for a weekend visit, and she'd had permission to go out with an aunt. She came into the lounge shortly after eight with two bundles wrapped in paper napkins—powdery doughnuts she'd wrapped up and brought back for Katherine and me.

She stood over me while I ate mine, all awkward solicitude, and then asked about Katherine.

I said, still eating, "She's helping some kid with a bulletin board."

Voka leaned forward, jaw sagging a little because she hadn't been able to make out my words. Her deafness gave her a stupid look that infuriated me even though I suspected it hid a pretty frightening intelligence.

"*Bulletin board*," I said crossly, not bothering to explain again.

"She has something to do then," Voka said, pretending I hadn't snapped. She turned from me with an almost maternal look, saying, "I'm so glad." She turned back for a moment, to explain. "Katherine sulks when she's kept in, unless there's plenty going on. Maybe this will cheer her up." She brandished the doughnut and then shambled off, good will in every angle of her frame.

"Thanks for the doughnut," I mumbled, knowing she wouldn't hear.

The building was almost deserted on Saturday mornings, with the nuns busy in the convent wing and several of the underclassmen out in town with a chaperone. I cleaned my room for as long as I could make it last and then wandered down the wide front stairs, still hugging the woodwork, brooding over bulletin boards and class portraits on the dark-panelled walls of the front hall. I went past the sign-out room, where girls checked in and out and asked permission each time they wanted to leave. I stared blankly at Sister Michael as I passed the door, hardly noticing as her image flicked into place in the frame of light. Then at the far end of the hall I saw Voka, coming out of the chapel door. She seemed to see me and hurried my way.

I found out later that she went to a movie with her aunt that day, sadly disappointed because she hadn't been able to find me and Katherine, to ask us too. I wondered whether Sister Michael remembered seeing me right before Voka came in to ask permission for me and Katherine, and what she must have thought when Voka said she couldn't find either of us. Even thinking it over I knew a movie with Voka wouldn't have appealed to me, but that didn't explain the quick, nervous jump I made into a doorway when she started down the dark hall, calling me and Katherine. Her expression, the way she peered into the dim hallway looking for us, the high-pitched deaf voice and the weight of her good intentions oppressed me and I held my breath, hiding from her.

As she passed me a classroom door opened across the way and Katherine stepped out, all innocence, just in time to see Voka's back. She stopped in mid-step and pressed herself back in the doorway, hiding, and then she saw me.

We waited without saying anything until Voka had gone into the sign-out room, biting our knuckles and hiding sheepish grins. When she had disappeared we stepped out, chattering like old friends because we knew we felt the same way about Voka and had found each other out, from the feeling itself to the shame we felt for it.

"What does she want?" Katherine said.

I shrugged.

"She got me up for Mass this morning and it wasn't even my day." Katherine had a wild look. "And she kept checking back to be sure I'd gotten out of bed." She rubbed her nose desperately. "She keeps coming *by* to be sure I'm not depressed."

"Did you get your doughnut?" I was remembering the moist look Voka had given me as I ate.

"Yeah." Katherine rolled her eyes upwards. "She just won't leave you *alone*."

"You can't just tell her to go away," I said.

"That's the trouble."

"And she's not doing anything, really."

"I know." Kat sighed. "She's just so damn *nice*."

Just then Voka came out of the sign-out room and we jumped back, into the same doorway this time, because neither of us had the strength to let her find us.

"If you see them tell them I'll wait," Voka said. She went into the elevator (she was allowed to use it, because of her health), and as the door shut and she went clanking upward we burst out of the doorway, giggling uncontrollably in our relief.

"What's the *matter* with you two?" Sister Michael said, standing over us suddenly, and she was a little crosser than she should have been, I think because she knew what the matter was and understood. We choked, laughing too hard to answer, and went to detention hall without complaining because this mild penance would help us forget that we had been unkind.

By Sunday night, at home in a shirt I'd worn for three days and a jumper full of crumbs, I greeted the returning boarders like an old hand. My feeling for the school had taken on a new color, because Katherine and I were friends.

We came to grips with the problem of Voka that December, on another one of those weekends, with Kat campussed again and me at school because my mother had gone to the Army game with some friends. We slouched in the lounge after supper, still insulted by the fish cakes and stewed tomatoes we had eaten, building up to a mood of revolt. We talked easily by then, because we were friends, but we didn't talk much that night. We were restless and iffish, weighed down by the prospect of three weeks at school before the Christmas holiday began.

"I don't know," Katherine said, fingering a hank of hair. "Maybe if I peroxided it would change my life."

I yawned. "The only thing that's going to change your life is getting out of this place." I had been in the school long enough to begin grousing too, to take part in the ritual of complaint that put a little edge of awareness on the days, making the classes, the uniforms, the whole business seem to matter more.

She looked at me suddenly. "We could redo you."

"Oh, come on," I said, impatient with her. "We redid me last week. And we did Caswell before Thanksgiving."

"I know."

We had a recurring daydream about taking one of our number and transforming her, the way they always did it in the movies, when the young man would take off the teacher's glasses and say with surprise, "Why—you're beautiful," or the girls in the boarding house would chip in for a new wardrobe and a platinum job for the mousy secretary and turn her into Betty Grable. We would pick on one of our classmates and imagine her taller, minus a few pounds. We'd think of just the right hair style and makeup and picture her emerging resplendent in evening dress from her jumper. Once we had her redone to our satisfaction we would send her out in imagination to do a little living for us, our champion, our proxy in the world. We would think of her (and by transferral, ourselves) at the center of a circle of men, and we took a vicarious delight in the imagined double-take when some man who had never noticed her before saw her, as we had rearranged her, and said, "Why—you're beautiful."

"Besides," I said, "all Caswell needs is to lose five pounds."

Kat moved over to the window, seedy-looking and graceful in a jumper that hadn't been cleaned since fall. "And all you need is some makeup," she said, appraising me.

"If you'd wash your hair it would do wonders," I said acidly.

"None of us have any *real* problems." She was swinging her head so that her hair flopped. "Either that or we're too far gone. I wonder which it is?" she went on, trying to pull me back into the game.

"We've *done* us," I said, bored.

She sighed. "I know. What we need is somebody new."

Just then Voka walked through the room, so alone in her deaf world that she didn't even notice us.

I looked at Katherine; Katherine looked at me and we began to laugh.

"We never did Voka," I said, feeling mean.

"Why not?" she said, still laughing. "I bet we could do a hell of a job."

"The hair would have to go first."

"Lipstick. If she'd only wear lipstick," Kat said.

"She probably needs some better underpinnings."

"And some new clothes."

"The hair is really the worst," I said. "If we could just get her to have it cut."

"Or she could keep it long, if she'd get a permanent." Kat was pacing now. Somewhere along the way we'd passed out of conjecture, and we were talking as if there was something we might do.

100

"And one thing—" I admit it—it was my idea. "She needs to shave her legs."

Kat had a visionary look. "That fuzz. If she'd only shave it off."

Suddenly we were obsessed by it. I slept in Kat's room that night and we talked about redoing Voka for some time before we fell asleep. All Saturday we took furtive looks at her, fixing on the dark hair that curled on Voka's legs, the veins that pulsated in white skin beneath. That afternoon we talked idly about getting her to wear makeup, or talking her into a permanent, but we were both thinking of the whole dark network on her legs and the skin that showed palely through.

We kept slipping into it in conversation, unexpectedly coming on the word "hair," or "legs," and beginning to laugh. Finally, after a Saturday night supper that only intensified our mood of dissension, we began to plan.

When the handful of boarders who were in that weekend clattered off to the movie in the auditorium, we set up headquarters in the washroom, drawing hot water and laying out towel, razor, soap.

Then we went for Voka. She was studying in her room.

"Hi, Voka," we said, going in without knocking.

"Denise," Voka said, with a plain, pleased grin. "Katherine." She looked so glad to see us that we faltered.

Then she went on about the poem she was memorizing, something we all had to know by Monday, which Kat and I hadn't touched. It was just enough to get us going again.

"I had this extra lipstick," Kat said fishing it out of her jumper front. "I wondered if you'd like to try it."

"It's a sort of a true red," I offered. If she took it, we were going to bring up the idea of a permanent, and the legs.

Voka was already shaking her head.

"It's very light," Katherine said.

"I don't think so," Voka said, and her jaw was broad and shining.

Kat and I exchanged glances. We were infuriated, I think, because she had the kind of character that didn't have to care how it looked.

Kat put the lipstick down on a table. "Well," she said, "in case you change your mind—"

"I know somebody who could use it," Voka said.

"Well, that's swell." Kat stepped forward. "But what we really came about—"

"What we really came about," I said, "is that there's something in the john."

"In the john?" Voka said, looking as if she thought her ears had betrayed her again.

Kat was at her desk, helping her to her feet. "It's moving."

I took the other elbow. "I think it's a kind of a bug."

"A bug?" Voka repeated, still not able to understand.

And Katherine mumbled something too fast for her to hear, and we began hurrying her down the hall.

We told ourselves we were doing it for Voka's sake, to make her better-looking, to help her out of herself, but I think we shaved Voka's legs in an attempt to change her in some more basic way, make her angry, perhaps, to scale her down to something we could understand.

At the washroom door she became suspicious suddenly, and dragged her heels. It was too late; we pulled her inside. Then Katherine, in a marvelous display of strength, got her down and I began to work on her.

I think we expected a fight. Kat sat on her stomach, holding her arms, keeping up a running patter about how it wasn't going to hurt and how much better she was going to look. I got the soap and razor and got to work, sitting on her feet. Kat and I seemed to realize at the same time that holding her wasn't necessary. I got up after a couple of strokes to rinse the mat of hair from the razor, and I saw Voka's face. She was perfectly quiet, suffering—not mad—just suffering, with quiet, inexplicable tears running down her cheeks. Kat looked down then and saw them too, and without having to look at each other or agree on anything we put the razor aside and let her go. She got up without saying anything, more remote than ever, and went down the hall to her room and closed the door. We could hear her crying, first quietly and then louder and louder, perhaps raising her voice because her deafness made it hard for her to tell how loud it was, and before we could think of hiding or trying to do something to stop her, the other boarders came back from the movie, with Sister Michael in the lead.

She looked at us briefly and then went into Voka's room. I know as surely as if I had been there that Voka didn't say anything about us, but Sister Michael had been in charge of that corridor long enough to know when somebody was at fault.

When she came out we were still lingering, half-hoping

to get it over with. Instead of accusing us Sister Michael passed by in silence, leaving us without even the benefit of a cold look. We trailed back to Katherine's room to sit out the rest of the evening, not relieved at having escaped punishment, just feeling sunk.

Except for a quick comment in Sister Michael's religion class, nothing was ever said. At the time, Sister Michael seemed easy-going and digressive, often entertaining us for the hour without opening the text. We might take in this idea or that without thinking it had any relevance, letting it filter in and lie half-forgotten until later that week, or some years later, when we had come to a certain point in life, and a sentence, an hour's talk would come back whole, and fit. That day she said, "Goodness is not always popular." She lifted her head because her glasses had begun to slip, and there was no question but that she was trying to explain something to Katherine and me. "Not many of the saints would have won a popularity poll."

I know now what she meant: the saints all realized something and realized it fully, in a kind of preoccupation that didn't allow for any softening, for any compromise. Most of us can't seem to cope with anything that ultimate, and we depend on each other, living on in our own way, day by day. Maybe I presume, but I think Voka was headed that way, and I think Kat and I did what we did because we sensed that saintly monomania, and being people—kids, but more important, *people* and therefore fallible—tried to pretend that we didn't, falling short, as we would time and time again.

Voka left us at the end of that year to join a contemplative order, and I heard later that the nuns were trying her case for some miracle of restored hearing, to further the cause of one of their dead members for beatification.

XI

When I'm bored I like to draw pictures full of creatures—lions and tigers coming over hills, snakes in trees, monkeys in the bush and birds in a sky filled with helicopters and the kind of airplanes we used to draw during World War II. There is usually at least one missionary in a cannibal pot, to keep things interesting, and there are plenty of hills, so that there is always the possibility of a new creature coming from just behind that last rise, where I can't quite see. The whole project can expand to fit any given length of time, from the span of a dull lecture to a long, empty afternoon. It helps me expand, too, in a way that makes boredom more bearable because my mind, at least, is busy with possibilities.

Boredom—rather, an intense restlessness—set in that spring. The corridor seemed like a hole, dark and close; the rooms contracted until they almost stifled us, and we spent hours staring out of classroom windows as if our whole lives were strung on trees just outside. By now I've been through enough boarding school springs, at the convent and again at college, to understand the feeling, but at the time I thought I would explode.

It was a time of discontent, of water fights and desperate practical jokes.

I was bent over a field of creatures—a real production—one afternoon when I caught a shadow out of the tail of my eye and stiffened, because I had thought I was alone. Because I was sitting down my eyes met the visitor at waist level, taking in the woven belt and the rosary and I jumped, because this was the first time one of the nuns had ever come into my room.

"Yes, Sister," I said, scraping to my feet, trying to look respectful and cover the drawing at the same time. And then I saw who it was and hit her in the midsection because it was only Katherine, done up in a choir robe and some towels and an official-looking rosary gotten Lord knows how.

"Hey," she said, "It's a sacrilege to hit a nun."

"You're not a nun." I yanked at the makeshift veil she had on her head.

"I thought you'd think it was funny," she said, ducking my hand.

"You scared the hell out of me."

She laughed. "You jumped a foot. Hey, let's try it on you." She came toward me, holding out the veil, and I jumped back almost reflexively, hitting her arm away. She was surprised by the blow, I think, and let the veil dangle, looking hurt.

I said "I'm sorry," not sure why I had been so violent.

"I just thought you'd look good in black." She began unpinning the makeshift wimple from her front.

I said "I'm sorry" again. "That thing just gives me the creeps."

"Apparently," she said, drawing back.

"Hey, look at my helicopter," I said, trying to make it up to her. She usually liked my drawings.

But she was already hanging out the window, waving the towel at someone in the garden below.

"Who's down there?"

"Feeney," she said, and stepped aside so I could see. "I hit her with a rock from here one day."

"That's sacrilege."

"Not yet." Kat elbowed me aside. "She's not a nun yet. Hey, Feeney. She sees me," she said, and waved again.

Across the court, on the far side of a wrought-iron fence that formed the fourth side of the quadrangle, Feeney barely raised one hand to indicate that she had seen. Then she followed the straight walk to the fountain at the garden's center, circled it and went off along another of the walks, toward the convent door.

She had become a postulant in the order only a year before, but the boarders talked about her as if she were legend and her shape intruded, a black memento mori, on days when their spirits got too high. Feeney was allowed monthly visitors and once Kat went to see her in the parlor, talking to her through the grate that separated them. She had permission to pass a book through the turnbuckle and when she came back that was the only detail she would give me, because the shadows of the parlor still seemed to cling to her. I found out later that she and Feeney had been close friends.

"You want a smoke?" Kat said, turning from the window. I could hear cellophane crackle when she patted her jumper front.

"Not me. I'm in trouble enough."

I had hit something the social workers like to call a down-hill spiral that spring. It happens easily when you're still in school. You get caught once, for something which may or may not have been important, and then suddenly you're in for a whole run of trouble because people have noticed you and you're on their minds; you're called down for every little thing because you seem to be available any time they're looking around for a culprit. I found myself buried under a minor avalanche, with an unexpected reputation for being trouble that wouldn't die until summer, when both the nuns and I would forget. A smoking offense had put me in jeopardy; one more demerit and I would be restricted to campus until June.

"Walk as far as the gate with me," Kat said, and I said I would.

Sister Bernard, the headmistress, was watching as we came into the court. She lifted her hand in a formal little wave but she looked so dark, so forbidding, above the vines that ran along the porch rail that I couldn't make myself wave back. Perhaps because she had all our records on file in her office and knew things about us that we ourselves didn't know, perhaps because she was brilliant in class, she had always seemed formidable, remote. We looked at her briefly and then crossed nervously to the gateway, going around a corner and relaxing only when we were out of her sight.

"Wv," I said, shivering.

"She's OK," Kat said easily. "You just have to get used to her."

"I've been here nearly eight months and I'm not used to her."

"If anybody asks I'm down at the gym," Kat said. Strictly speaking, it was true; we smoked under the bushes by the back wall, waving our arms to dispel the smoke.

"I never saw you," I said.

"Fine." She gave me a little push. "You better beat it."

I walked back into the court, surprised to find Sister

Bernard still framed in the vines, just standing, for once unoccupied. I hustled in a side door before she could see me and I would have to wave, carrying a dark after-image that seemed out of keeping with the rambling porch, the first green of spring.

There was a requiem mass for one of the kitchen nuns the next morning, and in a way I can't explain it colored the whole day, exaggerating moods and muffling actions, so that when we did anything, it was as if we were moving under water. Kat stopped by my door before it got light, waiting while I pulled the jumper straight and zipped it up. She hadn't bothered to change out of her pajamas; one pants-leg had already begun to unfurl. We were late and knew it (it was part of my pattern that spring to be late) and we came gasping into chapel just as the awful, pulsing *Dies Irae* began.

Afterward the nuns followed the procession to the grave-yard, walking to the measured sound of the chapel bell, and we hung out of the study hall window and watched them go. From the back, they looked like so many black tomb-stones, standing under the new leaves as the coffin was low-ered into the earth. The headstones in the convent grave-yard were identical, simple and somehow appropriate to the company of sisters who had lived out their lives to-gether in the cloister and would be buried within the convent walls, still in the same company.

"I entered when I was sixteen," Sister Michael said in class that morning. "The same day as Sister Theodore. We were scrubbing floors in the refectory the morning our class graduated."

We shook our heads and murmured, even though most of us had never seen Sister Theodore. Most of us were in iron tweed that morning, because we hadn't thought to change into gabardine, for spring, and I had already begun to scratch. I remember looking at Sister Michael's habit, dark and heavy in the sunlight, and thinking, I could never be a nun.

At lunch we were still subdued by the memory of the requiem, but Sister Theodore, who had seldom come into our part of the building, seemed more and more unreal as the afternoon wore on.

There was a bright breeze blowing down from the hill that afternoon, and somehow death seemed remote. Kat and I started a dozen projects and then abandoned them be-cause nothing seemed to satisfy us for long. We roved the building, going up and down stairs and into empty rooms and through seldom-used corridors, ending up outside the dining room long before it was time for supper, pacing in tight little circles until the bell rang and we were let in. By the time supper was over the building was too small to contain us, and as soon as the grace after meals freed us we broke and ran outside. Kat jumped the last few steps into the court and hit still running like a demon, ungainly and beautiful. I followed her, running hard across the court and out the gate. We didn't stop until we'd been twice around the perimeter of the grounds. Then we dove for the grass outside the gym, rolling over and over until finally we came to a stop on a little rise that overlooked the graveyard and the oblong of new earth.

We tried to talk but the air was too much for us and we snorted and giggled like drunks. On impulse I began running again, with Kat right behind me, and momentum took us all the way down the hillside and over the low cemetery fence. We dug in our heels as we came inside, coming to a near halt, quiet now. Kat stooped and kicked off her shoes and socks, throwing them over the fence without looking to see where they would land. Then she grabbed my arm, whispering.

"Look."

Right above us was the wall, and beyond it rose the science lab of the men's college next door. Now we were closer to it than we had ever been, because in all our forays down in hopes that some of the boys would hang out the windows and talk to us, we had never thought of coming into the graveyard before.

Kat gave a hoot and three of them looked out.

I hung back, trying to smooth my jumper into some sort of shape.

"Hey," Kat said, making a desperate attempt to fluff up her dirty hair.

One of the boys waved. "Hi, Miss America," he said, and the others, dashing in white lab coats, laughed.

"What's new in that jail?"

I got bold. "Beer parties every night."

"I bet."

Kat said, "Want to come?"

"Sure, beautiful," somebody said.

Kat elbowed me, grinning. "We're building a tunnel."

I wanted to be helpful. "Under the wall."

"Sure."

"I bet."

"Great," one yelled. "We can hardly wait."

We stuck out our chests like sirens, forgetting that the jumpers made us look like black oblongs with white sticks for arms. Talking to boys was heady stuff, and we would have kept at it indefinitely if they hadn't disappeared, as if on signal, to be replaced by somebody older—a teacher, probably—who looked at us balefully and then slammed the window shut.

"Oh well," Kat said.

I dug my toe into the ground, watching muddy water creep up into my socks. I bent and took them off, a little sad. "They were laughing at us anyway."

Kat spread her arms. "So what the hell?"

We turned, threading our way between the little mounds and white markers until we found ourselves posed, unexpectedly, like mourners at Sister Theodore's grave. We looked at the new, sharp initials on the headstone thoughtfully, and I don't think we noticed the first drops of a light rain.

Kat's voice was hushed. "I wonder what it's like to be dead?"

I looked down. "Somebody said she had cancer."

"She was sick for a long time."

"She and Sister Michael entered the same year," I murmured, trying to make something of it. "She used to make special Christmas pies."

"I think I saw her once," Kat said. "She had a limp."

We went on reciting crumbs of information about Sister Theodore, as if talking about her would make her death seem more real. When we thought we had run out Katherine came up with one more bit. "Mary Frances said she was very small." She looked at the grave pensively. "She'd have to be, to fit in there," she said, and then she walked up and down the rows of headstones, making measuring motions with her hands. "They must all have been."

I followed her. "Those graves are longer than they look."

"Want to bet?" Before I could stop her, Kat dropped on the ground, measuring herself against a green mound. Her head bumped, and she had to crook her neck so that it would clear the stone. "See?"

I flopped next to her in a fascination that had nothing to do with death, to see how much room the sisters had. It was a little like lying on a Japanese bed, with a block instead of a pillow, but I imagined it was more like the beds the sisters had, narrow, austere, without much room for turning.

Then I noticed the rain on my face. "It's raining," I said.

"Hey." Kat sat up, surprised, "It is."

We got to our feet, shaking ourselves off, and then we ran with our heads back, trying to catch the rain in our mouths. We almost forgot to pick up our shoes as we jumped the cemetery fence and headed back, to study hall.

We went by Sister Bernard's office window fast, like two shadows, hoping she wouldn't notice us.

"You look awful," Kat said, at the foot of the stairs.

I looked at the grass in her hair. "You've got the mud on your shirt."

She dangled her oxfords by their strings. "I guess we'd better change."

By the time we reached our corridor, word had come up that Sister Bernard was looking for us. Kat had gone into the washroom and locked herself in the end john, hiding, but I was too slow and Voka, beaming because she had a mission, fastened on me.

Sure that this was the end of the road for me, I bumped down the stairs and into Sister Bernard's office, wondering what I would do if she told me I was restricted until June. I stood in front of her desk, making up speeches, noticing with a pang of defeat that I'd forgotten to put on my socks.

She sat at her desk, bent over her assignment book. Waiting, I let myself look around. The office was stern, all dull colors and straight lines, with a lifeless, institutional look. The black of Sister Bernard's outline against the wall made her seem frighteningly large and I shifted miserably, waiting for her to lift her head and acknowledge me.

When she did look up her face was set, as if she had a whole speech planned. Too distracted to realize what I was doing, I curled my fingers and tried to comb some of the grass out of my hair and as I worked at it she looked away from me, to the window, maybe because she wanted to spare me some of my embarrassment. When she turned back she let out her breath and said mildly, "You know you ought to be wearing socks."

I scraped one foot against the other ankle and all my past offenses began to pile in, to weigh on me. I held my breath, wanting to get it over with.

Instead of lecturing she bent her head to her desk, making little circles in the margin of her assignment book. Then

110

she said, to no apparent point, "Anne Feeney was asking about you yesterday."

I squinted at her, puzzled. "Sister?"

"She saw you in the court and wondered who you were."

"Oh—" I couldn't make out what she wanted me to say.

"She was walking in the garden."

"The garden." I thought of the geometric pattern, the unswerving lines of the walks, and I said with unexpected bitterness, "Yeah."

Her head came up. "Is something the matter?"

"It's just—" my hands went wide in an uncontrolled gesture.

"Yes?"

I waved my hands again. "She's just a kid."

There was an edge to her voice. "We didn't kidnap her."

"I know—I mean—I just—" I could feel myself go pink, apologetic and confused. "I didn't mean—"

She smiled, smoothing it over. "I know. Just remember—it was her idea. It may not appeal to you," her eyes were steady, "and then again it may."

I felt my throat harden, but I kept still.

"She'll be getting the white veil soon," Sister Bernard said. I choked. "Uh—that's swell." A part of my mind had already linked Feeney and Sister Bernard and the graveyard in a way that I wasn't ready to explore, and I leapt for familiar ground. "Voka said you—"

"—wanted to see you about something." She tried to look stern. "I saw you and Katherine on the porch a while ago. Don't you know enough to come in out of the rain?"

I said "Yes, Sister," waiting for the axe to fall.

"You'd both better get into some dry clothes before you catch cold."

"Yes, Sister," I said, waiting.

She raised her hand in dismissal. "I think that will be all."

I hesitated on one foot, half of me already out the door, but something about the stark order of the room accused me and despite the fact that it would probably put me on the restricted list until June I said, "The graveyard. What about that?"

She was smiling. "Can't you leave well enough alone?"

I came back into the room, thinking, I wonder what we talked about Feeney for. "We were out there and all . . ."

When she took off her glasses her eyes seemed bright and young. "Don't think you're the first girl to try one of those graves for size." The cuffs of her habit were turned back,

111

and her wrists were smooth, like a girl's. "Those dry clothes," she said. "Make it pajamas."

"But—"

"I'll see that you're both excused from study hall."

"Thank you, Sister." I didn't comprehend that I was dismissed.

She closed her book. "That will be all."

And I dipped into a little curtsey left over from parochial school. "Thank you, 'Stir."

I found myself lingering outside the office, looking at the framed graduation pictures that lined the dark-panelled hall and overflowed, mounting the wall that flanked the stairs. Someone had pointed out Sister Bernard to me once at the beginning of the year but I hadn't paid much attention at the time, because the connection between the nun and this gallery of wide-eyed girls had seemed unreal. Now I started up the steps, going slowly along the rows of class photos until I came to Sister Bernard's class, a series of twelve oval photographs of girls who looked outrageously antique in chiffon drapes and deep-parted bangs, done in sepia and matted together, fixed as they had been photographed on some forgotten spring. There she was, third from the left, top row: Bernadette Reardon, looking as young as Feeney—or me. And there she was behind me, at the foot of the stairs, framed in the office door. It was her choice, I told myself, and then, Oh, God, please don't let me be a nun.

XII

A stained-glass window dominates the Naval Academy chapel, where God and Naval history seem all bound up together in a way that is appropriate, finally, because men who make their lives on the water accept death as a constant possibility, where John Paul Jones lies pickled in a great sarcophagus below. Within the frame of the window Christ walks on the water, for my father and all the others, for those who will die on the water some day.

I went to the chapel once as a child, to the wedding of one of my father's junior officers. If I noticed the window at all it was for the reds and blues and greens, the way the sun shot through the panes and spread in a splash of colored light. When I saw it again I was eighteen and my throat knotted so that I had to walk away from Katherine, pretending to look at an inscription, until I could face her again. We were freshmen at college that year.

Most of our class was at the Academy for a tea-fight, a mixer and dancing class for plebes. It was an earnest little affair, funny and slightly sweaty and hard to reconcile with the relics of gallantry, the list of Navy dead, the tattered flag that were our background in Memorial Hall. I trotted around the floor without noticing when one bright-faced boy elbowed out another and took me over with an air that was mechanical, cocky or romantic, depending on how polished and how old he was. I was too preoccupied to pay much attention to any of them and I barely managed to be polite as I looked over heads for Bunker, wondering if I would know him after nearly ten years.

He was a plebe that year. Mrs. Swift had written to my mother in that off-hand way that mothers are apt to adopt when they're going to ask you to do something hard. She had suggested that since we had been so close as children, I might look Bunker up.

It was simple enough; if I wanted to see him I could go to the main desk and have him called down. But I chose the dance, the anonymous kids in uniform, instead, with an unformed idea at the back of my mind that had to do with earning the meeting through ordeal. I wanted to find Bunker and I didn't want to find him. I wanted to find him in my own time, in my own way. I think I wanted him to find me.

Kat and I went to Annapolis together, crammed on the back seat of a WB and A bus. We didn't talk much because Kat was busy with a book and I was sunk into myself, uncomfortable in a wool dress that was too hot for early fall but flattered me, wishing morbidly that the fumes from the motor would make me sick so I wouldn't have to go through with it. I was nervous about the tea fight because I hated mixers, which called up the seventh grade in all its agony, when boys and girls stood on opposite sides of the dance floor and advanced stiffly, if they advanced at all. I faced the possibility of seeing Bunker again with feelings I wasn't ready to analyze; I tried to think about him as I knew him but all I could remember was the day the Swifts left us, with Bunker and his brother together in the back seat, and as if on cue the thought prompted a lonely ache.

I looked out the window morosely, watching the direction signs flip by, and then I poked Katherine hard, and pointed, because we had just come over the last rise and ahead of us, across the river, Bancroft Hall, the chapel dome, the whole Yard stretched out before us as if it had been set there a second before, for me to see at that moment.

"Oh," Katherine said, and put down her book.

Then we were on the bridge, skimming the Severn, and I took in quarters and quonsets and cars with official stickers with a feeling of homesickness not for this place, where I had never lived, but for the familiar, for Daddy in khakis and visits to the base. I tried to explain a little of it to Katherine.

"Um," she said, wanting to understand.

Kat got trapped by a lanky, disjointed young man who maneuvered her like a piece of farm machinery and when she got away from him finally she said, "Let's get out of here."

I turned away from the morass of dark uniforms, satisfied at last that Bunker wasn't there, that staying wouldn't make him come.

"Okay."

We clattered down the stairs and into the rotunda. A covey of midshipmen clicked past as if they had their minds on business but one or two of them looked back at Katherine. She caught it too, and I saw her hide a grin.

We came down the stone stairs and into the cobbled court. "The brick," I said suddenly, nagged by a vestigial memory.

"Huh?"

"There's something about a brick." I remembered it as something Daddy had showed me once, perhaps the day of the wedding, and it began to seem important.

"What are you talking about?" For a second Kat, in heels, looked like an impatient grown-up.

"There's a brick here with initials on it," I said, and the details began to come back. "Daddy showed it to me." I had to find it, to make Katherine see that I belonged.

Kat stretched, and was herself again. "Oh."

"I mean, it's the only one. They make plebes find it."

"Swell."

"Sometimes they're out looking for it for hours." I paced off the right number of paces from the stairs. "It's supposed to be right about here."

Kat came over, interested. "Let's see."

"To the left a little, maybe," I said, not so sure.

"I don't see anything."

It wasn't there.

I backtracked. I had to prove myself to Katherine. "Maybe it's over this way."

"Maybe you're making it up."

"I'm *not* making it up."

"You were only a little kid."

"But I *remember*." I motioned her over to another part of the court.

She hung over my shoulder, waiting to be shown.

"Oh, here." But the brick I had chosen was only cracked.

"Are you sure there's a brick?" Kat said in a way that irritated me.

"There's a brick." I walked bent over, like a peasant under a heavy load, staring at the bricks until they seemed to move.

"Hey, Denny, come on," Kat said.

"No, it's here. I'm sure."

"We'd better get going if we want to see anything."

I was stooping now, poring over the grey-faced bricks.

"Denny?" She touched my arm.

I shook her off. "Not yet. I want to show you. It's right here."

"Show it to me next time."

"I have to find it now."

"It doesn't matter," she said.

"It *does* matter. If I can't find it now I never will."

"Well, look. I'm going on over to the chapel. The bus leaves in half an hour."

I hardly heard her because I was looking at the bricks—all the bricks—now, staring until they seemed to move, like the elements of a kaleidoscope, changing and multiplying until they seemed endless, dazzling me. I looked up from them finally, helpless.

"Come on," Kat said, gently this time. She had come back for me.

I went with her docilely, caught up in a sense of something lost that primed me, in a way, for the chapel window, so that when I saw it I was ready for tears. I moved away before Kat could look up from the hymnal she had opened, and I got myself together before she could see me, walking the outer aisles, pretending to read the legends on the windows and the inscriptions on the plaques placed here and there. Without knowing how it had come to me I had the idea that Bunker was my link with the Yard, the window, the tradition, that I had only to find Bunker to make everything all right. I don't know now whether I was looking for romance or Daddy or simply a part of me that had been missing. I just know that at the time my idea of Bunker had something to do with a kind of completion, that even as I realized I expected too much I let myself think that things would be whole and right for me if only I could find him. I came back to the chapel door full of it, wanting to tell some of it to Katherine because explaining it might begin to make it clear but she had already gone down the steps to the sidewalk and was engaged in talk with an upperclassman, standing with one knee locked, under the trees.

The reunion, or what-have-you, came two years later, and when it came it was simple enough.

My mother greeted me at the door one evening that summer, as I came in from work. "The Swifts are back."

"No kidding?" I thought, Bunker, and my stomach tightened.

"They're living in Arlington. Jake is at the Pentagon."

"You talked to her?"

She nodded. "She sounds just the same. They're dying to see us."

"Gee, we haven't seen them since—"

"Since Florida. You and Bunker used to tear around like wild men." She seemed to be seeing us, and for a moment the air was heavy with the quality of that first winter in Florida. "You remember Bunker, don't you?"

It was the formula before we saw anybody we hadn't seen for a long time, a motherly prompting, but I was aghast at her even thinking I could forget so easily. "Well, sure."

"I thought we might call on them." She fluttered her hands uncertainly.

I looked at her then, touched but a little unnerved to see that she was apprehensive too. "Fine. When do you want to go?"

"I told her we'd come tomorrow," she said, and I had the feeling she'd put something over on me.

We didn't seem to have much to say to each other on the way to Arlington the next afternoon; we muttered over road signs and I smoked, wondering how much we all had changed, relieved that for this first encounter, at least, Bunker would be safely away at the Academy and I could break myself in gradually, starting with his parents. We pulled up in front of a series of brick row houses at four, the calling hour, and there was a little flurry while my mother went through her pocketbook for the slip with the house number. Then we smoothed the skirts of our summer linens, and went to the door.

"Jen!" Bunker's mother said, and I realized that I had expected her to loom over me in the old Cuban-heeled spectators, the droopy voile dress. Instead she was all freckles and shorts and long-legged informality, with hair shorter and redder than I had remembered it, and the fact that she and I were almost of a height now made her seem still younger, almost contemporary, so that I found myself thinking of her and Bunker's father by their first names. She looked at me briefly with an expression that called up that day in the shadowy upstairs hall and then she and my mother embraced.

"Denny," Jake said, and touched my hair.

After that first minute we were very gay.

We sat in aluminum chairs on the back screen porch, drinking—with both Swifts amused that I was old enough

—and the three of them slipped into talk so easily that I could begin to see the pattern of friendship remembered that had kept them close through years of not seeing each other, when they seldom wrote. They had begun the roll of old shipmates, the litany of Navy names, and the wraith of my father trembled at the edge of the talk, close, when Margaret Swift seemed to see where they were heading and got up suddenly, trying to shake off nostalgia and manage a hostess smile. "You haven't seen the house."

It wasn't until we followed her upstairs that I realized how completely I had managed to put Pearson out of my mind.

"This is Pearson's room," she said, opening the door on a rat's nest of papers and books, and closing it fast. "When he's home he does nothing but read. And even when he's not holed up in there he won't let me in to clean. Has a fit if I touch anything," she said, baffled but proud.

Pearson loomed in my mind, big and dark, and I remembered how much I had hated him. "He's—not here," I said, to reassure myself.

She shook her head. "He wanted to check on something at the Widener, so he's in Cambridge for the week. I know he'll be sorry he missed you."

I didn't say anything.

"Denny's sorry too," my mother said for me. "How's Bunker?"

"Don't let him hear you call him that. He made us drop the nickname when he got to seventh grade."

I don't know why, but I felt betrayed, and I knew I would never call him by anything but the old name.

"He's at the Academy," his mother said, knowing we knew. She opened a door on an immaculately plain room relieved only by blue ticking curtains at the window, a photograph of one of Jake's ships above the tautly spread bed. "This is his room when he's here."

"Oh," I said, and followed Jake inside.

The ship's complement had been assembled on deck for the photograph.

"That's me on the right," Jake said, and I recognized him at once, looking much the same, squinting in the sun that bounced off the whites he and the others had put on for the camera. His voice roughened. "Your dad is in the back."

And there he was.

"It was our first ship," he said, looking as if he wished he hadn't brought it up. "Ben wanted it for his room."

The curtains, the cruise box stencilled with Bunker's initials, even the air in the room seemed crisp and military and for some reason the jaunty young officers in whites had merged with Bunker in my mind, still young, always invulnerable, so that I was able to look at Jake and say easily, "He must love having a place to let down, after all those regulations."

"You'd be surprised," Jake said. "He never lets up." He showed me how the bedspread sprang back up under his hand. "He made that bed."

Then, before he could explain to me that Bunker was home on his first class leave, there was a sound downstairs.

"Here he is now. I was hoping he'd get back in time to see you." His mother leaned over the banister. "Ben, we have company."

Then he was on the stairs, and all the Bunkers I had imagined or remembered dissolved into a lean young man with hair cropped close to a spare, racehorse head. He came up, with a grin of instant charm, and surprisingly, kissed my mother on the cheek.

"Mrs. McLeod," he said.

"Well, Bunker," she said, pink and pleased.

"You remember Denny," his mother said.

"Hi." The grin again, and then a pause while he sized me up.

I remember thinking, I bet he's quite an operator. The meeting had been too quick, and I hadn't had time to match up this Bunker with the Bunker of my expectations. I tried to collect myself, and instead of saying something simple or even something I might say to another boy, to bring him on, I tried to recall things as they had been, to put them in focus, saying, "Hey, remember the war?"

And without a word of prompting he said, "PF 34 calling control tower. Control tower calling PF 34."

"Come in please."

"Hey, Ben, two minutes." A young man in khakis poked his head up the stairs.

"A classmate," Bunker said, explaining, turning away from my half-raised hand. "Sit tight."

"Oh, Terry." Bunker's mother said, following Jake and my mother down the stairs. "Go on up."

". . . cocktails in just a few minutes," Jake was saying. "It's a little class party. Will you come along?"

I heard my mother saying no.

"Don't rush off—"

"No, really, Margaret, Denny and I have to—"

"But we don't have to dress yet," Jake said.

"Not for an hour."

"No, it's time. Denise?"

"Be right with you." I bumped past Bunker's classmate, who had draped himself on the rail.

Bunker remembered his manners. "Denny, this is Terry Balin."

"Hi," I said.

"Well, hi," Terry said, properly attentive for a split second before he jostled Bunker's arm. "Come *on*."

"The boys have had this party arranged for weeks," Margaret was telling my mother in apology, "or he wouldn't be racing off like this."

"We're delighted to see him," my mother said.

"I'll see you," Bunker said.

"Fine."

"Ben?" Terry made it two syllables.

"Okay, okay."

Then my mother and I seemed to be saying goodbye.

"Hey," Bunker said, reappearing at the top of the stairs. "I'll call you. OK?"

I looked up, feeling so rushed that I wanted to go back and do the whole thing over. "That'd be fine."

Our mothers exchanged looks.

They couldn't know that Bunker and I loved each other, and would love each other for all that would happen, but in a way that has never had anything to do with romance.

The car seemed almost mournfully silent after that houseful of activity and talk. Neither my mother nor I had anything to do that night, and I suspect the contrast between the lives of the two families was beginning to weigh on us.

"Well," my mother said, to take our minds off it, "I guess we'll have to get used to calling him Ben."

I was thinking back. "He doesn't look anything like I remembered him."

"I think he's attractive," she said, waiting to see what I would say.

"He used to be so sort of sturdy."

"I remember now," she said. "He *was* stocky."

"I didn't think much of his friend."

"Balin," she said. "I bet he's Bob and Polly's boy."

"He doesn't *act* like Navy."

"The manners? He'll outgrow that." She turned into Memorial Bridge. "I bet that *is* Bob and Polly's boy. He looks a lot like his father."

I said, "So does Bunker."

"I know." She was watching the road, but I sensed that she was seeing something like the triple image I had seen, looking at the photograph in Bunker's room. To keep from having to talk about it, or having to think about the time when Jake and Daddy had been young and both families had been complete, she said, "You could have acted a little more interested in Pearson."

"I'm *not* interested in Pearson," I said.

"You were rude."

"I don't care." My face was stiff. "I don't want to have anything to do with him."

"You could have at least—" she began.

I had to explain. "He hit me once, when he shouldn't have."

She looked at me mildly. "But that was such a long time ago."

We came out of the park, onto Connecticut Avenue, and then she spoke again. "We don't have to be home for anything. Let's get a sandwich and go to a show."

XIII

Everything about the next four days was compressed, intensified, as if the days had been lifted up from the usual span of time and magnified, so that they would seem like entities. Bunker and his roommates had only that short time left before they had to report back to the Academy, and they did everything fast because they had to lay up a store of things done, things to be remembered, things different from the military routine which had so completely superimposed itself on their lives that their days at the Academy blended into each other in just the way that Mann describes, and time slowed down and extended itself only when they were away from the continuity of the military routine. My life was somewhat the same—patterned, with every day going by in much the same way, too fast to be marked or remembered—so that those four days stood out for me, apart, larger than life, and I think of the people of that long weekend as bound to me for life, even though I doubt if I will ever see any of them again.

The others and I look back on a short lifetime shared, and I feel as if I know Terry, Willie Laughton, who was Bunker's other roommate, and the admiral's daughter and the high school girl as well as I have ever known Pearson or Pat or Katherine. I am anxious still for any news of them, and I take a proprietary interest in the promotions, the weddings, the news of the high school girl's elopement and divorce, filtered through Pearson, who knows I keep track. I still have an affinity for the four of them; it's as if we have been through something momentous together, something which binds us, as the Titanic survivors are bound to meet on the anniversary of the sinking, year after year.

Part of this feeling of closeness in a given time has to do with the fact that the people involved are strangers. In such relationships there is no backlog of things known, no past and probably no furure, so that you may act more openly at such a time, telling yourself the whole incident is isolated from real life and you can go from it without being touched by it, back to being what you were, in your own time and place, without any break in the continuity. It's a what-the-hell feeling, but it's more than that. It's a revelatory time.

It might have been just that way; I might have come through those four days with Bunker and his friends untouched, like the others, if it had not been for the thing with Bunker in the parking lot, a matter of conscience which engaged me, and linked that time with the rest of my life.

I learned at the beginning that Bunker was interested in Iris Grisher, an admiral's daughter, that summer, and I didn't resent it in any way becaue Iris was pretty and appropriate for Bunker, and any feeling he might have for her did not infringe on the terms of our relationship, because we had agreed a long time before each to let the other be what he wanted to be. He called me on Thursday, the day after my mother and I made our call, and I was surprised but not hurt when he told me he had a date with Iris for a cookout at his house, and asked if I'd like to pair off with his other wife. His other wife turned out to be Willie Laughton, a middle-sized, awkward, sweet-faced boy from Nebraska who was not a Navy junior and had never even seen water before he came to the Academy. He was gangly and engaging, with a crew cut and helpless grin that made him look like Alfred E. Newman.

They turned up at our door in their idea of casual clothes: pale slacks and short-sleeved shirts, Willie's with a small print and Bunker's pastel green, neat and attractive, a little too well-kept and at opposite poles from Pat's idea of what was worn, what was shoe. My mother was pleased by their quick chivalry and I think she was delighted to see me leave the house with not one, but two boys.

"Iris is next," Bunker said when we were in the car. "Her father was in '27."

"I don't know her," I said.

"She lives in Chevy Chase."

I remembered that Terry Balin had been included in the plans. "Where's Terry?" I asked, hoping he'd been included out, because we had disliked each other on sight.

123

"He's picking up his—date," Bunker said, with an inflection that made me swivel to look at him.

"This high school kid from his block," Willie said. He had been humming under his breath, obviously delighted by the breeze on his bare elbow, by being free of the uniform.

"Kid!" Bunker said. "Willie's been staying with Terry. His folks are in—"

"—Nebraska," I filled in. "About this girl—"

They were like little boys about it, and for a minute I expected them to say "Woo woo," the way the boys used to in grammar school, rolling their eyes and giving it just enough suggestion to make it seem like the punch line of a dirty joke that is postulated on absolute lack of experience. I don't know that I can make myself clear on this: it's just that these particular boys had been lifted out of context at a certain time, when the rest of us were beginning to explore each other as people, and they still thought of girls not as people like themselves, imperfect and vulnerable, everyday and approachable, but in extremes, good and bad, as queens (and this is actually Academy slang for a beautiful girl) or as tramps, slinky and sinful, in a romanticism that gave them a peculiar innocence.

"Donna. You should see her." Willie shook his head.

"A sort of vest-pocket Monroe," Bunker said.

I said, "I'm not surprised," under my breath, and took out a cigarette.

Bunker heard me and grinned. "I didn't know it showed."

"It shows."

"Terry's all right," Willie said easily and his lower lip curved, just like the old illustrations of elves in children's books. "Poor Chumley hasn't seen a white woman in ten years."

"Mmm." I let Willie light my cigarette. "I bet Mrs. Grisher is going to be thrilled."

"She's not going to get a look at either of them," Bunker said. "Terry's waiting at home."

"He and Donna are getting the fire going," Willie said innocently, and we all laughed.

There was an easy, just-us-guys atmosphere in the car that had to do with Bunker's and my friendship as children, a certain equilibrium we'd hit when we'd decided, without having to think it out or discuss it, to continue the friendship on the same terms, dropping the mechanics of boy-girl games and telling each other what we thought. The feeling intensified when Iris got in because Iris was ultra-feminine, frilly and pale, and she always looked as if her mother had just finished dressing her. Her pretty face was just a little blank.

"Well, let's go back and check on the fire," Bunker said, for Willie and me, and then he fixed his attention on Iris, talking to her as if she were a queen.

"Mother and I took Tinker to the vet's this afternoon," she said, and began telling him about it.

In the back, Willie turned to me.

"You're in the Navy too, huh?"

"Well, sort of. My father—"

He seemed to know, and cut me off, so I wouldn't have to explain. "Yeah. But you're still in it, aren't you?"

I thought about Jake, and the picture. "I guess I am."

"Everybody in Washington is in the Navy," he said, looking glum.

"It just seems that way. I guess it's a little like being in a club."

"It's a lot like it." He gave a doleful, appealing sigh.

I found myself looking at him maternally. "It's kind of nice."

"Not for me. I mean—Ben and Terry—they have it made because they grew up with it." The curved lower lip drooped in a way that made him seem defenseless. "They know what to expect."

"I don't get it."

"The whole business. Getting through. I'll be lucky if I even make it through till next June. Ben—Ben's going to be an admiral some day."

I looked at the back of Bunker's neck, taut and neatly shaped, and thought he might very well. "If it's just grades, don't worry," I said, finally understanding what he was getting at. "They're out to help you, not cut you off."

"Like the rifle manual." He slipped into the recital with a certain familiarity, as if he'd made it many times before. "Ben and Terry knew it before I'd even heard of it. And little things, like the brick. Their *fathers* told them how to find the brick. I'm from *Nebraska*," he said desperately.

"You'll do all right."

"Ben—he hardly has to hit the books."

"He didn't pick *that* up just because he's a Navy junior."

"I know—everything comes easy for him." He picked morosely at the knee of his slacks. "It's just that this stuff—his father and all—makes it come even easier."

"Hey," I said, finding myself wanting to comfort him.

"I don't know—sometimes I don't think I'll make it."

"You'll make it," I said, reassuring him. It was shadowy in the car and I found myself wanting to make him feel better, patting his hand.

"I don't know," he said, taking my hand and holding it contentedly. "I just don't know."

Jake and Margaret were coming out the front door just as we got to Bunker's house, leaving for supper at the club. They greeted us on the front walk, pleased, I think, to see me and Bunker together, a continuation of a friendship they had prized. I stood with them for a minute, wanting them to stay, until Margaret, who seemed to see that I valued them too, took my hand and said, "We'd better run. Have a good time."

"Terry and his—girl are out back," Jake said and then added, significantly, "Better tell him we don't expect to be away too long."

Terry and his girl were sitting away from the firelight, nuzzling under a tree. She got up to greet us, sleek in a peasant blouse and black shorts rolled up to expose the curve of her thighs. She was one of those people who is always on, who seems always to know something that you don't know, and Terry, who had two years on Bunker and me, looked like a child beside her. She had a high school beauty queen gloss to her, a combination of mock seductiveness and hard-shelled sophistication that made her seem a little larger than life, as unassailable as the hundreds of girls like her who have followed it through to careers in Hollywood. I can't explain my feelings about her and the others like her, all the starlets and all the beauty queens, except to say that they have never seemed like *people* to me; they've always seemed like something more—or less. I felt awkward, like a child around the girl, even though I was nearly twenty-one at the time and she couldn't have been more than seventeen.

"Well, hello," she said, in an adult voice.

"This is Donna," Bunker said, and introduced Iris and me. I couldn't know what Iris was thinking, but I think she had the idea, even more than I did, that she was in over her head.

Then Bunker and Willie and I made a production of the fire, and Iris got busy bringing hot dogs, buns, all the rest of the paraphernalia out of the house and laying them neatly on the aluminum table Jake had set up for us.

The Swifts came home at ten or so, as they had promised, and chaperoned discreetly, going on up to bed because they knew it was enough that they were there. Terry and his girl left soon after, and I think the rest of us were relieved to see them go. Even Iris seemed to perk up, and talked to us all in that high, light voice that probably will never mature, hands folded on the sprigged print of her skirt. We knew we were keeping the neighbors up but we sat in the yard until the last coals died, laughing and carrying on in that exaggerated gaiety that comes when you know you're being watched. It's a form of awareness of the moment, the same thing that happens when you're riding around in a convertible, enjoying it mostly because you know that people can see you doing it, can see how much you are enjoying it.

In the car, on the way home, Willie put his arm around me.

"I'm the first one in my family to go into the Navy," he said.

"They must be very proud of you."

"They are." His cheek was against my hair. "I'm the first one to amount to anything."

I was pleased for him, and I touched his arm.

"But I just don't know if I'm going to make it."

"You'll make it," I said.

"I don't know." Our heads were close, and I could almost feel the vibration of his words as he talked. "I'm coming so close in a couple of things—three lousy years, and I still haven't licked it."

"Hey, it's going to be all right." The atmosphere in the car was dark and drowsy; the air was soft.

"I'm going to bilge out," he said.

"It can't be that bad."

He shook his head miserably. "I just don't know what they'd say—"

I kissed him to make him feel better, to shut him up.

Mrs. Grisher, who was in her sixties, older than most of our parents, gave us a dinner-party the next night, trying for an atmosphere of gaiety that she remembered from her debutante days, wanting to invest in us the qualities of the social crowd she remembered from her youth. We did our best and this pressure made the six of us—Bunker, Willie, Terry, Iris and I and even Donna, looming in her absence—seem linked, forged into a group. We sat in the living room after dinner, talking awkwardly over tepid drinks. Terry bent over the blind date Iris had arranged for him, his handsome head faceted like a diamond, charming her in a completely mechanical way. For all his ease, he was completely remote, alien, even to Bunker and Willie, who had roomed with him for the better part of three years. In the four days that I knew him, I don't remember that Terry and I ever talked. I could see Iris watching him, willing him not to make the break, but as soon as it was decent he excused himself, thanking Mrs. Grisher effusively and bending over Bunker to whisper, "I've got a late date," with the blood running close to the surface in his thin, dark face.

Iris told him goodbye at the door and then came back into the room anxiously, pleading with us not to let her party break up too soon. We talked for as long as we could, trying to pay extra attention to Iris's friend who had begun to look hurt the moment Terry had walked out. Finally it was time for us to go.

The boys took me to a Hot Shoppe afterward and we had orange freezes in the car, feeling cordial in the warm summer night.

The boys had hamburgers. "Bite?" Bunker said, offering his.

I shook my head.

"Come on. You'll starve to death. I know—you're slimming." He dug me in the ribs.

I had to defend myself. "I am not. It's Friday."

There was a slow change in his face, a remembered reaction so instinctive that he may not even have realized that it showed. "Oh, yeah. Hey, Willie," he said, "this girl's a member of your lodge."

Willie blushed and got all nervous, the way people do when they're reminded of something they haven't thought about for a long time.

"Poor Will," Bunker said, "he's been trying to forget."

I looked into his face then, trying to find something I could fix on, some objection I could answer, because I'd gotten old enough to want to answer, but all I could read was indifference.

"Wait till midnight," I said weakly, "and I'll eat the whole thing."

"Fat chance," Bunker said, and wolfed it.

The next night the boys picked me up in an aura of doubt that deepened when they stopped at the Grishers' and Bunker brought Iris out, mushrooming an umbrella over her because it had begun to rain. We were all in our best because it was Saturday night, the boys uncomfortable in light suits with shirts and ties that matched a little too well, Iris fluffy in a party dress.

There seemed to be an embarrassment over where we were going.

We were almost at the bridge when Iris said, "I thought we were going dancing."

"Tonight?" Bunker bent his head to her. "It's our last night."

I said, thinking I might as well, "How about the Eight Twenty-Three?"

"Can't." Willie tried a number of expressions, all of them unsuccessful.

Iris was watching Bunker.

"Party at Donna's house," he said finally, not surprising anybody but her. When she asked him about it, he wouldn't explain.

The house was almost dark when we got there and for a minute I was relieved, thinking there was no one there and we could go on without Terry and Donna. Then Terry was at the door, hailing us, ushering us in with the air of a householder. He excused himself almost before we were inside.

We went up the steps under one umbrella, the boys flanking Iris and me and pretending that they were being sheltered too, and we came into the living room like travelers cast together, a tight unit looking over its new lodgings. It was a little like the first act of *Outward Bound*.

The living room was dim and damp, with moisture entrenched in the yellow brick of the fireplace and the sisal rug that Donna's mother had put down for summer. The furniture was a combination of bamboo and flowered upholstery, and the room was without character, as impersonal as a room in a motel. I was touched to see a three-color photograph of Donna, taken some years before, angled on the mantel. For some reason I was relieved to see that there had been at least one attempt to put a stamp on the room. Iris arranged herself on a chair with an uneven little laugh and faced the door, watching it as if she expected the other guests to be arriving soon. She looked at me as if for reassurance but I wasn't sure what she wanted to be reassured of, and I turned away from her in a carelessness that I have since regretted, and pretended not to see. I found myself wondering what Iris was going to do. This wasn't the social life her mother pictured for her, and her puffy flowered dress seemed out of place in the careless, characterless atmosphere of the room. The three of us stood on a little island on the rug, watching her as if she were a cat we had sent into a strange place ahead of us, and whether we stayed or not depended on her acceptance of the place. She must have caught the feeling of the night just then, the character of our isolation, because she kicked off her shoes unexpectedly and sat on her feet, motioning Bunker to come sit by her chair. When he had settled himself on the floor by her, with his elbow up and one hand resting lightly on her skirts, Willie took my arm with a warm, I'm-here look that made us allies, and I followed his lead and sat on the couch.

Donna came out of the kitchen then, with a hostess smile that would have done credit to a TV commercial, jangling in a number of bracelets and an outfit that ended in black toreador pants. I had a pretty good idea that her parents had gone out somewhere before she got dressed, because her makeup was too thick and there were two thin gold chains looped around one ankle. She had on sandals that showed toenails done in an iridescent pink. Terry followed her, putting one arm around her shoulder in a mixture of proprietorship and mockery.

"Hi," she said. "Make yourselves at home. Ter?"

"Mmmmmmm."

"Come help me with the punch."

He followed her back into the kitchen, in a loose-jointed imitation of her walk. He came out with a fifth of rye. "You know what she was about to do? She was about to mix this with *orange* juice."

Bunker and Willie groaned.

Donna bumped him with her hip, pretending to pout.

"Don't worry, sweetie." He put an arm around her. "Daddy will fix."

Terry knew as well as the rest of us how things should be done, and he brought out a respectable tray—bottles, glasses, ice. We sat and talked fairly easily for the first two rounds, feeling our way. Then Terry became engrossed in Donna, and Willie and Bunker began mixing for us, getting heavy-handed.

I don't know what had fixed itself in Iris's mind, but I had an uncanny feeling that in part, at least, she mirrored me. Her eyes were bright and her hair was loose and somewhere along the way she had eased out of the chair and onto the floor next to Bunker, leaning against him, looking more relaxed than I would have imagined she could. She switched to ginger ale at one point, but her nose was already pink.

Willie and I had hit a new plane, where even the furriest little remark or the weakest little gesture signified great things and needed no explanation, talking in a mixture of friendship and manufactured self-pity that seemed to surpass understanding. As I talked I could detach myself and watch from a great distance, aching for Willie and his whole hopeful family in Nebraska, for the inadequacy of my attempts to reassure him. Terry and Donna disappeared without our noticing and when I looked at Bunker and Iris again they seemed removed, heads close, enclosed in their own small circle, which seemed to bear no relation to ours. Without knowing how it happened I found myself on the porch with Willie, pressed close on the glider, vaguely aware that there was a faint light coming through glass covered by curtains, because the door to the living room was closed.

For some reason, Willie was crying.

"Hey, hey—" I said. "Hey, Willie—"

"I am," he said. "Gonna bilge out."

"You won't."

"I will. I know it. What'll I do?" He pressed his head against me. "Be ruined. Couldn't go back."

I was rocking him. "Hey, Willie—hey—"

"My sister—" His voice was muffled against my front. "Sister got everybody to kick in—getting me a car. Graduation present."

"Great. That's great."

"Not great. I'm not going to make it. I'll never make it." He sat away from me for a minute, head drooping, elbows on his knees. "They all want me to. Know what I'll do if I don't make it? Kill myself. Just die—"

"No—no—"

"I will. Denny, I will." He almost threw himself on me for support, and I drew him to me because I wanted to give it, because he seemed so inept, so defenseless at heart. Then we were embracing, settling back on the couch in a growing, merging warmth. I felt myself drawn on, partly because he seemed so helpless, partly because a part of me knew I would probably never see him again, and if I was troubled by the dull knowledge that I had no business there, I was trying my best to fight it back. I can say in honesty that I don't know what would have happened if Bunker hadn't opened the door just then. We could still have settled back into darkness, pretending not to hear him, but the dull feeling in me snapped into focus at the sound of the door opening and I got up.

"Iris wants to go home."

There are times when you come so close. I wish I could say that conscience alone stopped me, held me back, that I faced it squarely and decided for myself, but it didn't happen that way. Conscience was involved, I think, but it was booted along by circumstance, so that I will never know for sure what I would have done if the choice had been left to me alone. I think now that there would have come a point when I would have stopped short, made aware of myself and what I was doing by the simple embarrassment of action, the reminder of time and place, but I can never be positive because circumstance robbed me of the decision. Knowing this potential in myself has tempered my judgments, made me much less sure of myself. And that makes me think these narrow escapes may be part of a design, some saving grace that saves because your intentions have been good most of the way along, and at the same time reminds you even more searingly that you are always fallible, as people are.

Iris stood alone, at the center of the living room.

Her lipstick was smeared and her hair disarranged, and she looked ready to cry. I noticed the hair first, and put a hand to my own, feeling frowzy and uncomfortable. The boys put on their jackets, trying for a conversation about where we could go next, and I noticed that their shirts were crushed, their summer suits all creaseless and rumpled.

Terry and Donna came downstairs just then, Terry natty in a tropical worsted and Donna dressed in a black sheath, with her hair redone, both looking freshly showered and too good for us. We stood in a grubby little tangle, watching them come.

"Where to?" Terry said.

Bunker shrugged. "I don't know. Iris wants to go home."

"Hey, Izzy," Terry said, "don't be a party poop."

Iris was in the middle of the room with her handbag pressed primly against her skirts. I couldn't make anything of her expression. She seemed to have tried on an old face of her mother's, found that it fitted, and decided to wear it until she got home.

She looked at Terry with dislike. "I have to. Mother is waiting up." She turned stiffly and went to the door. I admired her for the way she left, without looking to see whether anybody was coming with her.

"Hey, you don't have to go too, do you?" Bunker said, to me. His face was disorganized in a way that reminded me of the two of us, as children, he pleading for something and both of us knowing I would never say no.

I managed a smile, because of that, and shook my head. I wish to hell I had gone home then.

"We'll meet Terry at Szabo's, then," he said, and started for the door. "You and Willie riding with us?"

We followed him to the car, Willie finishing a rye he had poured in the fumbling silence as Terry came downstairs. He wouldn't look at me.

By the time we got to Iris's house, he was asleep. It was a silent little ride, with me knotted in the back seat and Bunker humming desperately, just to bring some noise into the car. Iris sat quietly, as unreachable as a carved white lady, and she relaxed the marble line of her jaw only long enough to say good night to me, to indicate that she held nothing against me, before Bunker took her in. I sat in the back, waiting.

The door on my side opened, and Bunker stood by it quietly.

Willie roused himself for a minute. "Yo, Ben," he said, and went back to sleep.

I got out and into the front seat, next to Bunker.

"When do you have to go back?"

"Tomorrow night," he said, looking tired.

"About time?"

He gave me a funny look. "How did you—yeah, I guess it is. Iris—parents—" He took a corner hard, and I realized he was drunker than I had thought. "There's just too damn much going on."

"In too little time," I said, trying to remember how long it had been since I had been home.

"And my damn brother—"

I can't be sure, but I think my hands went cold.

"—back from Harvard, all full of snot—" the car lunged. "—get the idea I'm not *good* enough for him."

"He was always like that," I said, wanting him to go on, to vindicate my hatred.

"And another thing—"

I waited.

"Two years in the Army, and his room is still a rats' nest."

I couldn't help it. I laughed.

"What's so damn funny?" The corners of his mouth seemed dragged down, and I should have been warned.

"You—he—" I couldn't get it out, at first. "He's such a— well, a bastard, and all you can think of—"

"All I can think of is what."

I shouldn't have pursued it, but I did. I think I wanted us to get into Pearson, to dissect him, to explain him, so that I would be armed in case I ever had to see him again.

133

"His—" I wasn't laughing, but I prolonged the sound, "His room."

"Why not his room?" Bunker set his jaw. "Two years in the Marines didn't even *touch* him."

"He was always hard to reach," I said, trying to get at something.

"It rolled right off him."

I tried another path. "He was always so—"

"He hated it," Bunker said, not listening.

"So hard to *get* to. There are people like that—all shield."

He may have said "Um."

"You try and try," I said, offering it. "And you never know if there's anything *behind* the shield."

Bunker was looking at the road and beyond it, his eyes bright with military pride. "If it had only been *me* in Korea—"

I hardly heard him, because I was trying to get on with the business of the shield. "Maybe it's something we all do—you know, prepare a face to meet the faces that you meet." I let it hang, wanting from him some understanding, some flash of perception that would unite us against his older brother.

He cut me off. "I would have shown the bastards."

"What?"

"In Korea."

His tone was so like the one I remembered from our war games as kids that at first I thought he was kidding and I said, with some irritation, "Didn't you get *enough* of that?"

He answered in a voice ragged with pride. "It's never over." Then, ignoring me, he began to talk about the things he had to do when he got back to the Academy, enumerating the bits of routine not for me, but for himself.

The air in the car had begun to go sour. I think it was simply because the weekend had gone on for so long at such a pace that something had to go wrong. Bunker and I and the others had been together for too long a stretch, and no matter what our feelings or our intentions, we were bound to part in an aura of fatigue and unpleasantness, like children who have played together for too long, past the point of pleasure, and can't help but quarrel.

Wanting to stave it off I let Bunker talk, murmuring every now and then when a response seemed to be in order. As I listened without interest it came to me that outside the country of memory, Bunker and I had little to talk about, and I was turning this over and over in my mind when I realized that I was supposed to respond.

"Huh?" I said.

"I said, I've been made a Batt officer," Bunker said, waiting for me to congratulate him.

"That's great," I said, grinning. If I acted pleased it was because I loved him, and when he began talking again I fell silent, brooding, trying to reconcile this Bunker with the Bunker of memory, with the idea of completion which I had carried, unformed, almost from the time we had said goodbye in Florida. I knew that no matter how many times we met he would always be remote, as he was that night, and it depressed me to think that no matter what the proportion of shared love, the backlog of experience, we would never have anything to say to each other. I was exploring this particular loneliness, engrossed in it, and at first I didn't notice that he had turned toward me, that he was watching, expecting some kind of answer.

"Huh?"

"Well, do you think you'd like to?" He was waiting.

"Think—I'd—like—to—" I was stalling, the way you do in class, when you haven't heard the question.

"Help me," he said impatiently.

"Oh, you mean—" I wanted to reach him.

"I was asking you to help me entertain the Robinsons Homecoming Weekend," he said with an edge to his voice. "But never mind."

"Oh, Bunker I—"

I reached for his hand, but it was too late.

"Forget it," he said sharply, and when he looked my way again his face was closed.

I sank into myself, hardly noticing when he pulled into the gravelled parking lot at Szabo's. It seemed appropriate that it was raining again.

Bunker roused Willie and got him under way, heading him for the glow of light at the door, and then came around with the umbrella.

"They're holding a table for us. Come on," he said, and I faltered, wishing there were some way we could stop the weekend then, before it went any farther, because there was already an edge of dislike in Bunker's voice, "Let's go," he said, prodding me.

I followed him inside.

We got Willie to a table, where he pushed a drink around

135

for a few minutes and then went to sleep with his head cradled in his arms. Terry and Donna came back to the table long enough to say hello and then went over to the circle of candy-colored light in front of the juke box, dancing, looking at each other with eyes so hot that I had to look away.

The waitress came back with a second round and I drank mine too fast, because the whole evening had begun to rush in on me and it was too much for me to handle. Across from me Bunker matched my speed, not saying anything, not even looking up. He seemed as lean and composed as ever, except that his eyes, when he did look across the table at me, had begun to open a little wider, like an owl's, and his head weaved ever so slightly as he faced me. He was drunk now, letting himself go as he never would if he had been in uniform, as he may never have done before, even on his first football weekend as a plebe, after the first long summer of restraint. I think he felt as I did the quality of isolation that seemed to enclose the weekend, to set it outside the stream of our lives, and took this chance to get completely, brutally drunk. I remember thinking, even if I wanted to I couldn't stop him, and feeling miserable. Willie slumped like a Zombie next to me, diminishing me even further, a souvenir of the scene on Donna's screen porch. I was troubled not just because Willie and I had come so close, but that I had come so close with *Willie*, when I didn't really love him, probably wouldn't care much about him beyond the weekend, when I hadn't even tried to tell myself that I loved him, at the time, to make it seem more reasonable. It was too late to do anything about Willie except be sorry, but Bunker sat across from me and I tried, once more, to reach him.

"Bunker, I—"

"It's Ben," he said, seeming for a second to snap to attention. Then as I watched his body suddenly stopped obeying him and his face changed in surprise, in a mixture of alarm and regret, like the face of a little boy who's been bad, and he said " 'Scuse me" convulsively, almost knocking over his chair, and lurched outside.

I remember wanting to call him back.

Terry brought Donna back to the table just then, and excused himself to go to the men's. Donna and I sat with Willie propped between us, looking artificial, like a stuffed escort, and we blinked at each other nervously because we'd never been left alone before and had never faced the need to make conversation.

136

"What are you taking next year?" I said finally, because it was all I could think of.

"Home Ec," she said, seeming pleased that I had asked. "If my grades are good enough I'm going to try to get in the U. of M."

"No kidding."

She looked at her hands self-consciously, and the effort of talking to me made her go pink under her tan. "The Miss America people like you to be in college."

"Huh?" Things were beginning to blur for me.

"You know—the pageant."

Atlantic City. "Oh," I said. "Oh, yeah."

"I can sing a little, and if I can just get through freshman year—"

"It's not so hard." I watched her outline waver.

"Mother says if I take Home Ec I might make it."

"That'd be swell," I said, looking down at Willie and thinking Lord, oh, Lord.

"But I'll have to win the state title first."

"Huh? Oh—sure."

"Willie's going to ask you to Homecoming Weekend," she said, with the air of someone doing me a favor.

"Swell," I said, finding it harder and harder to concentrate. I pushed my glass away.

"Terry—" she hesitated. "Terry hasn't said anything to you about me, has he?"

It would be too hard to explain why Terry would never say anything to me. Instead I mumbled something and hoped it passed for an answer.

"He likes me, doesn't he?" she said, looking at me hard.

"Huh?"

"Terry," she said in a voice as hard and practiced as a voice on a telephone, and then she looked up, all flustered, because there he was.

"Terry what," he said, sitting down and pulling her toward him.

I managed to escape then, to slip into my own thoughts and shut them out. Without wanting to I finished the drink in front of me and found that it tasted awful. I was detached from the couple across from me now, or thought I was, shut off and almost stifled by the weight of the past few hours, of the whole weekend, and when I looked up again I was surprised to find them still there, Terry even closer to Donna, picking at a spot of peeling sunburn on her arm. I stood up, almost sick with loneliness and revulsion, with the feeling that my whole world was out of joint, confused by liquor but driven by an overwhelming sense of chaos, thinking, *Bunker*, afraid for myself and for him. I turned in panic, and bolted outside.

I ran through the rain, calling, "Bunker," going from car to car in the gravelled parking lot, not knowing what I expected but frightened beyond bearing it, sickened with the idea that something was wrong and I had to find him. I ran blindly, drunker than I realized, oppressed by the foreboding which had begun gathering on that first day and now rolled in and almost overwhelmed me, so that when I saw a lump on the ground by one of the cars and found that it was Bunker, crumpled by a front fender, unmoving in the rain, it was as if this or something like it had been ordained from the beginning, as if I had known all the time that the extraordinary quality of the weekend as an entity would demand some painful finish and I bent over him thinking, "Lord, please Lord." I don't know whether it was this or the rain or the liquor, or that Bunker's head rolled on the gravel at a funny angle and his legs sprawled awkwardly, as if he had stopped caring, but—Lord, I don't now why—I thought he was dead, or dying, and I took some of the water that had collected in the pitted gravel at my feet, and I bent and sprinkled it on him, saying, "I baptize thee in the name of the Father, the Son and the Holy Ghost," crying because I was sure now that he was dead. He stirred, just as I finished making the sign of the cross and he raised himself on one elbow, saying, "What in the hell are you doing?"

XIV

I was surprised by sunlight the next morning, so relieved to find myself in one piece and things seeming much the same that I caught myself thinking "safe at last," like a mariner who wakes after a storm to find himself washed up on a sunny beach. Then I tried to move and found that I had a hangover, and that the hangover was overshadowed by a dull, thumping dread and I fell back, as the mariner must when he realizes that the trees lining his friendly beach are full of cannibals.

I've learned that I can get through such mornings—whether the hangover is real or emotional, whether I've drunk too much or talked too much or simply done too much on not enough sleep—by putting everything out of my mind but motion and moving slowly, like an invalid. I lay still for a minute and then got up slowly, coddling myself into a bathrobe and heading for the kitchen, trying to push aside the stripes of dust-flecked sunlight that lay in my path.

My mother looked up from her coffee as I came to the table, and without asking me whether I had had a nice time the night before, as she usually did, she put coffee and juice in front of me.

"Margaret called," she said finally, pushing the funnies across the table.

For a minute I was so busy with Mary Worth that I didn't seem to hear. Then my head came up so fast that I was sure my neck would snap.

"She wondered whether you wanted one of the boys to pick you up this afternoon."

The boys. Oh. Somewhere in the warmth of Thursday or Friday Margaret had invited all of us to the Swifts' house for a drink—a farewell before she and Jake drove Bunker and Willie back to the Academy. I didn't want to think too fully about Bunker, about any of the rest of it, so I set myself the specific problem, how to get to the Swifts' in Arlington to see the boys off and get back with a minimum of trouble. I had the idea that if I took the day one unit at a time I could shut out everything else and keep the totality of the weekend at bay. I reminded myself that Jake and Margaret would have to leave early to get the boys back on time, that they wouldn't have time to drive me home, and it occurred to me not to go. It would be more practical to skip it. But no matter how I pushed it back the order of the days stood in my memory and I knew that I would go to the Swifts' that afternoon because continuity demanded it.

Hell, I had to see Bunker again. I was doing my best to forget what I had done to him the night before, to minimize it, to pass it off as a gag or a drunken little accident, and I needed him to corroborate. I had to be reassured that everything between us was as it had been, that the thing in the parking lot was no more or less important than anything else we had done together, that we would both be able to pass it off.

"They said they'd see that you got a ride home," my mother said, prompting me.

"Oh. Iris, maybe." I had begun to connect this meeting, like my first one, with the idea of earning by ordeal, and because it would be harder for me I said, "I'll drive. Iris lives half way across town."

My mother was looking at me, trembling on the edge of a question but unable to frame it. "I had gas put in yesterday," she said instead and got up abruptly to clear the table, avoiding my eye as if she had seen something in my face that she didn't want to examine just then, apparently sensing that my morning would go to pieces if she disturbed a single element of my invalid's calm.

I went to the last mass of the morning making myself thin in my seat as the others went up to Communion, sitting like a shadow bent over the collection of holy cards that jammed my missal. I wasn't ready to think about it, but I knew that a number of things that had happened in the last four days would have to be examined before I thought about going up to the rail again. My mother had a steak ready, with a big salad—a convalescent luncheon—and I ate without saying much, picturing myself in the car, encapsulated, going over the bridge to Virginia and along the familiar route. I think it's to her credit that she never asked me anything about Bunker, Willie or any of the rest.

Everybody was already on the Swifts' screen porch, the boys neat and unfamiliar in uniform, the girls looking clean and fresh, a little sugary, like perfect candy dolls, in summer pastels. Margaret sat in the glider, smart in linen, looking at Bunker with pride, and Jake was making drinks with mint in them. Everything would have seemed ideal if it hadn't been for the fact that, Terry and his girl excepted, nobody would look at anybody else.

Jake joined Margaret on the glider, looking at us with pleasure, and I suppose we made a pretty attractive, scrubbed and handsome group. They may not have noticed that we were lifeless, hollow as Japanese figurines, because the weekend had drained each of us. Nobody was saying much. Conversation, despite the Swifts' efforts, was just a series of "wells," the way it is in a train station when you're seeing somebody off and run out of talk long before it's time for the train to pull out.

I stayed an hour, I guess, and then, hating to leave Margaret and Jake because something in them was so comforting, I got up and said, "Well—"

Margaret kissed me and Jake touched my hair. I said brief goodbyes to the others, who looked even more like strangers waiting for their trains, rootless and bored, and then Bunker escorted me to the car.

We hadn't said much up to that point, and perhaps I should just have said goodbye, and left the whole business alone. I'm no more brave or honest than the next person, but something was unfinished between us, and I knew I had to bring it up.

"Hey," I said. "About last night."

Bunker flushed. "I was smashed."

"Me too."

He shrugged. "So?"

"But then I—"

He broke in on an upbeat, a little quicker than he should have been. "Yeah?"

I waited for him to say something, to see how much he remembered, still hoping that he would tell me it was all right. But he stood, suspended, and I had to go on. "In the parking lot—"

He was shaking his head, not wanting to remember. "I was laid out or something."

141

"And I found you."

He pushed on, compelled as I was to bring it all back. "What in hell were you *doing*."

"The water—I—" for a minute I was halted by the totality of memory, by the picture of myself in the gravel, slobbering, and I could hardly speak. I forced it out. "I baptized you."

Bunker still shook his head, beginning to recall. "Yeah—you—I guess you did."

I stood, waiting for his anger, remembering that in all the years we had known each other, this was the first time I had intruded on the part of Bunker he had always kept to himself. I waited and then realized that he did not yet understand, and in the fact of his incomprehension I saw how far we had come in the past few years, how far apart we had drifted.

Because he did not yet understand Bunker looked at me directly for the first time that day, renewing the bond that had been formed between us as children, and in an honest effort of love he said, "Look, Denny, it's all right." He held his hands down, slightly away from his body, minimizing. "It was nothing."

And because I knew better than he what I had done, because I could not deny the gravity of baptism no matter how much I wanted to keep him, partly because I wanted to bring us closer in understanding I said, "It's *not* all right."

He stepped closer, comforting. "Hell, it doesn't mean anything—"

I may have wanted to let him go on thinking that, but I had to explain. "Bunker, I *baptized* you."

"Baptized—" He fell back a step, thinking. "That's when you come into a church, isn't it? Being stamped 'Catholic'?"

"Partly, I guess, but—"

"So what the hell?" he said, shrugging it off. "You can baptize me all you want, but that doesn't make me a Catholic."

I tried to say, "Not if you don't want it," but my voice was weak.

He forced a grin. "So let's forget it." He opened the car door in a graceful sweep, still talking. "Maybe we can get together at Christmas," he said, not meaning it, chattering on until I had to interrupt him.

"The baptism—"

"—get you a date with Willie," he said, trying to usher me into the car.

I faced him. "Bunker, look, I'm sorry and everything, but—" I hesitated, wanting to find the right words, and when they wouldn't come I went on anyway, in a rush of honesty. "Look, it makes you *different*."

He stopped then. He faced me squarely and I knew the look. I had seen it in him perhaps three or four times before. It was a look of pride, of surprise at privacy violated, of growing anger. He said simply, "Yes?"

I had to go on; I owed it to him. "It—look, whether you believe it or not, you're born again in a way, without the stain of original sin."

"Original sin," he said, spitting out the phrase as if he would have none of it. "Oh, sure."

"Look, Bunker, I had to let you know—"

His voice was sharp. "Just shut *up* about it."

Maybe if I had shut up we could have kept at least the pretense of friendship, but I couldn't. I had to make him understand, and I think he knew it. "I wouldn't have done it if I hadn't thought you were dying, or already—"

"Just what in the hell did you think you were doing?" His voice was low and even but he was trembling now, taut and furious, and I knew I had gone too far with him not as we talked but the night before, in the parking lot, and it was no particular comfort to me to know, as surely as I knew I was losing Bunker, that given the same circumstances, drunk or sober, I would baptize him again.

He was ablaze, electric. "Just who in hell do you think you are, trying to make me *different*."

In my misery I found myself clinging to a phrase from scripture, from the catechism, from somewhere—"unless ye be born again of water and the spirit . . ." and I offered it, knowing it would only make it worse.

"I know why you did it." He accused me.

"I did it for you," I said. "I *had* to do it."

"You couldn't leave me alone. You had to suck me in."

"Bunker, I thought you were—"

He went on, not hearing me. "You couldn't even leave me alone. You had to try to make a Catholic out of me." His voice rose. "You just had to cut me down."

As I remember it, I found myself suddenly calm, and when I spoke my voice came back full strength. "I just wanted you to—"

He cut in, not wanting to give me even that sentence. "—to be just like you."

"To have a *chance*." My strength left me then, because I had said it—I had said all I could say.

When he spoke again it was of the intrusion, of the baptism but more, it was of the alienation, the failure of understanding that had begun some time early in the weekend, perhaps even before, when as children we had said goodbye in Florida, and Bunker and his family had driven north. "What a rotten thing. What a damn, bloody rotten thing." He turned away from me without even saying goodbye, and started up the walk. I got into the car, not ready to shut the door on him even then, because I knew somehow that it wasn't over.

Midway up the walk he turned and came back. "Look," he said quietly, "I want you to remember one thing. I didn't ask for this. I didn't ask for it and I don't want it." He lifted his chin in a flash of pride. "I won't have it."

"Bunker, I—"

He stood thinking for a minute, trying to find some way to get back at me. "I can't just let this thing go by," he said.

I put up one hand, wanting to stop him.

"I'll *fight*."

I'm glad I'll never know exactly what my expression was just then. It must have been a mixture—alarm, fear, grief. It seemed to satisfy Bunker because he bent closer, pressing me.

"I'll tell you what, Denny." He bent until his face almost touched mine, glaring. "I'm going to do my Goddamndest to wipe out your little spell. I didn't ask for it, and the way I see it, I'm not responsible. The way I see it, *you* are."

"Bunker, please. Please—"

He seemed to be gratified by my protest because he jerked his mouth in the parody of a grin. "So I guess everything I do from now on is your fault." He shut the door on my protests, not willing to let me speak, and then he bent to the open window. "And I'm not going to be particularly careful about what I do."

Just then something reminded him that we were two friends on a street together, supposedly saying goodbye, and he made a stab at turning the whole thing into a gag. "Who knows, I might even manage to go to hell. I bet you'd *really* have to pay for that." He laughed unevenly. "Hey, what are some good sins?" He was trying to make it sound light, like a joke, but even this attempt was lost as he bent to the window in a final burst of bitterness.

"Don't forget—anything I do is on your soul."

"Oh, Bunker—" I opened the door, reaching out. Maybe all I hoped was that he would turn to correct me, to tell me it was Ben. But it was too late. He had already turned his back and was on his way into the house, impeccable in his uniform.

I bowed my head over the wheel then, knowing that for all that was still between us we had probably talked for the last time, that in my drunkenness the night before, in my fear, in trying to help Bunker I had broken the pact of privacy and had touched him too closely. I had marked him, whether he accepted the fact or not, and in so doing I had cut myself off from him forever. I pressed my fists against my eyes, just beginning to feel the complete, relentless weight of my responsibility for what I had done, for what he might do.

XV

Never mind what the next few days were like. I mulled over my trouble, immersed, almost suffocating in it, awash in a feeling of things gone wrong, a sense of regret that seemed to amount to something more than the sum of events, and a sense of apprehension that has eased some since but, despite my confession and the priest's reassurance, has not left me to this day. I wanted more than anything to be whole again, to put things right, and I prayed over it, knowing even as I did that there was only one way for me to begin, that as soon as I was ready to make my confession and say that I was sorry, God in His mercy was ready to forgive. Even knowing that, I was not ready because the whole idea of analyzing what I had done, of putting it into words for a priest, was too formidable to contemplate just then, and I kept wishing there were some other way. Yet I knew that one Saturday, if not that Saturday then some inevitable Saturday, my unhappiness at having cut myself off, my uneasiness and the need to put things right would outweigh my misgivings of the moment and I would nerve myself and go to confession. I looked forward to it with anticipated fear and embarrassment, and anticipated relief, wanting more than anything to have it over, but still not ready to begin. I may have guessed that even with confession and absolution the business of Bunker could never be completely over for me. My life has touched—really touched—only a few other lives, and it is still so closely bound up with these lives that I could never really separate myself from any of them; I could never separate myself from Bunker, from anything he might feel or do. And so in a sense I would have the feeling of being two people: myself, with my own way to make, and Bunker, who would fight God to spite me, whose defiance might never have been born if I had not been so drunk that night in the parking lot. It was almost too much for me to handle, and I did my best that week to put it out of my mind. I worked, twice as hard as I needed to. I packed for the fall term, getting everything in order two weeks early. I went to the movies. I slept.

Finally, because I had to, I drove over to see the Swifts. I don't know what I expected to find.

I found Pearson, bent over a book in the living room. He didn't know me at first.

I didn't see him when I first came to the door. I rang, and then poked my nose against the screen, trying to see inside. I was a little relieved when there was no answer and I opened the screen and yelled, to make sure there was no one home.

"Margaret? Jake?"

Somebody stirred in the living room, and then, as I called again, got up and came to the door, and unreasonable as it was my stomach shrank as I watched him come, because I had the idea suddenly that it was Jake, that he knew what I had done to Bunker and he was coming to accuse me.

"Yeah?"

"Huh? Oh." I stepped back, because it was Pearson, scowling at me.

"Yeah?" he repeated, obviously cross at being disturbed.

My first thought was that he was bigger, older, but that unlike Bunker he hadn't changed much in expression. His face had that same proud, black look I remembered from childhood. I was only surprised to see that he seemed smaller than I had remembered him.

"The—the Swifts. I wondered if they were here."

He let the hand with the book in it drop to his side. "They're not home," he said impatiently, with a look I remembered, and before I could help myself I was back in the house in Florida, outraged, hating him.

"I could take a message," Pearson said.

I was so taken up in remembering that I didn't answer him.

"I said I'll take a message," he said, louder. "They won't be back until late. I can tell them you dropped by," he said, drumming his fingers on the doorframe, waiting for me to go away. He prompted me. "I'm their son."

I looked him full in the eyes, perhaps more coldly than I should have, and said, "I know who you are."

He looked at me then, for the first time, and I had the feel-

147

ing that he'd just seen me as a person, something more than an annoyance at the door. "Oh, it's—"

"Denny." I set my jaw. "Denny McLeod."

"Oh—oh, sure." He was still puzzled, but beginning to remember. "I'm sorry. I thought you were one of Ben's girls." He opened the door. "Hey, come on in."

If I could, I would have turned and gone, but I was still eaten by worry about Bunker, and I had to stay until I'd heard a little news of him. "I don't know," I said. "If you're busy—"

"Hey, don't go!" He made a sudden motion, as if to hold me, and I saw that he was lonely.

"For a couple of minutes," I said.

"Great." He opened the door wider, waving an arm in an awkward attempt to usher me in. "I haven't seen you since Florida."

He led the way into the living room, talking jerkily. "—just moved in two months ago. Dad's at the Pentagon. I guess you know," he said, turning to be sure I was following. "Dad said you were over when Ben was home."

I nodded and sat down.

Once he had brushed the paper out of his chair and we were both seated, there was nothing to say.

He grinned at me, sort of well-here-we-are, apparently pleased to have company but without any idea of what to do with it now that he had it. I could see him looking at the magazines on the coffee table, his papers, the title of the book he was reading, trying to think of something to talk about and I let him flounder, not ready to help him out. He drew in his breath once or twice, about to say something, and then thought better of it and lapsed, jiggling one knee nervously.

I began to look around. It was the first time I had been in the living room for any length of time. I found myself settling into it, feeling safe in some way because it was crowded with reminders of a time when we had all been safe—pictures of Bunker and Pearson as children, furniture I remembered from childhood—and it was almost as if I had come in from the world for a minute, as a child will come in to be comforted. Even Pearson, sitting across from me, seemed to be left over from childhood, and at the time I wanted to keep him in the past, to keep intact the hatred for him which had been a larger part of my childhood than I would have cared to admit. If my fear for Bunker hadn't forced me into the Swifts' living room that day I might never have divorced Pearson from the year when Daddy was lost, or let myself know him in a time when we were no longer children. I might have kept him static in time, compartmentalized in a part of my life that was already past, cherishing a hatred that was obsolete. As it was, Jake's souvenirs from the war and Bunker on the mantel, pictured in whites, called me back, and I was reminded of the time and my reason for being in that place.

"Bunker got away all right?" I said, because I had to know.

"Ben," Pearson said, reminding himself. "Yeah. I saw him Sunday before he left. I got back from Cambridge late, so I only saw him for a minute."

"How is he?"

"He's—" Pearson shrugged, as if he hadn't really thought about it, and wouldn't know if he had. "He's fine, I guess. He's going to be a Batt officer this year," he said, no more interested in it than I had been, but relieved to have something to talk about.

"He's OK, then."

Pearson had a wry look. "He's always OK."

I pushed my luck. "—No different?"

"Different?" He looked at me sharply. "From when you saw him last?"

I had the uncanny feeling that he was on to me and I retreated, flustered. "Oh, yeah. I guess I did see him Sunday." I was gesturing vaguely. "I forgot."

Pearson was watching me now. "He's quite the officer."

I don't know what more I thought I could learn, but I withdrew for the moment, determined to wait him out, to begin again when he didn't seem to be listening so attentively. "What are you doing these days?" I said, bringing him on.

"Pre-med," he said without enthusiasm.

"Where?" I knew, but it would keep the conversation going.

"At Brown."

"Your father said something about the Army." I wasn't sure at the time whether it had been the Army or the Marines, but it didn't matter.

He nodded. "Two years. It wasn't bad." His voice died. He seemed to have run out of things to say.

I gave myself back to the room. The ship's clock on the mantel struck two bells.

"Well—" Pearson said, a little desperate. "How about you?"

"English," I said, and named the college.

"I never heard of it."

I stuck my chin out. "It's small, but it's good."

"You going to teach?"

I hadn't wanted to show him anything but a blank face, but every time I mentioned English the question came up, and by now it irritated me. Before I could think it out I snapped, "I wouldn't be caught dead."

For the first time he looked amused. "What are you going to do with it then," he said baiting me.

I shrugged, not giving him anything. "I don't know."

"Good."

"Huh?" I stopped short, because he had hit a nerve. At the time I didn't know what I wanted or what I was going to be, but until that point every person I had told had resisted the idea. People would try to push me into something, to suggest and settle things for me, and when I said I honestly didn't know what I wanted they took it with resentment, maybe because they didn't like the idea of any person they couldn't plan for, file in a certain slot under "Occupation," saying "there," with satisfaction in a matter closed.

"Trade school," he snorted. "If you want to make people happy you go to trade school."

I couldn't help grinning. "Yeah."

"Tell them you don't know what you want to do and they eat at you. Tell 'em you're going to be a lawyer, a steeple-jack—anything, and you shut them up. Funny what makes people happy—"

"You get this kind of thing?"

"I get it in spades. Everything has to be *for* something. If you have half a brain they push you into a course so you can *be* something." He snorted. "Like Ben. When he finishes he'll be an officer."

"He seems to want it."

"Big deal."

"I guess I'll be a nothing," I said, distracting him, out of some loyalty to Bunker.

"Great," he said. "You should be able to do things for the hell of it. You know what? If I wanted to *be* something I'd be a plumber. Good money and no degree."

"D.P., maybe," I said.

"Doctor of plumbing?" He laughed.

"But you *are* going to be a doctor," I said, remembering the pre-med.

"Oh—yeah." His face lost expression. "Well—" he waved a hand. "You've got to shut them up."

"Not if you don't want to," I said, wanting him to fight.

He turned on me suddenly. "What do you know about that?" He slouched in his chair, looking at nothing, and when he spoke again he was already lost in some black vision of his own. "Crap," he said, on a new tangent, already forgetting that we'd been on the same ground a moment before. "It's all crap."

"Huh?" I was confused.

"None of it matters." His gesture took in more than I would have wanted it to, and when I saw his face I began to realize that I might still be on the simple level of education and occupation, stuff that Cardinal Newman had already justified to me, but that Pearson had gone on past me, that he was lost and swinging somewhere beyond my reach.

"It—" I hesitated for a moment, because I had carried my own old, set idea of Pearson for some ten years and I wasn't ready to be sucked into something new. Yet I saw how completely he had deserted me, the room, the conversation, and because I had to I tried to draw him back. "It probably matters."

"Um," he said, not even listening.

"It probably matters," I said again, too loud.

"One thing is as good as another." It came familiarly, like an old catechism phrase that has long been committed to memory.

I think I yelled. "It's *not*."

"Funny." He threw one leg over the arm of his chair, engaged again. "That's what my parents say." He levelled his eyes at me. "You can't always know whether people mean what they say."

I thought of Jake and Margaret, struggling to say the right thing to their dark, diffident son. "Why shouldn't they?"

"Why should they?" He seemed to be waiting for something, for me to make a certain statement or ask a certain question that would let him go on, that would let him get out some of the things that were on his mind. Maybe he was simply testing, to see whether I cared, whether I was really listening.

But I let it pass, satisfied simply to have him back in the room. Maybe it was a failure of understanding, but I think it was more a matter of memory, of my reminding myself that this was Pearson who had hurt me in Florida, and not wanting to be pulled into anything that would disturb my idea of him—I began gathering up my wallet and my keys and when he tried to go on, I wouldn't look at him.

"It's just—" he said and then saw me fidgeting and de-cided against going on. There was a silence.

I sat looking at my hands, waiting him out.

"Oh, by the way," he said finally. "Ben gave me a message for you."

I tried to keep my hands still. "Yes?"

"One of his damn gags, I guess."

For a minute I let myself think it was going to be just a gag. "Hysterical, I bet."

He went on, recalling. "He said tell you he'd found a couple of neat sins."

"Oh," I could feel my breath seeping out, like the air out of a balloon. "Thanks."

"You're a Catholic," he said with no particular emphasis. I think he was just reminding himself.

"Yes." My face had gone stiff.

"Yeah," he said, nodding, and I could see that the only difference it made to him was that it explained Bunker's remark. "I guess it had something to do with that."

"Yeah." I knew now what I had come to find out. It had been as bad as I thought it was going to be. I could go.

"He always was a little bigot," Pearson said, trying me.

But I knew what I needed to know. I think I believed I was through talking to him. "Well," I said, ignoring the remark, "I'd better go." I got up.

Pearson was watching me.

"I have to be home by six," I said, backing out of the room.

"Oh, sure."

"Yeah." I found myself flustered, wanting to explain. "My mother will be waiting supper for me."

He was waiting.

"It was swell talking to you." I was almost at the door.

"I bet." His voice stopped me. "Hey."

I turned.

His face was congested, red and black. When he spoke it was a statement, even as it was a question. "We weren't ex-actly friends."

I found myself meeting his eyes, shaking my head.

"It was—that business in Florida," he said painfully. "I —" he was making himself recall. "I hit you."

I nodded.

His voice was low. "I thought you remembered." There was a silence as he grimaced, trying to get himself organized. With an effort, he said, "I—I was sorry as soon as it hap-pened, but I didn't know what to *say*."

"Oh." It was as if somebody had taken a prop out from under me.

He got up, involved in the whole business now, hating this kind of self-exposure but bound to see it through to some sort of finish. "I was a little bastard."

When I saw how much it cost him to say it, I shook my head.

He was considering. "I don't think it was really you I was hitting. It was—" The motion of his hand brought back not just that day but all the rest of it, the anxiety of all the days, the fears we had never let ourselves frame.

Knowing now that he was right I said, "I guess it wasn't."

We were caught in silence then, me just on the verge of something, Pearson contorted in embarrassment, waiting. I thought of him hitting, of me hating, and it came to me that it had never really been Pearson that I hated, and I was surprised to find myself almost crying. "I—I had to hate something for what happened," I said.

"Yes?"

"It—happened to be you."

He nodded, satisfied, and sat down.

I stood in the shadows for a minute, grateful to him for giving me this time to collect myself. Finally I said, "I'd better get going."

He got up then, and came to see me to the door. We were both surprised, I think, to open it and find that the day outside had not changed. The sun was a little lower, but the street was much the same.

We stood at the car for a moment, disconnected, trying to find a new basis.

"Give your parents my best," I said.

"And Ben?" He was waiting, receptive, giving me a chance to tell him what had made me so disjointed, so touchy about his brother, so obsessed.

"I—" the whole thing came back to me, engulfing me, and I shook my head, no more ready to go into it for him than I was ready for a confessor.

There was an awkward pause.

He tried to make it better. "I mean—"

"Never mind about Ben."

He gave me a short nod, apparently understanding. In all the times we were to meet after that, we never discussed his brother except when I set the terms, bringing the subject up and laying out explicit boundaries. "You're leaving for school soon?" he said.

"Two weeks."

"Then I guess I won't see you." He said it smoothly, as if he was trying to approximate one of his brother's dating relationships, knowing as well as I did that it wouldn't work.

"You're pretty busy—"

He tried his hands in his pockets, seemed dissatisfied and took them out, for want of a better gesture examined his nails. "I'll be in Cambridge for a couple of weeks on this project. You'll be gone by the time I get back."

"It's all right," I said, wanting him to relax.

"Well—"

"Uh—"

"Well—" He managed a passable smile. "If you ever get to Providence, look me up."

"I'll do that," I said. "I have a date up there this fall—"

"Bring him along," he said, and I think he was relieved to find us on that footing, to know that we would be simply friends.

"Have a good year." I started the motor.

"Tell your mother I said hello."

"I will," I said, and drove away. In the rear view mirror, I saw him wave.

For a few minutes after I left him, I was comforted. The glimpse of the chaos within him made me feel a little better about myself. My own worries—and by now I realized that they included the hatred I had carried for him for so many years—could be pinned down, defined, and I had only to muster the guts to do something about them, to get to confession and ask forgiveness, to have them dispelled. I hoped there would be some reparation exacted, some way I could begin to make up for everything, because I wanted more than anything to clear the books. Confession next Saturday, I told myself, thinking furrily, driving sleepily through streets drenched by afternoon sun. Then it will be over— except for the consequences, I thought, and went cold, because no matter what I did there would still be Bunker, fighting, Bunker, whom I could neither touch nor control.

XVI

Fall came on in a rush that year, all brilliant air and whirling foliage and golden tones, in a full-scale parody of all the September issues of al. the fashion magazines. I bought clothes in earth colors—yellows, greens, rust—and wore them on overcast days in early Semptember before it was really late enough in the year for anything but cottons. Maybe I exaggerate, remembering, and the only good thing about that fall was that I was free of summer, but I don't think I've ever seen an autumn so beautiful. I fixed on each change in wind, in temperature, in the color of the air or the quality of the evenings with delight, hurrying with change toward winter, pretending for the moment that the past had changed too. I rushed the season, getting back to school hours before anybody else because unpacking, putting books and clothes away in the room Katherine and I would share for our last year at college, I could forget for the moment the preoccupations of August.

Katherine would be along soon. We would change into sneakers and skirts that were exhausted after a solid three years of sitting—a sort of cloak of invisibility—and slouch through the halls, looking so disreputable that people ushering new students and their parents around, trying to give them a good impression of the place, would pass us by, pretending not to see us, for fear they'd have to stop and introduce us as seniors, pretty nearly the end product of the place.

As I recall I was too restless to wait for Katherine and too restrained, for one reason or another, to go down and watch for her at the main door. Instead I bounced a little, almost flapping my elbows (fall is the time of year when you want most to fly) and then I made a tour of the floor, following the U-shape of the building to the tip of the far arm, drawing tight the cloak of invisibility so I would not have to speak to any of the people who were beginning to open rooms here and there. At the far end of the corridor I turned, because there was no place else to go, and started back.

A door opened at the apex of that side of the U and as it opened I stopped because Sister Thomas, who had her office on that floor, crossed the corridor, so tall, so changeless that for a moment the sight of her stopped me in my tracks.

She had a master's degree in journalism from Columbia and she had been a reporter on a Philadelphia paper for three years before she joined the convent. By all rights I should have wanted to talk to her—about my courses, the school paper, any simple bit of business which would have restored the continuity of the old year and let the new term begin.

As it was I was put off that day, perhaps because the sweep of her veil kept her from seeing me and I could not bring myself to hail her, perhaps because her silhouette was so sharp, so black and constant against the moving colors outside the window that she seemed to me almost alien, remote from my concerns and my life as I knew it. I only know that for all her intelligence and humanity, for all my own loneliness, I was not ready to talk to her, perhaps because I had not yet put things right and knew the contrast between us would be too great. It seemed to me then that no matter what we might have to say to each other there would be the habit, the ordered life she had chosen, a certain awareness, to mark the difference between us, to make her too tangible a reminder of eternity for me just then. I remember trying to explain it to myself in another way, muttering, "What could she know?" Then I waited without moving until she had posted a note on the bulletin board and returned to her office.

When I got back to the room Katherine was there, strewing her things abstractedly, straining toward the window as if she would never get enough of the splash outside.

"Hey, Kat," I said.

"Hey," she said, looking for someplace to throw her suit jacket.

"You didn't write."

She grinned. "I never write, but I don't change." She twirled the jacket on one finger and sailed it at a chair. It missed, and we were at home again.

I waited while Kat changed into her worst shirt and skirt

156

and then, without having to consult about it, we went outside. A light, ceaseless wind moved the leaves and pushed us along, so that we seemed to be taken from one place to the next, going without effort. We could see friends under the trees in front of the building, toiling with suitcases from car to room to car again, but for some reason we wanted to keep them as they were, framed in leaves at a distance, and we turned without waving and went down to the gulch where we had been sneaking cigarettes for years. We could have gone to the smoker, I suppose, but it didn't fit in with the day.

We sat and smoked, looking at the tumble of rocks, and because Katherine didn't seem to have anything to say I began going over old ground in my mind—Bunker, the baptism, the confession I had not yet made—so taken up in the familiar landscape of my preoccupation that when Katherine finally did speak I was actually surprised to find myself in a new place, with the season changed, not alone, as I had been for so much of the summer in Washington, but with Katherine. My mouth went wet and for a second I was so moved that I almost spilled the whole business to her.

But she was talking, and I saw something which I had known from the first minute in the room but had not marked—she was in a funk.

"Pat's coming tonight," she said. "He's on his way through to New Haven."

I said, "Great." I liked Pat better than anybody else I'd seen Kat date.

"No." She ran her fingers through her bangs, undoing the set her mother had commanded for the first day of term. "It's not great."

I pulled my gaze back from the trees. "What's the matter?"

"I don't know if I can explain it," she said, still combing the bangs with her fingers.

"I thought you were seeing a lot of him this summer," I said, trying to give her a place to start.

"I was. That's the trouble."

A thought skittered across my mind, but her next sentence made me discount it.

"He's in love with me or something," she said, picking the fuzz off one of her heavy wool socks.

My first instinct was to be pleased for her. Kat had talked about a lot of things—joining the convent, joining the women's Marines, writing in a hovel somewhere, but from

157

the beginning she had been made to be loved. "Hey, that's great." My voice was uneven because I knew as sure as I was sitting there that she would be married—soon, if not to Pat to someone else—and whether she wanted it or not, it would mean the end of our long childhood together.

There was a silence, while Kat scratched at the dirt with her heel, making a little trough.

"I don't love him."

I was arguing for Pat, who wasn't there. "You don't have to marry him."

"I—I couldn't."

"Well you don't have to drop him either."

"You don't get it, Denny." The bangs were sticking out now. "I do have to drop him."

"You like him," I said. "He's a good guy. For now that should be enough."

"That's what I told myself all summer." She punched out her cigarette in the trough her heel had made and stood up, in that horse-blanket skirt and the socks like bandages, looking incongruously like Liberty, or Joan of Arc, and said, "It's just gotten to the point where it's not fair to Pat. He's got all that charm, all that drive—hell, all that sex—and it's wasted on me because I know I'm never going to marry him."

There didn't seem to be anything I could say.

"He ought to be out spending himself on some girl who's going to love him." She turned her back, staring across the gulch. "I've been feeling cruddy all summer. Like an emotional gold-digger. I've been taking advantage of him."

I thought of Pat, who thought he was pretty worldly. "I bet he doesn't see it that way."

She turned slowly. "That's the point. I've got to make him see it. I'm going to get it over with tonight."

She seemed to stand out from the background of moving leaves, soft, almost luminous, and I remember thinking quite rationally, with a pang for Pat, that elbows and horse-blanket skirt and disordered hair be damned, Katherine was going to please some man a great deal, having to swallow hard before I could say, "It's your ball game." Then a whole month's worth of worry and rationalization began to tumble in on me because Kat's concern over something which another girl might not even have considered a matter of conscience had set some wheels going in my own mind. It's senseless, because these things aren't relative, but I measured Katherine's conscience against my own, against what I had done, and began to feel worse than ever, even smaller, for putting off an accounting for so long, and I said, "Hey, Kat. Go to town with me?"

She must have seen that something was troubling me because she said without question, "Sure."

So we trudged off to the bus stop without bothering to sign out or to greet any of our classmates and Katherine stood around outside the Cathedral, where the priests heard people twice a week, while I went to confession.

I went through everything: the business with Willie, my being drunk, and finally Bunker and the baptism, in a sequence I had begun to formulate the day after everything had happened, and had pruned and pared and perfected and repeated in my mind a hundred times since then, against the day when I would finally bring myself to get it over with. I knew I would have to have something, in this case a memorized formula, to go on before I would ever be able to begin.

". . . so I baptized him. I am sorry for these sins and all the sins of my past life."

There was a pause. I could hear the priest on the other side of the grill, shifting, perhaps trying to form words.

When he did speak we talked at length, with him asking questions, me doing my best to answer, and once the business was clarified he gave me my penance and began, in Latin, to give me absolution. When he finished and said "God bless you," expecting me to go, I tried to get up but couldn't, perhaps because for me it would not be over until I could find some positive action to take.

In the silence I could hear my breath.

Finally, seeing that I was still kneeling, he said, "No one can foretell the future. You honestly thought the boy was dead."

The weight was still on me. "Father, I think—I hope I did. I was drunk. How can I know?"

His voice was gentle. "You're going to have to believe that you thought the boy was dead."

"But *baptizing* somebody, when he doesn't want it—"

He cut me off. "You did the right thing for the moment."

I bowed my head.

He was still trying to reach me. "Remember, you can't be responsible for the future. No matter what the boy says." Then he said, a little louder, dismissing me, "God bless you."

I said, "Thank you father," ending it as I had ended every confession since grammar school, and blundered my way out of the box, to kneel at the altar rail.

When I came out of the cathedral, the afternoon sun hit me hard. The wind was a little quicker now, and the whole street seemed to be in motion. I yelled, "Hey, Kat," and hurtled down the steps, sweeping her up and heading for the bus stop at a dead run. We got off at the bottom of the hill and ran the rest of the way to our building, racing in a flurry of leaves, I running as if all hell were at my heels, Katherine running for joy.

Pat was parked in the turn-around.

"Oh, geez," he said, sensing some of the currents that crackled around us, and got out of the car. "Oh, geez," he said again, taking in Katherine's militant sack. "Back in uniform."

She grinned. "Yeah."

He took her by the elbows, face bright. "Well, hi."

I stepped back. "Hey, I'll see you guys."

"See you, Denny."

Kat turned. "See you at supper. Sign me out, OK?"

"I thought we'd eat out," Pat said. "I don't have to be on the road till ten."

She was shaking her head. "Pat, I—"

He didn't seem to see what was coming, and I found myself shuffling in the gravel, wishing there were some way I could make it easier for him.

Kat had one hand lifted, trying to explain. "Pat, I—hell, let's go."

There was nothing to do for it, so I left.

I went slowly until I rounded the corner of the building and then I walked faster, picking up speed, hustled along by the wind at my back. Then, because I couldn't help myself I ran again, taking the long way, foot after foot pell mell, going faster, drunk on the air. The confusion of color, the brilliance of the afternoon dizzied me and I began going in great leaps, made uneasy and finally so frightened by the dazzle, by my impetus, by something I could not understand that I turned suddenly into a dark doorway, still running, and went inside. I raced up the stairs, fleeing now, not sure why I was afraid but shaken, like a small rock in the midst of a glitter of gems, tossed like something caught in a kaleidoscope. I could feel the wind at my back and I stopped only when I reached the top of the building, the hush of the upper hall. I might have gone on even then but for Sister Thomas, who stood at the window near her office, set against the reds and yellows and browns like a black stone at the center of the same kaleidoscope, fixed in a way that seemed reassuringly quiet and sure after the quick wind and shifting colors of the day outside.

I came to a halt beside her, at rest. " 'Lo 'Stir."

She seemed to see the blaze reflected in my eyes. "I saw you tearing up the stairs."

I was still panting from my hurry, and something in me resented her calm, so that I said, with a freshness that surprised me, "Don't you wish you could?"

"Some people prefer discipline," she said drily, and opened her office door. "You'd better come in and do something about your hair. It's a mess."

After I'd made a few passes at my hair with a comb, going by my reflection in the window glass, I sat down by her desk.

"I saw you skulk past today," she said, rattling the papers against the surface of her desk. "You looked like a spook."

I bit my lip, embarrassed. "I was just sort of—"

"—ducking people," she said.

"I'm sorry, Sister." I must have looked guilty. "I had something on my mind."

Her eyes were clear. "I thought so."

I sat back for a minute, taking in the neat, spare office, the order of the desk, the bookshelves, the crucifix above the door and for the first time since the business with Bunker, I began to feel comfortable. "I think it's over now," I said, because she seemed to be watching me.

She looked at me steadily. "I'm glad."

Bunker and his anger were still quick in my mind, and without wanting to I found myself saying, "Except for one part." I may have felt I owed her something, for avoiding her that afternoon.

She pretended to examine a pile of blue books on her desk. Finally she said, "Maybe it's not as bad as you think," and seemed willing to let it go at that.

I looked first at my hands, then once more around the room, still compelled to explain. I began looking for a way to tell her about the baptism, about Bunker and the feeling of responsibility for him that I could not shake. "If a person doesn't want—" I stopped, and tried to begin again. "How responsible . . ." I waited for her to make some remark, as she might in classroom discussion, to help me get on with it.

Instead she shook her head. "You don't have to tell me anything."

"I thought you might—"

"You don't have to explain anything to me," she said. "It would probably be better all around if you didn't try."

Respect made me keep on. "I mean, since I ducked you this afternoon, I thought you might want to know the reason."

"I don't need to know," she said. "I only need to care."

She said this quickly, trying not to make too much of it, but I saw that even though she had removed herself from life as I knew it, even though she spent most of every day in this small office and left the college grounds only once or twice a year, Sister Thomas was in touch, and this understanding moved me as I had been moved earlier that day, being with Katherine. I could begin to imagine the scope of Sister Thomas's concern, the tendrils which touched a number of lives, and in that moment I saw her as one life in a network of lives, with the nuns, her friends, people she had known and people she would know, all interlocked and interacting in a way that would give continuity to everything she did. I remember a certain joy at being able to sit there, with my own sense of order restored by the afternoon's confession, at being able to talk to Sister Thomas without constraint. I knotted my hands and looked down, because it would be a minute or two before I could trust my voice.

She said, "You might like to see that collection of Punch cartoons," giving me a chance to recover myself. "It came in the mail yesterday. You might as well borrow it before somebody else takes it off and I never see it again." She put on a tone of mock complaint. "I lost twenty-eight books last year."

I said, "Maybe you ought to make people sign for them."

"Or charge fines." She shook her head. "People either return books or they don't, and all the paper work in the world doesn't make a bit of difference."

By then I was able to grin. "You could chain them to the wall or something."

"I saw Katherine leaving with a young man," she said, seeing that I was myself again. "Was that Pat?"

"Yes Sister," I said, and we began to talk about them.

We talked until dark, ignoring the clack of heels, the voices of girls and their parents, coming in droves now, the cars pulling up outside. We talked about the paper, about my summer, about what she had been reading and a number of other things of no consequence, stopping only when the bell called her to the convent for prayers before the evening meal.

I went down the hall to my room, slopping along in my sneakers at no particular speed, waiting for Katherine to come. In a few minutes she would be back with the business of Pat finished, for her, and we would eat and pass the evening in talk, catching up. The next morning Kat and I would get up while it was still dark to go with the others to the first Mass of the school year, and when the time came I would be able to join the others at the rail for Communion. Then there would be breakfast and the first class bell of the day, and the year would finally begin.

XVII

"Denny, this is Pat."

"Where *are* you?" My voice must have leaped, because Netta Freeward stopped typing and looked at me.

"Somewhere downtown. Norty wanted to see the cherry blossoms."

"You idiot," I said, a little pleased at the way it sounded, going over the phone. "That's not till spring."

Across from me, Netta was watching. I was at the museum, as usual, at my desk, as usual, in the fall of my first year out of school. I hadn't seen Pat since the visit to Katherine's.

"When can we see you?"

"I don't get off till four-fifteen."

"Meet you at your place," Pat said.

"What?"

"See you."

"Some friends," I said to Netta, when I was sure Pat had really hung up. This was the first time my private life had intruded in the routine of the office, and Netta was watching with interest, apparently waiting for something. I mumbled a little, trying to think of some way to explain my delight. "Just somebody I knew from school."

She nodded, pleased for me, wanting to believe more than I told, and when I didn't say anything more she bent to her work, moving papers from under the cast of a fossil that she kept on her desk. It was she who nudged me a few minutes before quitting time and said, "Why don't you go ahead? If Mr. Rankins says anything, I'll say you wanted to take it off annual leave."

I almost caught my hand in the metal door, shutting my typewriter away. "Well, thanks."

She made me stop for a spray of perfume from an atomizer in her purse, twitching at my collar in such a way that I hadn't the heart to say that this was nothing more than a visit from friends, and then she made me stand off so she could look at me before she let me go. I was her champion in some way, her emissary in a world she had declared closed to herself, and I would have to come back Monday with a matchbook from some Washington club, a trophy she could take with a feeling of something accomplished, something won. As I left she was turning the fossil in her hands, scanning the manuscript beside her with lips moving as she tried to find her place. She looked up one last time. "Have fun."

I was starved for the sight of a friend, no more, no less, but I couldn't disappoint her by letting her know. "I will," I said, giving it a lilt, and then ran for the elevator.

They were at the apartment when I got there, flattering my mother and bouncing like a couple of kids. In some way that I didn't have an opportunity to think out just then, Pat had arranged it with my mother so that they were spending the weekend with us.

Pat met me at the door in a sort of embarrassed, affectionate tangle and then he stepped back so I could see Norty, still done up for the road in khaki shorts and a Navy polo shirt. I said hello, wary of him. Behind him I could see my mother making little mouths because she liked him and she could tell by the set of my face that I wasn't altogether ready to be polite.

He must have been well-briefed. He was funny and engaging, and he remembered me this time.

"My dear," he said, "I haven't seen you Since."

"Um?"

"Bon voyage to Bridgeport and all that."

"Oh, yeah. The Survival Kit."

Pat laughed. "I was touched. I mean, touched."

"I brought you a Little Something," Norty said, and offered it with a grin.

It was just that—a Little Something, ceramic, in four colors and indescribable.

"An elbow rest for tired hunchbacks?" Pat asked.

"A pet for people who don't like things that crawl," Norty said.

"A denture dish for a Martian?" Pat picked it up and investigated it from underneath.

I took it and turned it around. "I don't think so. I think it's a statue of an amoeba," I said, and set it down.

My mother was hiding a smile, and something in her look reminded me of the last time I had seen that smile, on another weekend, when Willie and Bunker had been kidding and scrapping like boys, making themselves at home in our living room.

"The hell," Pat was saying. "It's Norty's id."

She was laughing now. "You're too much," she said, already in love with the idea of both of them.

I don't know whether it was meanness or some need to remind Norty of himself or simply because I saw my mother laughing and I had to warn her, so she wouldn't pin too many hopes on us and be disappointed again, but I found myself turning to Norty, suddenly, in an overpowering need to make it plain how things stood. "Where's Glenda?" I said, surprising myself. Then I explained, "Norty has a family," for my mother, and waited for him to respond.

It took him a minute. He had been so busy playing the boy that I honestly think he had forgotten her. He blinked, as if he didn't particularly want to be reminded. "Fine. She and Sarah are at her folks's."

"You have children," my mother said, adjusting.

"A daughter," I told her, wondering what blind hope I had imagined for her, who I had thought I was protecting. I knew only that it was important for me to show that the two of them were no more carefree than anybody else, charming but no less vulnerable, handsome but no more nearly perfect, that I expose them somehow before her eyes dazzled.

"Sarah," Norty said grudgingly. "She's three."

"That's wonderful." My mother was shifting easily into a new attitude. She said, parent-to-parent, "You must miss them both."

Norty frowned, looking at me. Then he saw that she was still waiting, politely, for what, for another father, would have been an easy response. "Uh—yeah." He scraped one foot against the rug.

At the window Pat coughed, and I saw that he was watching me. I think he must have had some idea of what I was getting at because he looked away from me, at something on the sidewalk below, and when he turned back he said, "Hey, some kid out front's got a pogo stick," asking me to let them be what they wanted to be. Because things had been made plain and that was all I asked, I said, "No kidding," and went to the window. Norty followed with what sounded like a sigh of relief. Like children again, we crowded each other, all elbows. In a few minutes we would be out on the sidewalk, trying to make a deal to borrow a pogo stick.

We had spaghetti in an Italian place in Georgetown and went to a movie nearby. We were disgraceful in the movie, eating ourselves sick on popcorn and Jujyfruits, passing them back and forth because I hated green ones and Pat wouldn't eat any of the blacks, holding them up to the light to see what color they were. Norty and I had a fight over the last two in the box, digging at each other and whispering like little kids.

I have never seen Norty more charming. He seemed to cut loose after the movie, putting on a gentle, garrulous one-man show for us at the place where we stopped for a beer, not trying to show off for the rest of the place as he usually did, or even for us, keeping his voice down and going into monologues on Norty in investment banking, Norty in J. Press, Norty in the old days in ROTC, with no more aim in mind than to keep us entertained. The nasty streak I had seen in him from time to time was hidden, as if it had never been.

"So I admitted I was color blind," he finished, "and they kicked me out."

"You'd have paid them to get rid of you," Pat said. "I don't know. Over There and all that stuff." He managed to look wildly quizzical. "Maybe the Army is a home for me."

"You don't *like* your new job," Norty said.

Pat snorted. "It didn't like me."

"You mean you're—" Norty said, feeding him his line.

"Unemployed."

"Oh, Pat," I said.

Norty made a mouth. "Your friend must be delighted."

"Oh, sure," Pat said, choosing his next words with care. "If it matters, it matters. Tough rocks."

Norty laughed. "There are more where that one came from."

"Shut up," Pat said, with some embarrassment.

I opened my mouth, about to ask a question, and then withdrew without saying anything more because I knew, and I don't know to this day how I knew for sure but I knew, that Pat was sleeping with some girl. It didn't matter who, in particular, or how long this one would last because from now on there would always be a girl; this was the first of a series of girls Pat would take up without caring to pass the time, sleeping on, beyond the point where he might have married, perhaps even beyond the point of potency, without any real interest and probably without love, in a bleak and endless bacherlorhood, because he had made his choice some time since the last visit to Katherine, and he was playing the game.

"Tell her to bug off," Norty said, waving his glass. "Tell 'em all to bug off."

"Forget it," Pat said.

"Tell you what," Norty said expansively. "Got just the solution."

Pat didn't seem to want Norty to go on. "Um."

"Antarctica." Norty drew himself up. "You can count icebergs and serve your country at the same time. You know—" he prompted Pat, grinning. "The geophysical year."

Pat reached for the check. "Well, great." He hesitated for a minute, giving me an oblique look, perhaps trying to gauge how much I had picked up from Norty's talk and whether I would want to follow it up.

"Let's blow this joint," I said, and we left.

Norty excused himself as soon as we got home, going on to bed in the spare room.

Pat and I sat up over bitter coffee in the kitchen and talked. I said, "Norty's in good form."

He looked pleased. "He's doing all right, isn't he?"

"My mother thinks he's great," I said. "She thinks you're both great."

"I *thought* this trip would chirk him up." Pat was hinting, wanting me to ask him more.

"The trip's for him?"

He nodded. "He's been living with me for a week. For a while there I thought he was going to kill himself or something."

"He and Glenda are . . ."

"I don't know what exactly." Pat turned his cup in its saucer until the angle of the handle struck him right. "He's having a rotten time."

"I thought she had more room to complain," I said, remembering Glenda abandoned at parties, Glenda scratching around the house for change.

"Her father can . . ." Pat shook his head.

"What happened this time?"

"I don't know. Something happened and Norty just took off. I don't think Glenda even knows where he is."

"*Pat.*"

He looked down, a little ashamed. "I couldn't rat on him.

168

I thought I'd better keep the hell out of it, anyway. It's not my business."

"Norty's living with you."

"So?" Then, because he wanted to remind me that he was doing something about it, he said, "Maybe this trip'll cheer him up enough so he'll want to go back."

I shook my head, thinking of Norty on the pogo stick, Norty giggling in the show. "I don't know. Anyway, you were good to do it for him."

He folded his hands modestly. "Not such a bad idea, huh?"

"Pat, you're a promoter."

He grinned, flattered. "Besides," he said, "I wanted to see you."

I hardly heard him, because a couple of lines of remembered dialogue had clicked in my mind. "Hey," I said, "If Norty's living with you, how come he didn't know you lost your job?"

"Oh, that." Pat grinned. "He knew."

I set my cup down too hard.

"He was just having fun."

I was thinking of Norty contriving, trying to embarrass us both. "*Wait* a *min*ute—"

"You know what your trouble is?" He leaned over the table. "You take things too seriously."

"Oh, come *on*."

"You do." He toyed with the idea of taking my hand. "You ought to ride with things more, Denny. Take them as they are and not get all involved."

"I try to, up to a point." I was trying to find some way to explain. "I— " I began, and then saw that he was watching me with amusement, that he'd brought out the eternal verities the way somebody else might produce a Monopoly game, and he was bringing me on.

"We'd better get to bed," I said. "It's late."

"Denny, I—" In the door to the hall, we passed close. Pat's eyes had a mechanical glaze and I think that for the moment he'd forgotten I was me, Denny, that he was seeing me only as *girl*, maybe simply one more to add to his series. I touched his hand.

"Good night, Pat."

"Denny—"

"Night."

In my room I found a note from my mother. "Pearson

Swift called. He's leaving a book by for you tomorrow after lunch."

I'm not sure now what impulse of loneliness brought Pearson Swift to our house that day, when we hadn't talked for nearly a year and I had written only once or twice since the weekend in Providence, and had gotten a couple of post cards from him after graduation, when he was hitch-hiking across the continent. He was living with his parents now, reading, not doing anything in particular. It may have been that he remembered us talking, and there were few people he was able to talk to, or that he sensed as I did some inter-locking of our families, joined in so many common mem-ories, and found this visit to my house appropriate. His pre-text was a book.

When he came, Pat and Norty were just getting up. Norty had waked just after noon, in a bad mood, and my mother had served him scrambled eggs, setting his place and seeing to his coffee with an air of bewilderment. Norty was trim-ming his toast now, lips puffed slightly, face plump and but-tered, in a flash preview of the way he would look when he began to age. He was stacking his toast and bitching at Pat, who blinked into his coffee, ignoring him. By this time my mother had fled to the store and I sat behind the morning paper in the living room, trying not to laugh.

When I answered his knock Pearson must have been sur-prised to see the two of them behind me eating, framed in the dining alcove.

"I'd better come back another time," he said, already on the retreat.

"No." I pulled him inside. "Come have coffee with us."

Pat got up, eyes bright with curiosity, as I brought Pearson to the table. I think he was interested, as I have always been, to meet a friend of a friend, a stranger who has noth-ing in common with me but this particular friend, who meets my friend with a familiarity that I have always thought of as my right alone.

"Pearson, some friends of mine from New York—Pat Cas-tine, Norton Jarboe. Pat, Norty—Pearson Swift."

Pat nodded as he sat down and Norty grunted something through his toast. Pearson settled himself unhappily, book still on his lap, watching Pat and Norty eat.

For the most part, Pat and I talked. Twice I tried to draw Pearson into the conversation but he had come with one thing on his mind, whatever it was he had been going to tell me about the book, and he couldn't seem to think of anything else to say. I was uncomfortable for him, and threw myself into talk with Pat with a feeling of relief, glad there was somebody at the table who would chatter easily. Pat was animated, drawing me into talk along the lines we had laid out for our friendship, pulling me into some of our old routines. I think he meant to show Pearson that he had a right to be at my table, even as he waited for Pearson to show his own credentials.

Finally Pat said, "You live in Washington?"

"Arlington," Pearson said. "Rather, my parents do."

"You work for the Government?" Pat said.

Pearson shook his head.

"Oh, then what—"

"I haven't made up my mind." He stared blackly into his coffee, stirring it without any intention of drinking it.

"Well—" Pat said, and let it trail off. I could see him taking Pearson in, not sure what to make of the somber suit that would not have fit him properly even if had been well cut, the flicker in his eyes and his black, uncompromising air.

"Have you known Denny long?" Norty said, coming to life suddenly. I think he had decided it was time for Pearson to leave.

Pearson shrugged and mumbled something.

"Our fathers were classmates," I said for him.

"Oh, a *long* time." Norty still fixed on Pearson, trying to get a rise out of him.

"We grew up together," I said, wary by now.

"Oh." He smiled pleasantly, showing his teeth. "Not for years but for life."

Pearson twisted his hands in his lap.

"You might say so." I was uncomfortable for both of us.

"Isn't that wonderful," Norty said softly. "Childhood romance." He turned to Pearson, all solicitude. "And we come busting in—"

"Norty," Pat said, but Norty wasn't listening.

"—when you'd probably rather be alone."

Pearson was still staring stubbornly at his coffee, shoulders set. Pat jiggled in his chair. I think he was impatient with Norty, impatient with Pearson for not talking back.

"Norty—" I began.

"Oh, we'll go, we'll go," Norty said, as if I'd asked him to. "But first . . ." He teetered in his chair, looking down his nose at Pearson. "First I think we ought to ask this young man what his intentions are."

Pearson flushed darkly, not knowing enough to pick it up and carry it a step farther, to disarm Norty by playing his game.

"Norty—" By that time I was miserable.

"All dishonorable," Pat said suddenly, and he gave Norty's chair a backward push.

"Wha—" Norty began, and then got all involved in trying to right himself.

We began to relax.

"You'll have to pardon Mother Jarboe, here," Pat said, giving Norty another push. "She comes from a long line of marriage brokers and she can't help herself." He grinned easily. "It's a kind of a tic." Then he looked up, with an air of victory, because he had made Pearson smile.

"The Baudelaire I wrote you about," Pearson said under cover of Norty's squawks at Pat. "I found an extra copy in San Francisco and got it for you."

I took the book, the first thing Pearson ever gave me and the only thing I ever saw him give anybody, and murmured some kind of thanks.

Before I had finished, Pearson was on his feet. ". . . so I guess I'd better go."

"Hey don't," Pat said unexpectedly. "Come excurd with us."

"Huh?"

"We're just here sightseeing, so why don't you come along?"

Pearson moved stiffly, settling his jacket on his shoulders. "I'd better not."

"No, seriously." Pat got up, moving between him and the door. "Denny's taking us to the zoo."

Pearson hesitated. "I can't."

"Come on," Pat said. "When was the last time you went to the zoo?"

"If he doesn't want to he doesn't have to," Norty said.

"Shut up."

"You're going to be busy," Pearson said, to me.

"No, come on." I was delighted by the idea. "We're just going to be fooling around. Unless you have to be somewhere . . ."

He shook his head too quickly.

"Well, great," Pat said. "Norty can loan you a sweater, so you don't crud up your suit." He meant that he was a little embarrassed by the cut of Pearson's jacket, that he would be more at home with him if he could make him look a little more like other people he knew.

I could hear Norty beginning to protest, but somehow Pat was in front of him, too, so he couldn't say whatever was on his mind.

Pat produced the sweater a minute later and Pearson, a little helpless, hypnotized by Pat's charm, took off his coat and tie and put it on.

Pat got Norty up from the table before he had finished his coffee and herded us all out the door with a satisfied little grin.

I think it was the smile that won Pat, that made him decide to make Pearson a project, like Cheering Norty Up. At the time I was glad to have him interested, and I may even have thought we could do Pearson some good. Maybe we did help him, superficially, by giving him some fun, but we may have suspected even then that while the superficial Pearson could be pleased, pliable and almost amiable, there was beyond that an intellect which would always set him apart from us, a part of him which we would never be able to meet or comprehend, and that this part of him which needed our friendship most was beyond our powers to help. I may have begun to understand this at the zoo, when I saw that we could move toward him as much as we wanted to but that nothing really came of it until he relaxed his own high hopes and came part way to meet us.

At the time we tried to make him like us, and for a while it worked.

We were off from the others a little with our elbows on the guard rail, watching the seals. We were both drinking orange freezes and Pearson was poking at his with a straw, not really tasting it, not really seeing the seals and the water and the trees rising beyond. I hooked my elbows on the metal, pleased enough to be there on that day, and drank my orange freeze. I was surprised when he spoke.

"Maybe some time we can *really* talk."

I jerked around to look at him. "Huh?"

"You know, without everybody mucking around." He flushed, a little embarrassed at having spoken.

"If you want to say anything—"

"Hell, it's hard enough to say anything to anybody, but here—" With one gesture he dismissed the zoo, the whole quality of the day.

The breeze was soft around me and I was still feeling a

little muzzy in the sunshine, just happy to be where I was, light and inconsequential as a piece of fluff. "What's the matter with being here?"

He snapped to. "It's not *enough*."

I remember looking at the heavy trees, the seals, Norty and Pat just starting down the winding path from the bear cages. "You don't—this—"

He looked around bleakly. "It's nothing. If we could just talk—"

I remember wanting to forestall him, wanting him not to hope for too much from me. "What makes you think if we talk, there would be any more?"

He made an impatient, chopping motion with one hand. "There has to be more."

"Look," I said, getting angry. "It's a nice day. We're having fun."

"And you're willing to settle for that."

I stuck out my jaw. "Yes."

He gave me a quick, fierce look. "When it isn't *enough?*"

Because I was mad I said, "Nothing's ever enough for you, is it?"

"Hell no it isn't," he said on the same angry note, and then his expression began to change. "Hey," he said, and his voice was uneven. "You *knew*. How did you know?"

"You don't have to understand everything." I was conscious then of Pearson in memory, of our lives past and present touching in a way that made it possible for me to know this about him. I found myself aware of all the others I had ever cared about, beginning to be joined somehow, and I may have wanted to explain something of this to him, to make him see it, but there seemed to be nothing I could say. I said, "I just knew."

He nodded, almost as if I had explained and he saw it all, and his face was bright with pleasure.

Pat and Norty rounded the last curve of the path just then and came ambling toward us, eating ice cream, light-haired and fine-looking in the sun.

Pat yawned. "So what else is new?"

"These seals," I said. "They're great."

"That big one over there—" Pearson said, beginning carefully because he was playing directly to us. "Watch what he does when the little ones splash him."

The old seal swatted one of the little ones, as if on cue.

"The old bastard." Norty bent closer, laughing.

174

"He's been doing that for ten minutes," Pearson said, grinning now.

Pat pulled a face. "He has his rights."

We watched for a few minutes, shoulder to shoulder, hanging over the rail. Then Norty said "Enough of this. I want to see the reptile house."

"Off to the *rep*-tiles," Pat said, heaving to. Norty swung about smartly and the two of them led the way.

Pearson hesitated for a split second and then, in an apparently conscious decision to join us, he took my arm. "Off to the *rep*-tiles," he said, echoing Pat's tone, and we followed Pat and Norty up the path. I think for that one day at least, Pearson had decided to settle for what came and to be happy in it, and if he gave some, in accepting us on our own terms, he was grateful to us for letting him.

I see us in a series of tableaux, like snapshots taken on a sunny day: Pat, striking a pose in front of the lion's cage while we spot him at once among the seals, high-spirited and inconsequentially handsome, sleek and gay. Norty, fancying himself a cinnamon bear and the rest of us, at the time, believing it is so. Pearson pointing to a turtle submerged in a tank with its legs going madly in the water because its head is stuck in the drain. (At the time he said "Me," and grinned, but I didn't see him there.) The three of them taking me from cage to cage, making me turn my head at this angle and that in front of the brown-eyed hooved animals and the restless cats, not being able to agree which animal I am.

I remember talking a lot, bringing Pat out for Pearson, Pearson out for Pat because it pleased me to see the lives of my friends overlap and interlock. It gave me a sense of solidity somehow, as if I were weaving a net or forging a chain of friendships, of incidents shared which would sustain us all, a powerful specific for loneliness.

When we came away from the zoo even Pearson was laughing, but when Norty began to needle him and when Pat made some reference to Glenda in the car Norty snapped, from habit, "that bitch," and my images of the afternoon began to change. I thought back over the four of us in front of the animals, trying to remind myself of Norty as he had looked to me in the zoo, the teddy bear, but despite his charm and his kindness to Pearson the rest of the afternoon I was troubled by the persistent, lunatic vision of Norty as a sloth, long hair matted, tail curled under, blind face turned to the sky.

XVIII

When I look back I'm surprised to see that Pearson and I actually talked no more than a dozen or so times in all after we reached our twenties. Our battle from childhood, the continuity of my resentment, must have given him reality in my mind even in the years when I didn't see him because I can't think of a time, even in the convent boarding school when I was probably most removed from Florida and the war, when there wasn't Pearson. When we met again we may have been carried along by the impetus of the childhood feeling, or I may have been traveling, more than I realized, on the strength of my ties with Bunker, or it may simply have been affinity. I only know that our lives intertwined, that the threads will never be separated and straightened out, and I think this is just as well. I'm only sorry for the times when I failed Pearson, for the fact that there was no way to make up for all the years I took away from him.

I saw him once or twice during the year when he was still in Washington, and I may be one of the few people who reacted without resentment or surprise when he dropped plans for graduate school, turning his back on his talents without any plan or rationale, rejecting the idea of a job, and began to drift. We talked on the phone a couple of times and despite the fact that we lived less than an hour's drive apart, we wrote. Then I changed jobs, for a few months, leaving the museum for a Catholic social agency, and by the time I got used to the routine of house calls and reports and tried to get in touch with Pearson he had taken off for New York.

For a while, it looked as if I might be in New York too. I thought of taking a job there when I found I didn't have the stomach for social work. They told me at the agency that they were sorry to see me go, that some of the families had begun asking for me. I said I had to go. I didn't have the cheerfulness, the short range of vision necessary for work like that. If the rest of them realized fully what they were fighting, and I think they probably did, they had managed to forget the enormity of the enemy, and deal in particulars. I didn't seem to be able to manage it that way. From the beginning anything any of us did seemed to me like a drop in the bucket, measured against the droves of unwed mothers and unkempt kids and unemployed husbands and poor, trapped families, and I found it impossible to see only the immediate problem, and see it as something I might be able to help. And I could never leave the whole business behind me, as the others suggested, when I went home. I was dogged by growing, shifting images of a million families, a million problems multiplied, moving in a grey photomontage of misery. The people I saw may have sensed this, and I'm sure it didn't help. They needed someone who could come in with confidence and give a quiet measure of assurance, but I went into their homes already oppressed by the growing feeling that even when I had given all the help I could, when all the people in a position to help had given all the help they could, there would still be too much to fight, too many enemies, and even if we did away with all the poverty and dirt, the material enemies, in too many cases we would be brought up against a deep-seated enemy, within ourselves, within the people themselves. I wanted everything for them, right away, and I wanted it perfect. I tried to explain this to the head social worker when I left, and I think she saw that I simply didn't have the guts to attempt a partial solution. Maybe I'm not reading it right, maybe I'm just trying to justify myself. I don't know. At any rate I begged off after the first few weeks of it and went to New York to look for a job.

It seemed natural, after I'd gotten in touch with Pat, for the two of us to look up Pearson. We found him in Washington Heights, in one of his famous furnished rooms.

I was giddy, bouncing and idiotic, released from the enforced adulthood of the social agency, and when Pat picked me up at an aunt's place I made him take me to Reuben's for cheesecake and then to the Museum of Modern Art to see The Moon.

"I told Pearson four," I said, when we came out.

"Forget it," Pat said, and took my arm. "If we get there

late enough, maybe he'll feed us. Besides, there's something I want you to see."

I had confessed to Pat at some point that I had never seen the Metropolitan, and he put us in a cab and took us there. We started at the beginning and went up and down stairs, into this gallery and then the next, so that I was almost glutted when Pat brought me to a final turn and made me wait for a minute before he gave me a little push and I went around the corner, through a doorway and into a room.

If I said anything at all it was a sound, not a word.

"How d'you like that?" Pat said. "The sun."

It was almost an hour before he could get me away from the network of gold wires that dominated the room. I walked around and around it, beginning to change and spin with the wires and when Pat finally took me down and out through the front doors I burst outside wanting to yell, and I made him run with me for a couple of blocks.

We were both laughing when we stopped.

Pat rewound my scarf and pulled me together. "Twenty-three years old and running like a maniac. You're a disgrace."

"Sorry," I said, making a face because I wasn't.

"What would your friend Swift think?"

"I think he'd probably like it," I said.

Pat slowed. "I don't think so. Did I tell you he called me up?"

"Pearson?" I stopped to look at Pat. "He doesn't strike me as the type."

"I was surprised too. It took me a couple of minutes to figure out who he was. He was so jumpy I thought he was going to ring off before I could find out."

I had lived with my own idea of Pearson for so long that it gave me an uncanny feeling to hear him described by somebody else. Thinking back, I said, "He must have liked you. I can't think of many people he would have called."

"Hell, he only saw me once, that time at your place in Washington."

"He does things for keeps."

"He said he'd been in town for a month," Pat said, "but I got the feeling I was the first person he'd talked to. Funny."

"He gets lonely, I think. Anyway—"

"Anyway, he asked me to get him this appointment at the network—with Personnel." Pat resettled his coat on his shoulders. "Then he never showed."

I shook my head, trying to figure it.

"When I called him to find out why, he sounded so down

178

that I had to have him over for a drink." Pat looked exasperated. "He was there for a whole hour and he never explained. He just sort of moped around, staring out windows and mulling over my books. Glenda came by with Sarah and he looked like he was dying to stay and talk to her but as soon as she sat down he got that miserable look, the way he does, and took off."

I wanted to apologize for him, to explain, but I realized there was nothing I could say.

"He skunked himself with the network," Pat said. "He'll never get inside the door, now."

"I can't quite see him—" I began.

"What the hell," Pat said with a careless wave of the hand. "He doesn't belong in that kind of setup."

"He needs to be somewhere using his *brain*."

"I don't get him," Pat said. "I just don't get him. Anyway—"

"Anyway—"

"Anyway, if we leave now, we'll be there by six. Time for a Little Something. D'you think he can cook?"

I had to laugh. "I wouldn't put money on it."

Pat drooped. "You're right. I can tell you're right. Besides, if he's not working, he probably can't *afford* to cook. Let's take a CARE package for him. If we're good maybe he'll let us have some of it."

I hesitated for a minute, thinking of Pearson in his dark pride, turning us away, but I knew that Pat would be able to carry it off and so I followed him into a Chinese restaurant to order won ton and egg roll and egg foo yong and sweet-and-sour pork and for an incongruous finale, Napoleons from the pastry shop next door. Then we took the cartons to Pearson's room and spread them out with great ceremony, arranging them on the crate he used for a desk.

If I expected Pearson to be embarrassed by the display of food and to refuse it out of some hurt pride, I was surprised. He let us in with an air of detachment and waved us to chairs almost without speaking. Then he sat by, preoccupied and distant, while we rustled drinks for ourselves and foraged in his cabinets for silverware and dishes for the food.

At first, Pat and I tried to jolly him along. We found ourselves clowning, jumping around and making inept little comments, like paid jesters, trying desperately to cheer him up. He sat back with the air of an invalid, like somebody who can barely lift his head from the pillows and let us bring the food to him, saying "Egg roll? How about some

179

of this neat shlimp flied lice?" rattling and giggling and getting more and more exasperated by the minute, scraping around for jokes and leading questions to draw him out. By the time the food was served and we were ready to begin eating we ignored him, muttering to each other through sub gum and talking about people we know without bothering to explain to Pearson who they were. We split the extra egg roll and haggled over the last Napoleon without caring whether he was interested or not.

"How long are you in New York?" Pearson said unexpectedly.

For a minute it was as if he hadn't said anything. We exchanged looks, surprised, and then turned to study him.

"I mean, is it a visit or are you looking for a job?" He went red-and-black, stiff with the effort.

"Well," Pat said softly.

"I thought you might be looking for a job too," Pearson said, holding his ground. Warmed by the food, or by our prattle, or whatever, he was trying to give.

"I am, sort of," I said finally. "They want me back at the museum, though. If nothing good comes along I'll probably go back."

Pat grinned. "How would we get along without you?"

I let him have it, trying not to laugh. "How have you managed all these years?"

Pearson was smiling too. "Living at home is cheaper anyway."

Pat nodded. "But not nearly so much fun."

There was a pause.

"Ben's ship was in Brooklyn last month," Pearson said finally, just to keep the conversation going. I don't think he expected to see my head snap around as quickly as it did.

"How—how was he?"

He shrugged. "The same. Fighting the war."

"The war." Pearson and I had never talked about it, but I knew exactly what he meant.

Pat looked from Pearson to me, puzzled.

"World War II," I explained, for him. It wasn't strictly true, or complete, but it would give Pat a place to start in whatever talk was to come. I hesitated, in the fullness of memory. "We—we all took it pretty hard."

Pat made a wry little face. "The war. I kind of miss all those funnybooks. Dad had to convert his plant to tank parts," he said, almost nostalgic. "Some kid in my class had a Commando suit."

Pearson began, "You weren't—" and then made a helpless little gesture because there was no way for him to describe what the war had been to us.

"I had a plane-spotter's book," Pat said, beginning to understand. "The maid used to let me mix the oleo. You remember those bags with the thing the yellow comes in?" He looked apologetic. "I guess that was just about it."

Pearson nodded. "Probably just as well."

Pat looked at him sharply. "You—"

His voice was dry. "We were a little more involved."

I was looking hard at Pearson, engrossed in the discovery, the confirmation of something I had never known him well enough to assume for him. "It did get to you then," I said, because I had to hear him say it.

"Yeah."

"You were so much older. We were never sure."

"It was the same for me," Pearson said.

I found myself caught in memory, explaining, not for Pat but for myself. "Our fathers were in it—it was all around us —it was all there was."

"Some of us are just now getting over it," Pearson said. "Denny's father—"

"Oh, yeah," Pat said, flushing because it embarrassed him to have to be reminded.

"I got over it in Korea," Pearson said. "You know something, Denny? Korea didn't seem like a real war to me. I don't think there will ever be a war as real as that one was." He got up abruptly. "And it's over."

"It's over," I said, echoing him. "But you know what?" It was a confession. "I still have trouble talking to a Jap."

"Ben," Pearson said with dislike. "Now Ben will never get over it."

I wanted him to deny it. "No?"

"No. Why else would he make the Navy his life?"

I was thinking of Jake, of Daddy, of the tradition and the triple image of the fine young officer in his whites and I said, "A lot of people have made the Navy their life."

Pearson's face was dark. "Sure, but they're defenders. It's different with Ben. He's looking for a place where he can stand and fight."

Wanting to stop him, to keep the triple image intact I said, "Oh, Lord, you don't think he's still fighting the war."

"Some war." Pearson was at the window now. "Not our war. Any war. Just war. That's the difference." He was

181

thinking hard, and finally he said, "We only had it in us for one war, and that's over now."

I sat back, with a feeling of relief. "Yes."

"I don't—" Pat began, but he stopped because he saw that we had almost forgotten him.

"But that guy—" Pearson glared into the street and then pulled the shades. "I don't know what he's fighting, but he's still fighting."

I was thinking of our estrangement, of the baptism, and even knowing Pat was listening I ventured, "Me, maybe."

"Huh?" Pearson said distractedly, and he answered carelessly, as if it were of no importance. "I don't think so. I told him I'd seen you and he didn't even have a message for you."

So there it was. I let out all my breath, relieved and at the same time disappointed because I had expected some word from Bunker; I had expected to know, at least, whether he still hated me for the baptism, whether he still hated me enough to hate God for it. I was still troubled by what I had done, by a sense of responsibility, but somehow the fact of no message, the idea that I had lost touch with Bunker, was almost worse. I sat back without saying anything, because I was exhausted.

Pat made a couple of false starts and then, because he saw that I was miserable, he subsided too.

"Well," Pearson said, apparently remembering that he was the host. "You were great to bring the food."

"It was fun," Pat said. "Thanks for the booze."

"I've been working on something that might be in your line."

"No kidding?" Pat looked up, polite.

"You're doing something with scripts?"

Pat managed to look professional. "I'm story editor for one of the anthology shows."

"That's what I thought," Pearson said, and he thrust a sheaf of papers into Pat's hands. His voice was taut and he had a tremulous, anxious look. "I wanted you to see this play."

There is a certain etiquette about writing, and about showing it to other people. I know this from Katherine, who would drop a poem on my bed with the air of someone who couldn't care less, and who always managed to look as if she'd just as soon throw it away.

Pearson was pressing Pat, leaving no doubt that he *cared*. "It's—pretty important," he said. "It's about a lot of things I have to say."

"Well—I—" Pat said, and then handed the sheaf back to him, put off by Pearson's willingness to expose himself, honestly baffled by Pearson's untidy hand.

"You have to read it," Pearson said, as if everything hinged on it.

"Uh—" Pat had drawn his elbows close to his sides, embarrassed because Pearson was so intent, so importunate.

"Maybe it would be better if I read some of it." Pearson sat down, looking over the papers at us. I don't think he was trying to sell the play to Pat, or get us to praise him. I think he was honestly trying to give.

It was brilliant, plotless, incomprehensible, so tied up in philosophical considerations and the intimations of darkness that had dogged him for as long as he could remember that Pat and I were confused, swept up and tossed down, overwhelmed and almost gasping when he stopped reading finally and said,

"What do you think?"

"It's—" Pat looked like he wanted to flee. "It's pretty interesting," he said and then, because he hated anything overt —the play, the naked look on Pearson's face—he said, "Needs work," and then withdrew.

Pearson turned to me. "That business about the pulley. The character who is the chorus for the chorus, telling what they really think. The one who is no more than someone else's motives—" He was pleading with me for some kind of understanding.

I did the best I could. "I'd have to read it more carefully, maybe hear it again."

"Sure," he said, "Oh, sure," and wadded the whole business into a carton. "Well, what else is new?"

Pat looked at me and I looked at Pat.

"How's the job-hunting coming?" Pat said.

"Oh—that." Pearson's smile was no more than a grimace, ugly and uncontrolled. "I'm all taken care of."

I said, "What kind of thing?"

"Hamburgers," he said abstractedly. "I'm in hamburgers. At the bus station, twelve to eight a.m."

"Hey," Pat said, "If that's the way things are, why don't you—"

"I'm satisfied," Pearson said, almost belligerent. "What the hell?"

"Oh, well," Pat said feebly. "You can always cop a free meal."

I wasn't much help. "All the mustard you can eat."

"Screw it," Pearson said, and then he stuck his chin out, waiting for us to try again.

We made a few more stabs at conversation, but we were at some kind of impasse. From time to time Pearson would smile, as if he was really glad we were there, but he didn't seem to be able to get it across in words. I think he wanted us to stay but he couldn't seem to say or do anything that would make us want to stay. Pat and I went into one or two of our old routines but then stopped, because we didn't have the heart for it. Finally we were so depressed that we left. Some other day we would try to make amends.

We bounded down the stairs like a couple of freed wallabies and in an orgy of disloyalty, in our relief at being away from Pearson we went to a neighborhood movie and laughed and laughed and laughed.

When we came out, Pat said, "D'you mind if I put you in a cab? There's—somebody I have to see," and I told him it was all right because I knew from his expression, from what he didn't say, that he was going to spend the night with one of his girls.

XIX

I taught for a while, in Washington, filling out the term for a teacher who had been sick. By the time the job carried me into summer and I found myself at loose ends again, I was ready to go back to the museum because I had learned, if nothing else, that I could be just as restless in an eighth-grade classroom as I could among CLAVICLES, PLEISTOCENE, or on the trail of a glamorous job in New York.

I went back to a slightly better job but to the same office, the same people, the same desk. I remember feeling guilty that first day, as if I should apologize for something I couldn't quite grasp, when I saw Netta Freeward's face. She greeted me with a look of disappointment, and I think now that she wasn't disappointed for her own sake, because she had given herself to the stream of time past some years before, but for mine, because she remembered how passionately I had tried to pull her out of it, and she saw my return as a kind of defeat. She couldn't know that if I was back it was because I wanted to be back, because one place had begun to seem as good as another to me. I was drifting, in a sense, as Pearson drifted, but I believe I was drifting happily because everything I did in those days seemed to tie in with my idea of preparation, and while I didn't know at the time what I was preparing for, I did everything I did with a certain feeling of content.

Pearson visited me at the museum that summer, atremble with energy and a feverish sense of purpose that shook me and left me frightened even though I told myself over and over that I should be glad he had hit on something he thought he wanted to do.

"Denny," he said over the phone, "Take some time off and meet me downtown for lunch."

He sounded so gay that I abandoned my desk without even shutting away the typewriter and gave Mr. Rankin a casual excuse. As I recall it I waggled my fingers at Netta just before I left because she expected it of me, and I saw her brighten, imagining a promising afternoon.

We met in a dim, dark-panelled ice cream parlor on F Street and sat for two hours over lunch, chattering almost without stopping to eat. I was starved for news and for once Pearson was full of it, telling me all about Pat, who had taken it upon himself to drop in from time to time wth leads on job openings and cartons of exotic, inedible food, about the people in the hamburger joint and what had happened the day he quit his job. He was full of plans too, but he held them back, dropping hints with a subtlety that I had never seen in him, amused to see me so curious. I talked too, about my job, about everything I had read for months, about one or two lonely visits to Jake and Margaret, when we had sat in the quiet house, trying to cheer ourselves by bringing up the names of absent friends, of Bunker, of Pearson himself. I talked about teaching and about what my mother was doing and about dreams and about funny lines I had overheard and moments of embarrassment that had slipped by because there was nobody there to laugh with, going on and on in that spate of logorrhea that comes when I have gone too long without talking to a friend.

"Hey," I said finally because I was pleased to find us talking so fluidly, because he was smiling. "You really look great."

He grinned. "I *am* great. You don't know how great."

He seemed so confident that I waited with a funny, left-out feeling as if he had outstripped me somehow. "What's up?"

"I'm on to something," he said, and then stopped, as if he was too engaged in it to have time to explain.

"Something new?" I answered him with what may have been a touch of jealousy because I had the idea that he knew something I didn't know, because at the moment he seemed so happy, so *sure*.

"Yeah," he said. "It's what I came to tell you about."

"Let's hear it," I said, wanting to be caught up in it, whatever it was, and carried along.

"Not now," he said, drawing back with a maddening air of secrecy. Whatever he had on his mind, he seemed to be saving it up. "Hey, let's go back to your place, and you can show me around."

I stood up, because I knew there was no point in pressing him.

We went from chamber to chamber in the museum, looking at rocks, specimens, gems, artifacts, stopping in front of rock-browed prehistoric men and Ming vases big enough to hold two of the forty thieves, with me making little speeches about each display and Pearson listening but more interested in the secret he was nursing, so that most of his attention was turned inward, on it. He seemed to decide the time was right, finally, in the hall of dinosaurs and sabre-toothed tigers and mammoths, and he stopped there in the shadow of the huge, brooding shapes.

"Now," he said.

"Now."

"I'm getting ready this summer," he began almost modestly. "It starts this fall."

"Yes?"

"It's a kind of an absolute—or as near to one as I think I can get."

I didn't understand, but I knew better than to interrupt him.

"You know how I've been—always wanting things one way or the other." He stared past me, sorting his words. "I think this is a field where I can hope for it."

He paused, apparently caught up in the idea and I repeated, "—hope for it," trying to hurry him along.

"It's not like medicine at all," he said. "You know—you have one case and that case lives or dies and then there's another and so on, so that none of them really counts and you can never even count them—"

I found myself wanting to protest but Pearson had already raised one hand to stay me.

"This is different. One case can be all. You know—set a precedent. It came to me last winter," he said, "after a night I spent drinking with Pat. He may even have put me onto it." His eyes were alight, and he looked as if he thought he had said enough, as if I already understood everything and there was no need for him to go on.

"Put you on to *what*?" I said, more impatient than I should have been.

His smile was almost tolerant. "The whole business. The idea that there is an area where things can be one way or another." He looked at me directly for the first time. "I've always wanted to *know* exactly how things stood. Now I can have some part in determining it. It's a place where I can find things out."

If he hadn't seemed so smug and so mysterious, I might not have snapped. "What in hell are you talking about?"

He laughed. "It's something I can begin—and settle, in a way, each time—but *there's no end to it.*"

"Pearson, for Lord's sake—"

He was still laughing. "Denny, don't you see? I've found the one place where I can be *sure* things are one way or another. I'll be able to say, and it will be so."

"Well, great," I said, hurt, and turned to go.

"Denny," he said, pulling me back. "I thought you'd know. Look, I'm talking about the law. Get it? The *law.*"

"The law." I was strangely disappointed. "But you were talking about that last year."

"This is different. I understand it now."

"Law. You'll be going to law school," I said, slowly, because I realized that for some reason my disappointment, like his excitement, was out of all proportion to what he had just said.

"I've been picking up some night courses at City College so I'll be eligible."

"Well—great," I said, reminding myself that I should be pleased to see him interested in a career. Maybe it was that he was *too* interested. I only know I was not comfortable with him that day.

He looked down modestly. "I'm accepted for this fall."

I thought of the reading involved, of the judgment it would take and for a minute I was able to convince myself that he had hit on something demanding enough to engage him. "It sounds really swell."

"I'll be at the best in the country."

"Columbia?"

"Yale."

"No kidding?" I grinned then, pleased at the idea of Pearson in New Haven.

He relaxed a little, satisfied that I was following him. "The Yale part was Pat's idea. We were gassing one night—he was making lists of things I could do—ditch digging, lepidoptery, prostitution—you know."

I smiled, because I knew Pat.

"Anyway, he got around to New Haven, and how we could get me into the Culinary Institute. Then he started listing professional schools—drama, forestry—you know—

and all of a sudden, there it was. I didn't even realize it until after he had gone home."

"Yale Law," I said. "It's a terrific place."

His chin went up. "They've got some of the best men in the country."

Something in his tone made me uneasy, but I wasn't yet sure what it was. It seemed important that I keep him at the level of particulars. "The best clerkships go to Yale people."

He passed it off. "That's not what's important."

"I always thought—"

"It's what I'll be doing. The way I'll be working—I don't know—I think it's going to solve a lot of things for me." His hands went off in different directions and he watched me, willing me to say that it was so. "These guys are taken up in something with endless possibilities. I'll be able to *talk* to them." He waited for me to agree.

I knew then what bothered me. It was not the idea of law as a career for Pearson, or even as a way of life, but the fact that he hoped too much.

"Don't you see?" he said, and his face was suffused. "They're all going somewhere and I'll be going too." He leaned forward as if he were already in motion.

"Pearson, I—" I began, wanting somehow to slow him, to hold him back.

"Ben laughed," he said thoughtfully. "He hated me for drifting from thing to thing. It's worse for him," he said with a sudden sharpness. "He's stuck."

"He's got the Navy," I said reflexively, defending Bunker.

"Not really," Pearson said. "It's nothing to him, except a place where he can fight. He's so stuck in that, in his pride, that he can't move. Don't you see?" His eyes were ablaze. "At least I'm *moving*."

"If this is something you really want," I said cautiously.

"All you need—" he said (and I was shaken by the finality of his "all you need") "—all you need is a framework. The law is mine—" he flung out his hands in a jerky oratorical gesture. "Hell, Denny, it's a place where I can *begin*."

He stopped, breathing hard, trembling like a flame in that dark hall. Behind him rose a hulking stegosaurus and beyond it sprawled a diorama, and at his back I could sense—no, see—pre-history rushing into history and as I watched it came to me that the two of us were static, embedded somehow, and that time parted and flowed around us and hur-

189

ried on beyond, leaving us caught, suspended, like specimens hanging at the bottom of some murky tank, and I saw that I could not help him, that despite all the hopes and all the friendships I had tried to shore up against it, in that way, at least, I was as isolated as he. I saw all this and I saw at his shoulder something more, something that may only have been the shadow of his disillusionment, the moment which was bound to come when he found that actuality could never meet his vision, that it could not and never would be perfect; it may simply have been the inevitability of his disappointment, the natural antithesis of his joy, his vibrant hope, or it may have been some intimation of his death. I only know that I was frightened, that I wanted to warn him in some way, but he seemed so happy that I knew it was not my place to speak.

When I did say something it was weak. "It sounds wonderful, Pearson," I said.

After we said goodbye I went back into the chambers and wandered until closing time, not knowing who I could tell or what I could say, mulling it with no real understanding of the danger or the enemy. When closing time came and I groped my way into the late afternoon sunlight I had only the idea that something was wrong and I'd better pray for him.

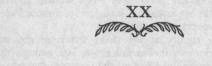
"Katherine's dead," I said to Sister Thomas, dropping it on her desk like a bomb, almost accusing her. I don't know what I expected her to say or do, but the news was fresh and I think I still had the idea that there must be something somebody could do.

She looked at me. "I know."

"*Chicken* pox." I pushed a chair around with my hip so that it faced her and slammed myself into it. "She picked it up from one of the kids. You know what? The twins have it now. They're still in bed with it." I'm still ashamed to remember the laugh I faked then. "You know those kid diseases. One kid gets something and it goes right through the family." I was after Sister Thomas, dogging her, trying to get something out of her. "What do you think of that?"

She wouldn't take me up. "How's Jim?"

"Oh, he's great. Just great. All alone with three kids."

She took in her breath, about to say something, but then looked at me and decided to be still.

"It had to be somebody with four kids," I said, hammering at her. "Somebody like Kat." I wanted the whole business to cost her something; I wanted to exact some measure of pain, if nothing else some effort of anger. "Why somebody with four kids? Why not me?"

I had already gotten some satisfaction out of her, some unhappiness, in the moment when I had clicked into the office as I had on a dozen other visits, very much the young adult in town clothes and I. Miller shoes. When she had tried to introduce me to that year's newspaper staff, a bunch of children in old sweaters and baggy skirts, I'd been barely civil, not even trying to smile. I had stared stubbornly, not saying anything, until she had turned with a look of embarrassment and dismissed them.

Ordinarily we would have been at ease now, with me smoking, using an ashtray she would have produced from somewhere with an air of conspiracy because college rules barred smoking in the building. The cigarette always set the tone of informality, marking me as an old girl, no longer touched by college rules. It was an emblem of the change in our relationship, of my promotion from student to friend, and once it was lit we usually talked freely, almost like colleagues, until it was time for me to go.

Today she sat rigidly at her desk, watching me, and I stared out the window. It was fall again, late enough in the year for the sky to be dead and all the trees drained of color. There were streaks of brown leaves still plastered to the trees and the streets were dragged with brown, flattened on the pavement and festering in the gutters.

When I turned back to the room it seemed circumscribed, almost unbearably small and I was fighting it, even as I fought Katherine's death, when I said, "It's rotten. Just rotten," and waited for Sister Thomas to say something I could attack.

Instead she said, "She's with God." I had known she would.

I knew it too, but I knew it only intellectually, and it didn't make Katherine's death any easier for me to take. "But why her," I said, unwilling to give up.

Sister moved impatiently, so that her veil crackled, but she kept her peace.

I knew she was unhappy for me but by that time I couldn't stop myself. "It had to be her. It could just as well have been me."

I could see that I had reached her.

I bored in, forgetting everything in my anger at Katherine's death, railing at it. "She had so much—I've got nothing to lose."

She stood up then, furious but controlled. "At this point I think you have a lot *more* to lose." She slammed a book on the desk and went over to the window, standing so the curve of her habit hid her face.

I could feel myself turning to liquid in the chair, sick with embarrassment, with something more fundamental than embarrassment because Sister Thomas in her anger had touched a certain part of me and touched it surely and profoundly. She wasn't a simple woman. She wasn't trailing flowers, or telling me to count my blessings. She was telling me that

Katherine, fulfilled, might very well have been ready to die, while I, in my preoccupations, in my resentment, was not. It was as if she knew about the lives which were bound up with mine, the matters yet unfinished as certainly as if I had told her everything. She seemed to understand before I did that I was hanging between past and future, with the matter of Bunker unfinished and a number of other things—even to my own life—undecided, that I carried the responsibility for Bunker with me still and that I wouldn't feel myself ready to die, to go anywhere, until I had found some way to redeem it. I put down my head, too overwhelmed to cry.

She came back to her desk and pretended to riffle through a book, not looking at me.

"I'm sorry," I said when I could talk again. "It's just that with Kat gone—"

"Never mind," she said, closing her book. "Tell me again about that time you and Pat went to see her."

At first I was reluctant. "Maybe some other time."

"No, I'd like to hear," she said with a certain firmness I did not mark at the time. "You said she wanted to be so soignée—"

"Oh, yeah." I found myself smiling. "You should have seen her when she met the train—she looked about twelve years old."

Sister Thomas looked up. "I suppose she had on that terrible raincoat."

I nodded.

"I was hoping she'd burn it before the wedding. Especially after it kept her home from the college press conference."

"Schrader went instead." I made a face.

Sister nodded. "Sister Martin was convinced she'd wear that raincoat to Chicago, and disgrace us all."

"I always liked it," I said. "It was a kind of a badge—"

We talked on, talking until it was easy to talk about Katherine, not about Kat dead but about Kat as she had been, in classes, at home, telling each other about Kat in the graveyard at boarding school, Kat on the day of her wedding, piling memory on memory until Katherine seemed to glow in the room.

"She's always so—" I began and then stopped, surprised to find myself talking about her in the present tense.

Sister Thomas moved a paperweight from left to right on the glass surface of her desk. "You see?"

I thought of Katherine, complete in memory, and began to understand. I nodded, grateful to her for reminding me of that gift of memory, the reality the dead will have for the living until there are no more people to recall them, no more moments to recall.

I think now that she was showing me something more but at the time she looked at her desk, not saying anything, not trying to press her point.

"It's funny," I said, remembering. "That time Pat and I went to see her, she knew she was going to have Jimmy—the baby—and she didn't say anything."

Sister Thomas leaned back. "I doubt if Pat could have taken it just then."

"I know. I probably wasn't ready either."

"How is he now?"

I shook my head. "He called, right after he heard. He still feels pretty terrible."

"He doesn't have much to fall back on," she said, because she knew almost as much as I did about Pat. "He's still a little in love with her, isn't he?"

I looked up, surprised that she had picked up something I hadn't seen for myself. "Gee—I guess he is. He never said—" I thought back. "He'd probably die before he'd admit something like that. You know how he is."

I stopped then because I saw that she was amused, because she had never met Pat and probably never would, but we both seemed to take it for granted that she knew him.

"Well, you *do* know him."

She shook her head.

"If it's not knowledge what is it?"

She said simply, "It's more a matter of concern."

"But you're in here, and still you—"

She stopped me. "We don't lock ourselves away from people when we enter."

"But why do you have to—"

"We help each other," she said.

I bent my head, thinking on it.

It's hard to explain how she knows them but she does know Pat and Pearson and Bunker (up to a point) and perhaps a dozen others in my life, and probably dozens of others in a dozen other people's lives, and in her concern they have a continuing reality, even as Katherine does, so that limited as she is to the college grounds, to her office and the convent, Sister Thomas will always be in touch. I think now that her awareness of these lives acts on her awareness of

God, sharpening it, even as her awareness of God makes it possible for her to touch all these lives, meshing and moving with them in a purpose which strengthens her and makes her whole and content. I remember beginning to grasp this, wanting to reach out.

I must have been staring because she called me back with a gesture that seemed to take in the room, the building—more, the community of nuns—saying, "We're all interested in the same thing," and then she switched on the gooseneck lamp on her desk.

It was natural for me to begin telling her about Pearson then.

"He bugged out of law school last month," I said. "I found out last week when I called his parents. They think he's in New York. That's another reason I felt so terrible when I came in here."

"He was doing all right last summer, wasn't he?"

"He had a government job. I think he got it because he'd had one year of law. I thought he was doing fine, better than I'd seen him—" I stared at the glass top of her desk for a moment, looking at the reflected clutter of papers, the inkwell, the calendar. "I think I know what got him."

"You said he was so excited about it last year," she said, and I knew she remembered how troubled I had been.

"It just—wasn't enough," I said. "Nothing is."

"—for him," she said.

"For him."

Near supper time there was a knock at the door and Sister's student editor came in, as militantly unkempt as I had ever been. She was a little grinny, as people still in school seem to be in the presence of old grads returned, mixing respect for the advanced state in life with impatience for the alumna who is already obsolete and on the verge of making an Old Fool of herself by pretending that she still has some part in the life of the college.

We talked for a minute or two, with me telling the girl what I was doing now, and asking her how things were, and then I stood up. Sister Thomas looked over her student's head at me. "I'm glad you came."

"I—" There was no way for me to say what came to my mind. I grinned and said, "So I'll see you."

"Come back soon."

I hung on the door, just for a minute. "I will." Then I turned and went into the darkness of the hall, setting my feet carefully on the polished brown linoleum.

XXI

I didn't see Pat again until late June, when I met him in the Yale Club because he wanted to show it off to me, and we had our sad little exchange about Katherine. We picked up, as we always had, without any sense of the lapse in time, but for once the continuity of our talk didn't do much to cheer us. We didn't start out with bathos in mind, but every path we took seemed to lead to some reminder of time passing, or a friend gone, or a life not going according to plan. Norty Jarboe had left Glenda and was in California. According to Pat, he was making her file for divorce. When Pat asked me about Katherine's kids I had to tell him they were living with an aunt, because Jim hadn't been able to find any way to keep them with him. I turned to Pat's classmates, asking about Mack Glendauer, whom I had dated when Pat was still going with Katherine; Pat said Mack's father had cancer. Even Pat was unsettled, troubled for the first time by the spectres of a number of things he should have done and would never do, so that he turned to me finally, wanting reassurance, and said, "So how the hell are *you?*"

"Okay."

"What are you doing in *Bronx*ville," he said, hoping I would be able to make something funny out of it.

I wasn't sure myself but I said, "Living with my aunt, until I get settled."

"How's the job?"

"It's a job." I pushed my dessert plate aside. "It doesn't really matter."

"Um?"

"I'd been in that museum too long. I'd been in Washington too long. Hell, I'd been living at *home* too long."

"You save money that way," Pat said, beginning to lose interest. "No rent."

I looked at him and went on, because I was pretty sure he had stopped listening. "It just seemed like time to cut a few ties."

"Où sont les neiges," he said, staring past me. "Où le hell sont les neiges."

For want of anything better to say I said, "Let's go."

We forgot ourselves for a minute or two when we hit the street and stared like children, digging in our heels and watching the variety of people until Pat, made self-conscious by the glare of an old lady in a mink cape, said, "Let's have a drink."

We settled in a booth in the back of a narrow bar on Third Avenue, balancing this subject and then that in a delicate juggling act, trying not so much for gaiety as for a more comfortable mood.

"The sky is falling," I said, trying to make fun of us.

"Denny, you're *too* depressing. Maybe I ought to get you drunk."

"I'd just get maudlin," I said. "How about a flick?"

"We'd have to find a paper and check the times, and then we'd probably get into a fight about which picture to see. Then we'd have to *get* a cab, and *get* to the theater, and *get* a ticket, and *get* a seat, and by that time . . ."

"By that time we'd be exhausted," I said. "Oh well. It was a thought."

"We could take in a ball game." Pat knew I hated baseball.

"Or get arrested."

"Or call California collect." Pat inspected his nails for a minute and then said, "If I hadn't packed him off to New Haven, we could call up Swift," producing it like an entertainer bringing on the pièce de résistance.

"Pearson?" My quick gesture must have gratified Pat.

"The same," he said, pleased with his effect. "He's working for this friend of my father's this summer. I lined it up for him." He bent his head over his nails, all modesty. "The firm is one of the best."

I put out a hand. "Wait a minute. I thought he was through with the law."

"He was, until I pulled him out of it." Pat grinned. "I thought you knew."

"I didn't know," I said, a little cross at him for holding out on me. "I haven't heard a thing about him since I saw his

197

parents at Christmas. For all I knew he was still hanging around the city."

Pat hesitated, stretching the pause maddeningly and then he said, "He might still be, but I ran into him in December, and sent him back to school in time for the second term." He brought off the line with a flourish and waited for applause, smooth head bowed.

"You didn't," I said, managing to sound incredulous.

"Why not?" In the dim light his pale hair shone. "He wasn't in any academic trouble. He'll lose a semester, but he'll graduate. You know what? By the time I finished he was all fired up about it."

Something in what he said struck an echo, and the memory of Pearson, hot with enthusiasm, gave me pause. "He was all fired up before."

"Only trouble is—" he began, and then thought better of it.

"What," I said, prompting him.

"Nothing."

"You said something about trouble," I said, and despite the fact that Pat hadn't come out with anything, I could feel my hands go cold.

"I don't even know if it is trouble," Pat mumbled, not wanting to crab his act. He must have caught something in my expression because he tried to minimize it. "I only have this one guy's word for it."

"Word for what?"

"Nothing—oh, I don't know." He centered his glass in front of him. "I ran into this classmate of mine, who's working in the same office. Jack Griffin—he finished Yale Law last June. I saw Jack at a party, and he said—" Pat paused, trying to remember what had troubled him. "He didn't say anything, exactly—I just got the idea that he thought there was something *creepy* about the guy. He said he wasn't—"

"Wasn't performing?"

"Oh, he's doing his work. I don't know—" Pat made a little circle with his glass, and brought it back to home. "Jack didn't say much, but I got this picture of Swift floating at the edge of things, sort of hanging, like a spook. If he hadn't been a little bit that way when I saw him, I might not even have picked it up."

"You didn't tell me—"

"There wasn't anything to tell. At the time I thought he was just jumpy about being out of school. He's so damned hard to *get* to."

"I'd like to see him," I said.

"Hey," Pat said, raising his glass halfheartedly. "Cheers."

I tried to grin, and failed. "Sorry."

Pat shrugged. "We're really a swell group." He pushed his glass away again, moving it slowly, and then brought it back. "Hell, with Kat and everything—what could we expect?"

We stared around the bar then, beyond trying to be gay, getting older as we sat. Pat had his chin in his hands, staring at nothing. I withdrew to a point somewhere within myself and began to enumerate the losses, diminished by Kat's death, by the new worry about Pearson and the old worry about his brother, which would never leave me, troubled even by the news of Mack Glendauer's father whom I had never met. I could almost feel myself aging, touched by so many things that I could never hope to be the same again, and I examined the feeling, experimenting, not entirely unhappy in it.

Then Pat said, "Tell you what," arresting the process for that night at least. "We need a party."

"Oh, sure," I said. "We can go as death's heads at the feast."

"Don't be a nudje. It'll be a great party, and we'll even get points for doing a good deed."

"Who are we good deeding?"

"Glenda," he said. "She's all alone out there at her parents' place with nobody to talk to but that kid. She must be depressed as hell." Cheered by the sound of his own voice, Pat went on. "What if we gave her a party, to pull her out of it?"

"Who can afford a party?"

"That's the great part." His eyes were alive now. "She can. I've always wanted to have a party out there." He drew himself up with a look of mock importance. "We'll just be in charge."

"Well, Grover Whelan," I said, and we both began to laugh.

When Pat put me on the train that night Glenda had already agreed to a party and the wheels were in motion. Pat had an officious look and a handful of lists. He'd spent two hours on the telephone, checking names and discussing wines and foods with Glenda, getting acceptances from Mack Glendauer and some other classmates while Glenda, at her parents' place on the Sound, was calling up everybody she knew. We had stormed Pearson by long distance telephone, making him promise to rent a car and drive down from New Haven for the event. It seemed to be important that he come, and Pat hung on the telephone until he had agreed. I think Pat had the idea that if he got enough of us together, and made the evening gay enough, he might be able to stay the rush of time and so stave off the aging, the inevitable change, the measure of pain that were implicit in it. He may even have thought that he could answer, for the time being at least, some need he seemed to sense in Pearson, in Glenda, even in me, and in himself, that getting us all together might make things different.

Glenda's parents' house looked like Oz, with a domed porte cochère and turrets and mazes of leaded windows and I somehow expected to see all flags flying, fluttering green from every peak and crenelation along that high, improbable roof. It was to his credit that Pat had managed a yachtsman's cocktail flag and a series of bright arrows pointing the way to the dock.

I had the cab driver let me out at the porte cochère, and found my way around the house alone. There were a handful of people already on the dock, in bathing suits: Mack Glendauer, who greeted me as if he were really pleased to see me, and introduced me to his wife; two classmates whom I recognized from parties in New Haven, and a couple from Bridgeport whose name I didn't catch. Pat was with Glenda under the trees, superintending the setting of a long, white-covered table for buffet, which would come later, and rearranging bottles on the smaller table which would be the bar.

"Denny," he said, waving me over. "You remember Denny McLeod," he said to Glenda, and she nodded.

She was glossy and tanned from a month of sitting by the water, and she was so beautifully turned out in sandals and a white bathing suit that I wanted to throw my raincoat over my head and retreat before she saw me in the boy's shirt and faded madras shorts I had brought.

She stepped forward and stayed me with one hand. "Thanks for coming." She grimaced, whispering, "I don't know half these people."

I grinned. "Neither do I."

"But it was a great idea, don't you think?" She seemed pathetically glad to have me there. "Wasn't Pat a doll to think of it?" she said, and then made me go around with her and inspect the table setting, the sliced turkey and cold meat on ice in the summer house, the bowls of chilled fruits and the chocolate pies, saying, anxiously, "Do you think this is going to be enough?" and "Do you think I ought to have Pat phone for more gin?" and "Hey, did Mack and Jenny look like they were having a good time?"

When I had told her again and again that everything was marvelous, that everything was beautiful she smiled, not much relieved, and said, "This is my first party Since—" and then said, "Oh, gee, let me take you up and show you where to change."

She hovered while I changed from my town clothes, offered me a bathing suit and when I declined offered me a series of hats from Jamaica and wouldn't rest until I had accepted one.

"Look," I said, wanting somehow to reassure her. "Everything's going to be fine."

She gave me an uncertain, grateful grin and then excused herself to welcome the next set of guests.

I found my way back to the dock, glad to be in sneakers again. I wanted to talk to Pat, but he was busy on a ladder, rearranging the Japanese lanterns. I remember watching with a little pang as he bent to catch something Glenda was saying, and then laughed. Pat and I talked so easily and seemed so close that it always surprised me to see him on a similar basis with somebody else. It must be a blindness within me that makes me want to believe that my friends are mine alone. I know, simply because I am divided among several friends, that they are divided similarly and that I expect too much of them, but I like to think of them as compartmented when they leave me, and of our friendship as unique. Even though I know it's impossible, it seems true when we meet, and perhaps this is enough. That particular day Pat said something to Glenda and she seemed so grateful that I didn't interrupt them, but hurried on.

"What have you been *doing?*" Mack Glendauer said, making a place for me on the dock.

I began to tell him, and then said, "How about you?"

He made a face. "Still in graduate school. It's peanut butter and pasta until we finish."

Jenny must have decided I was all right because she said, "I've been thinking about going on relief."

"You're going to teach?"

"Yeah." Mack squinted at the water. "It's the only way I can support what I want to do, which is paint."

"I think it's terrific," I said.

201

"His beloved classmates think he's crazy," Jenny said.

"They're all in investment banking," he explained, "or just out of Harvard Business School, and getting rich."

"So what?" Jenny said. "You're going to be discovered some day."

"Tell that to the brokers. They say I owe it to the kids."

"What, making money?"

"Something like that," Jenny said. "I think they're jealous because they never have any fun."

"I hate to be corny, but what's money?" I said.

Their grins were warm and it seemed natural for us to spend most of the afternoon together, soaking up sun on the dock. Near dusk we wandered back to the Japanese lanterns, lighted now. Pearson must have come while we were out walking because he stood off to himself behind the drink table, in a suit much too dark for the occasion and much too heavy for June. His face was drawn and he was glaring, which I took to mean that somebody had asked if he'd like to take off his coat, or undo his tie. He looked relieved to see me.

I introduced him to the Glendauers because I liked them, trying to make him feel comfortable with them, but he wasn't giving an inch. He seemed to fight me, digging in his heels and setting his jaw, saying nothing more than the bare minimum. Finally Mack looked embarrassed and said maybe they'd better go get out of their bathing suits, since Glenda had changed into sleek white duck trousers for the evening and a couple of the more elegant classmates were done up in shorts with coats and ties. I nodded and said I'd be along to get into a skirt in a minute, and then turned back to Pearson, wondering how I would ever get *to* him, whether it had been a good idea to drop him into the middle of this particular group.

"How've you been?"

He shrugged. "Fine."

"Pat said you were back in New Haven."

He jerked his shoulders again, as if it couldn't matter less. "Yeah."

"How do you like the summer job?"

"It's a job." He seemed to be looking right past me.

"Well," I said weakly, "It looks like you've got a career."

He sighed. "If you want to call it that." Then he made a series of faces as if something were troubling him and he wanted to tell me about it but couldn't come up with any way to begin.

202

"Look," I said, "is something the matter?"

"No," he said, and I could almost see him withdraw.

"Look, Pearson—"

"I said *nothing's* the matter." He was glowering.

I was at the point of losing patience when Pat came up. He put out a hand. "Well, Swift."

Pearson seemed glad of the distraction. "Sorry I was late."

"No problem," Pat said easily. He took my hand and from the way he moved I could tell he was a little drunk. "You don't mind if I borrow Denny for a minute, do you? There's something I want to show her."

Pearson was already turning away.

"Pearson, I—"

"He'll be all right," Pat said. "They're bringing on the food. Hey, there's something I want to show you. Come *on.*"

He led me across the lawn to the house, moving with an air of mystery that seemed to dissolve as I followed him up on the wide front porch. By the time we had walked the length of it, he seemed to have forgotten why we had come. We came to a stop at the far end of the porch where the rail came to a bend, and I looked at the water, almost able to pretend that we were on a ship. I waited.

"Well." Pat grinned foolishly. "How d'you like the party?"

I remember thinking that they were beginning to put the food on the trestle table, and being a little annoyed that I hadn't had a chance to change into a skirt. "It's going great guns." I was still waiting. "What was it you wanted to show me?"

"Huh?"

"You were going to show me something."

"Not really," he said with a charming, guilty grin. "I just said that. Hell, I wanted to *talk* to you."

I couldn't help being flattered. Then I remembered wanting to talk to him at the beginning, and finding him busy with Glenda, and without being able to help myself I said, with an edge of sarcasm, "I've only been here all day."

"But I've hardly *seen* you."

"That's not my fault." My voice was so sharp it surprised me.

Pat looked at me closely for a minute, seeming to take some meaning from my tone.

We had been sitting side by side on the rail and now we seemed to be moving together, simply easing along without any particular design, until Pat turned me to him with one hand and kissed me. I slid into his arms, returning the kiss with an affection that gave way to a sense of loss even as we embraced because nothing had come out of the kiss—no new closeness, or knowledge of love—yet I knew it marked a change in our relationship. I remember bowing my head against Pat's chest for a moment, sorrowing, because the same part of me that had wanted our friendship to be unique had wanted it to remain unchanged, knowing it was too late because Pat was ready to move on.

He slid off the rail and landed lightly on his feet, still holding my hand. "Hi," he said, grinning, and he tugged gently, trying to edge me toward the door and inside the empty house.

Even without the grounding in faith and the force of conscience, a certain selfishness of friendship would have kept me from going with Pat that night. I knew without having to analyze it that our friendship could never be supplanted by love and in my selfishness I wanted to remain a friend, unique and unchanged, and not become just another of Pat's girls. Another side of that same selfishness must have moved Pat to hustle me on toward romance, to add another facet to our relationship. We seemed to be at an impasse that night and I think a joint stubbornness, or strength of will kept us where we stood, he drawing me by the hand, insisting, me holding my ground with the knowledge that it was too late, because something was already lost.

"Oh Pat," I said.

"No, huh?"

I shook my head.

He murmured, "I didn't think so," and dropped my hand. When he looked up again, he was trying for a new footing, and his tone had changed.

"The trouble with you is—"

"Yes, Doctor?" I said, going along with him.

"You were too well brought up." He wanted us to fall into the old pattern of kidding and he said, "What *is* it with you convent girls?" pretending bafflement.

"Hey, don't blame the convent," I said, to help him keep it light.

He dropped his guard for a minute. "Kat—you—what else can I think?"

"I—" I faltered, remembering Katherine. The whole new line of talk seemed to be going wrong somehow, and I couldn't see any way to stop it.

"Anyway, what is it with you?" he said, kidding but not kidding. "You're like so many brick walls."

I mumbled something, beginning to be embarrassed.

"Is it the church, or is it you?" He was fishing now, partly because he was interested, perhaps more because he could see that he was making me uncomfortable.

"How can I—" I began, but he wouldn't let me go on.

"The funny part is, I always thought you were a pretty sophisticated Catholic." He brought it off with a grin but he was challenging me, almost angry at something he couldn't seem to deal with or understand.

I picked at the hem of my shorts, biding my time. "What do you mean, sophisticated?"

"You know," he said, with a disorganized gesture. "Enlightened. Seeing that there's some room for latitude." He leaned forward, pressing me.

I looked blank. "I don't know what you mean."

"Well, like—" He thought it over for a minute, and I could see him wondering how to get at it, at me, what he was going to say. "Like Sunday," he said.

"Yes."

"You're on the road to Washington for an important dinner party and you either skip church or turn up at your dinner an hour late. What do you do?"

My answer was automatic. "Be late."

"Well." It was a little setback, but he went on, sure he was on the right track. "Well, all this Friday stuff. You really go for that?"

I nodded, and said, "Fisheater, remember?" just to help him along.

"Yeah. OK. Botulism." He grinned, a little more sure of himself. "You're in a hamburger joint on Friday and there's botulism in the tuna fish. There's no place else for miles around where you can eat. You'd have a hamburger, wouldn't you?"

"Grilled cheese," I said, and I must have made a terrible face because he laughed.

"I don't know," he said, still trying me. "The whole thing. It's not *that* big a deal, is it?" He was looking at me squarely now, wanting me to say it was not.

"Yes."

"Denny, Denny." He pulled a wide, despairing sweep of the hand. "You poor dear. All those rules."

"Pat, that's such a small *part* of it."

"I don't know. It all seems so drear."

I looked at him, considering. All of my childhood in the faith, even to the wish that I could be something easier, came

crowding in on me along with the sure sense that I would
never have had it any different, that I would rather be a
Catholic, even a poor one, than anything else anyone could
offer me. "It only seems that way," I said, and I knew I could
never explain to him.

"You know your trouble?" He was only pretending to
kid now, and his voice was ragged and unsure. "You're so
hung up in the rules that you don't have time for the real
thing. You know something?" He hesitated for a long minute and then brightened as if he had really come up with
something. "I don't believe in anything but I bet I'm more
religious than you."

I think he was trying to get a rise out of me but there was
nothing I could say. I waited.

"What I mean—" He stood with the moonlight bright on
his hair, looking at the water, and when he turned back to
me his face had changed. "I bet I worry about God more than
you do." There was a certain seriousness in his look, some
hint that he wanted to reveal himself. It was almost as if
he was waiting, tentatively, for some sign from me. But at
the same time his tone was light and his mouth moved in an
involuntary grin; he may just have wanted me to agree, and
so give him the evening. I don't know.

I only know I couldn't help what happened next. It came
out of all the times I've talked to Pat, knowing he was trying
to bring me on, and out of all the times when in self defense
I've tried to make him laugh. Maybe I've done him an in-
justice. I can't help wondering now if there isn't something
behind all the talk, if he may not be offering up little bits
and pieces of himself in hopes that someone some day may
respond with some single truth, something he needs to hear.

At the time I knew only that we had already said too
much and when I snapped back with "What do you mean,
worry?" it was as reflexive as the punch line to a joke.

Pat must have seen my nervous grin, for all I tried to hide
it, because he snorted, "Denny," and stalked into the night.

I said "Pat," then, but my voice was so thin that it hardly
left my lips. I watched him go, already sorry for the moment missed, for the misunderstanding. I pressed my head
against one of the porch supports for a minute, stiff with regret, because our talk, even Pat's kidding, could not have
gone differently; it had not rung true and I knew then that
no matter what I said or how I tried to make it up to him it
would not help because we were through talking together;

we were already changed, and our lives would never really touch.

I remember greeting Pearson with timidity when he came onto the porch that night because I was almost overcome by a desire to stay where I was, as I was; I had already done too much that day. I knew as soon as I saw his face that it would be impossible. His eyes were smouldering, not with elation, as they had that day in the museum, but with some consuming urge to learn, to explain.

He was all motion, quick, awkward, as he came up the steps and started across the porch. "I have to talk to you."

"Pearson," I said. "Hi." There was something in the concentrated, hurried angle of his body that made me want to stay him, to slow him down. I looked out at the sky, the pale light that crumpled the water, and made a wide gesture, wanting him to understand or at least to acknowledge the quality of the night. "Pearson, look."

"Huh?" he said, still coming.

I was offering all of it. "*Look!*"

He was confused for a moment and when he turned to the water in mid-stride he turned too quickly, catching one foot on the other, and almost fell. He faced the water obediently, with all the attention he would give a subway poster, and then turned in on himself, already talking, so fixed on his own grey inner landscape that he could not see anything beyond. "We haven't talked for a long time."

"Not since you told me about the law."

"At that museum—what a place!" His eyes mirrored the procession of gigantic animals, the almost visible flow of time. "I was close to something. I've never felt more—" He seemed unable to describe it.

"You were so—so *up*," I said without conviction. I couldn't let him know how his excitement had frightened me, because I had known how soon and how completely it would leave him.

"I thought I was on to something," he said, and his face went dark.

We sat quietly for a minute or two, in splintered, high-backed chairs that might have come from the porch of an old hotel. I wanted to lose myself in the sky and the water, in the gentle party sounds rising from the yard beside the house, but I was too aware of Pearson, taut beside me, restless in the shadows.

He turned sharply, anxious and intent. "Remember how

it was when I told you what I wanted to do? You understood, and the fact that you did—that *somebody* did made—the whole thing seem real. It seemed worth trying."

I flushed, wanting to warn him somehow, to stop him because he imagined too much for the rest of us, because he still refused to realize that when he went into the country of his ideas he went alone. I said, "Maybe you put too much into what I said."

"No." His eyes were bright. "Look, Denny, I wouldn't even have come today, but I had to talk to you."

I put up my hand, trying to forestall him. "I can't—"

"If I can just talk to you about things again, make you understand again—" His eyes were bright now, with a blind faith that I could do something for him.

I barely whispered "Yes?" already as frightened by this new trust as I had been by his surge of joy in the museum. I wanted to beg him not to expect too much from me, from any of us, not to hope for too much.

He seemed not to see my hesitation. "—then some of it might be worth something again."

I remember leaning forward, saying, "Then nothing is worth anything now," afraid to hear it confirmed.

"No. But when I tell you—" He let it dangle, waiting, hoping for something.

"Pearson, I—" I began, and then it came to me that there might be some way for me to warn him, to show him that I was no better than he, and he had no right to expect me to be any surer than he about anything. "Look," I said, "did Bunker ever tell you—" The rest of the sentence trembled in air.

"Ben," he corrected absently, stopping me in mid-stride.

"Did Ben tell you anything about—" I began again, wanting to get the business of Bunker and the baptism, the business of this particular failure out into the open, to *show* him how it was. I had to show him that he had no reason to place hope in me. My voice was faint because I needed some sign from him, some place to start. "—about the last time I saw him," I said, teetering.

Then I saw he wasn't listening. Someone had put on a record and the sound came out the windows of the sunporch —Ella Fitzgerald, singing Cole Porter in a voice softer than air. A breeze had caught Pearson off guard, lifting his hair and distracting him. He seemed suspended now, almost as unwilling to go on as I had been. In that second he seemed to catch something of the atmosphere, to be aware for the first time of the evening around him and he stood up quietly, taking in the gentle quality of the air. "Hey," he said, expanding to meet it. "Have you eaten yet?"

My breath came out in a rush. I wanted to go on, but he had made it easy for me to stop without changing anything between us, to keep the evening as it was, and I wasn't strong enough to begin again. "No," I said, and added, like a subdeb, "I haven't had a thing."

He may have known I had something I wanted to tell him and I think now that he did, but apparently he didn't want to hear it just then. He may have sensed that it would interfere with his hopes, that he would have to abandon them and with them the evening, because he turned as if I hadn't begun anything or left anything unsaid and took my hand, almost gay. "We'll talk later. Let's eat."

And because I needed as much as he did to let the matter slide, I followed him.

We piled our plates and shambled over to join the Glendauers and another pair of marrieds in the children's trampoline. The others had gone off into the darkness by twos, leaving Glenda to fret over the platters on the table, solitary in gleaming white. Pat came out of the house and touched her arm, drawing her over to the trampoline. We crammed to give them a little space and then sat eating, just a few inches above the ground, slung in a swaying seat that made me think of a lifeboat swinging at the side of a ship. We mumbled through our food, slipping into a mood of quiet good humor, and I was pleased to see that Glenda was laughing with Pat, that Pearson, with his collar undone and his sleeves rolled up, looked almost like one of the group. Mack began a low, rambling commentary on the activities of those who were missing and soon even Pearson began to laugh. After a time our talk trailed off, leaving only the sound of the water and Pat's voice, light on the air.

"Has anybody seen our, anybody seen our, anybody seen our ship."

The breeze picked up and it grew chilly but still we sat together, not minding cramped legs or occasional slips when someone would lose his balance and fall against somebody's plate. There were pebbles, a dusting of sand, little bits of cole slaw in our canvas sling but we were comfortable and we rocked in safety, suspended in air, in time itself.

I don't know just when it happened or how long it took us to be aware of it but we stopped short suddenly, silenced by a hush in the air—a vacuum, like the still at midnight, when the wind is just about to change—and in the stillness I found myself looking around at the others, to find them looking at me. Mack Glendauer glanced from Pearson to me and then, with an exquisite, unnecessary tact, scrambled out of the trampoline and gave Jenny his hand. The other couple followed dutifully, quick and gentle and willing to leave the place to us. We watched them move off quietly, two by two, until the darkness closed after them. Then Glenda, beset by some nervousness, skipped her feet over the edge of the frame and lit on the ground to stand uncertainly by Pat's corner.

"I got a letter today," she said to Pat, as if they were alone.

Pearson was so involved in his own thoughts that I don't think he even heard. I bent my head, pretending to be engrossed in the darkness, the dead calm of the night.

"How do things look?" Pat said.

"He's met somebody." She pulled at the lacings of the trampoline.

Pat tried to pass it off. "He's always meeting somebody."

"But this time—" she began, and her face was on the verge of crumpling.

Pat looked at me acutely. "Wait a minute," he said, and hitched himself over the side to stand next to her. He tried to hush her but she rushed on, murmuring insistently.

"—so it's really over this time."

"Hey, that's not so bad." Pat soothed her, moving with her to the trestle table, where it would not be so obvious that Pearson and I could hear.

I knew him well enough to know that he was trying to spare us the discomfort that would come when she realized she'd said too much in front of us. I noted this and looked down, pretending to be too far away to hear or even see.

Her voice rose. "But everything's *over,* and I'm not even twenty-four."

Pat's monotone had a reassuring sound, and I hoped he'd be able to quiet her.

She said, "But it's not *fair.*" She went on at length, ending with a phrase that went up at the end, like a question.

I looked up just then and was surprised to see Pat gesturing toward me. "Twenty-six."

"And she's still got it all *ahead.*" Glenda was about to cry.

I didn't want to hear Pat's words; I didn't want to hear any of it, but I think I apprehended it before he brought it out because I could feel my blood slow even as he said, "Don't be so sure," going on in complete honesty. "Don't be too sure about any of us."

He turned then, because she was crying, and put an arm around her shoulder. Without looking back he led her back to the house. He would turn her over to the housekeeper, who was sitting out the summer with her.

Pearson shifted his weight unexpectedly and I jumped because I had almost forgotten he was still sitting there.

"Finally," he said, and I knew he had heard nothing, had noted nothing except that the others were gone and now he would have a chance to talk. "Denny—"

I held my breath, willing him to stop.

"Denny," he said again, "help me sort things out."

"I—don't know if I can."

"You did last time." His eyes burned.

"All I did was listen," I said, shaking my head. "Maybe if I had said something more—"

"No. It was just right. It was great." His chin was up and even in the stillness his dark hair seemed to move. "You understood."

My "No" may have been too weak to reach him, or he may have refused to hear; as I remember it he drew himself up as if I hadn't said anything, preparing himself to go on. I could feel my stomach tighten with apprehension, but I knew there was no way for me to forestall whatever was coming.

"It's just that the thing we decided on wasn't enough." His words were coming in little bursts. "I've got to keep looking."

"Yes," I said, because he seemed to be stalled.

"I've got to find out what I want."

I nodded, to show him I understood.

"I've got a couple of things in mind. You always make things seem so *rational*—"

"Pearson—"

"Let me try this new idea on you."

"Pearson," I said again, with a feeling of helplessness, "don't expect too much."

His voice was low. "I always do."

There was a little flurry in the air just then and Pat came back to the trampoline. "Mind if I join you?"

Pearson stiffened.

"Be my guest." I giggled a little in my relief. "How's Glenda?"

He shrugged. "She'll be OK. She'll look as perfect as ever by the time everybody comes to tell her goodbye." He hopped the metal frame and landed in the canvas with a little bounce. "Well, Swift. How's the job?"

Pearson looked at him then, with an almost beautiful grin. "Intolerable." He paused long enough to give his next words weight. "I'm going to quit."

Pat straightened. "The hell."

Pearson set his jaw. "Why not?"

Because I had to, I went to his defense. "It's his life."

"You *can't*," Pat said, getting red.

"I'm going to."

"Why shouldn't he?" I could feel my hackles rising.

"Look, I told lies to line up that job," Pat said. He was pink with exasperation. "D'you think I'm going to let him bug out now? How would I explain?"

Pearson looked at him coldly. "You don't have to explain."

"He can take care of himself," I said, knowing as I said it that I should keep to myself because our turning on Pat would put the two of us in league as surely as it bound two kids, ganging up on a third.

"I made you out to be another Joseph Welch," Pat said. "What's the matter with it? It's a damn good job."

Pearson said simply, "It's not what I want."

"Dammit—"

I said, "Leave him alone, Pat, it's his business," and regretted it as soon as I had spoken because Pearson had fixed on me again, blinded by hope.

"Denny knows. I've got to try a couple of things—*important* things."

Pat snorted.

"Look, I've been reading, trying to systematize things. If I can get them down, figure out a scheme—" He left the trampoline to stand in front of us, gesturing, trying to carry us along with words.

Pat slouched, not wanting to listen.

"It's so simple," Pearson said. "It may take me a lifetime, but when I finish I'll have a place to start. I have to *know* before I can *begin*."

He began to lecture us, face burning first red and then white, and as he talked he unfolded a mad, complex scheme for systematizing all knowledge, bringing it into some shape, of working for years on some vast, almost limitless compendium and when it was finished releasing it to the world.

He talked on and on, losing me, then Pat, so caught up in the power and scope of his own ideas that he didn't seem to realize that neither of us was able to follow, to comprehend.

"Well?"

He had come to the end, and he was looking at me.

I bit my lip and looked away from him.

"Well, what do you think?"

I was baffled, and he must have seen it. I tried for a word —anything—but nothing came.

He turned to Pat, boring in. "How about you?"

"I—" Pat began, but couldn't go on.

"Do you think it's valid or not?" He was angry now. "Shall I go into it?"

"Pearson, I—" I shook my head. "I don't even know where to *begin*."

"You know," he said with a fierce, concentrated look. "You just won't tell me what you think. Why are you holding out?" He faced Pat. "The web of philosophies. Shall I go ahead with that, maybe publish it separately?"

"How the hell should I know?" Pat said, angry now because Pearson had left him behind without even intending to.

"You should *know*," Pearson said, and his hands went out of control in a quick series of angry gestures that he didn't seem to be able to help. "Denny," he said again, pleading with me. "You—"

"Pearson." My throat filled with the words and they came out slowly, with force. "I can't help you. Nobody can tell you what to do."

"You're the only person—the only thing—I can count on." His face was black and his whole outline seemed to shimmer with the intensity of his words. "You *have* to—"

"I can't help you," I said, offering what came next because it was all I had. "I can only *care*."

He tried to smile, to hide the look of raw disappointment that changed his face and even as he said "Thanks" I wanted to weep because I knew that he was too restless, too exacting in his vision to settle for anything any of the rest of us could offer.

Then, before Pat or I could stop him he launched into the whole plan again, the complexity of areas and planes, the morass of a hundred philosophies and the geography of a dozen sciences, repeating it in a deathly determination to force it on us, to make us understand, running down gradually, until he came to a stop and we sat, uneasy and off balance in the shifting canvas, waiting for what we knew must come next.

"You don't understand what I'm trying to *tell* you." His voice was bleak.

I could feel Pat rustling nervously at my side. We were allied now, facing him. Somewhere I found the guts to shake my head.

"No."

He dropped his head then, aware for the first time just how alone he was. He stood, taut and unmoving even when Pat stepped out of the trampoline to stand beside him talking evenly, all charm, all good intentions, anxious to pull Pearson out of himself and bring him back to us.

"Hey," Pat said in a gallant little attempt to save the moment, "The law isn't such a bad place to start." He knew Pearson hardly heard him but he seemed to need to keep on talking, to send his light voice into the air. "Sit out that degree and *then* make over the world."

Because the silence was intolerable I said "Look at it this way—it's a living," and managed a shaky little laugh.

Pat tried to grin. "When you're an LL.B. we'll get you into the smartest firm in New York. John W. Davis, maybe."

"Or Debevoise, Plimpton and McLean."

"You can live in the *smart* East Seventies." Pat made a face, trying to jolly him along.

"And eat at the Plaza." I wanted to build on the joke. At the time it seemed the only way to turn.

Pearson shifted slightly and I think we let ourselves believe that we were reaching him.

"And meet the right people." Pat stepped off and pretended to survey him. "We'll have to get you a few things at Press."

"Maybe we could get you into the Union League Club." I grinned as if my life depended on it, trying desperately to pull him into laughter, into some more familiar framework that would make him easier to deal with, perhaps easier to understand.

"Or the University Club," Pat said.

"All you have to do—" I began.

"Is go back to work Monday morning," Pat finished with a flourish, blinking at him.

I was sliding in the trampoline, trying to right myself. I kept talking, nervous and compulsive. "Well—what do you think?"

"Yeah," Pat said. "What d'you think?"

Pearson stood like a dark monolith for the space of a minute and he seemed to swell, furious in his isolation, holding his breath until I was afraid. Then, when we could not have borne another second of silence, he spoke.

"Sure," he said, smouldering. "Oh, sure." Then he turned away.

"Hey," Pat began, but he could not go on because he knew we had failed.

Pearson was already walking away from us, straight and uncompromising, unreachable.

I wanted to run after him, to call him back but there were no words for it and I was still hung up in the trampoline.

By the time Pat had helped me to the ground Pearson had slammed the door of his rented car and started it with a roar. We could hear the motor's growl above the trees as he raced the car around curves and turned onto the main road.

"I'll be damned." Pat's voice was weak.

I fell back, sick and shamed by the failure of our understanding, and bent my head.

"Damned nut." Pat's sigh trembled on his lips. "He left his coat."

XXII

That next week I called Pearson at the office a number of times, and each time the girl at the switchboard told me he hadn't been in and they didn't know when to expect him. For some reason I put off trying to reach him at his room, probably because I already suspected that he was gone and there was no way to reach him, and the only way I could keep the suspicion—the premonition, or sense of gathering darkness that threatened me—at bay was to put off knowing for sure. On Friday night I nerved myself and called him at his rooms. His landlady answered the phone and I caught something in her tone that reminded me of the landlady I had met in Providence, helpful and protective but baffled by his fierce air of privacy. She hadn't seen him all week.

I found out later that he had spent the week in a little hotel on the Sound, apparently trying to think things out. I still wonder if there was anything I might have done for him.

When I did hear it was from Bunker. It was late Sunday, and we were at dinner. My aunt went into the hall to answer the phone and came back and called me.

"It's long distance," she said, and stood over me until I took the telephone from her and closed the door.

"Denny?"

"Yes."

"Dad wanted me to call you."

"Yes?" For a minute I didn't recognize his voice.

"Denny, it's Ben."

"Bunker," I said, and I remembered that my voice leaped with a lightning hope for new beginnings, things mended.

216

At the same time I was already crowded with apprehensions, with shadows of scenes rehearsed and played out before in the early years of the war when we had all waited and not waited for news that would change everything. My throat was dry. "What—what's on your mind?"

"Perry," he said, and his voice was controlled.

"You mean Pearson." I remember resenting his new use of the nickname he had always refused his brother. I think I wanted to stop him and make him call Pearson by his right name. I may have wanted to quibble about it, to put him right, to put off what had to come.

"They thought you'd want to know about him."

Without answering I let myself down to the floor, so that I sat in that narrow hall with my knees up and the telephone at my side, already trying to prepare myself for something that had not yet been said. I pressed my back against the wall and waited for him to go on.

"He drowned Saturday," Bunker said evenly. "He was swimming in the Sound and he went out too far."

"He—"

"Drowned. He just didn't come back to his hotel. They found him today." He went on mechanically. "Mom and Dad wanted you to know."

"Oh." The second time I said it there was no sound to it— it was no more than a rush of air. "Oh."

I think we talked on about plans. He would be buried privately, in New Haven. They didn't expect me to come, but they wanted me to know. Bunker's ship would be coming into New York at the end of the summer, and maybe he would see me then. Maybe we could talk about his brother.

"You knew him better than I did," he said, and I don't think he was even aware of what he was saying. "After we got big I hardly saw him."

"I—" didn't know him at all? "Yeah," I said.

His parents were taking it pretty well. They sent their love. They just thought I would want to know.

None of it seemed real until I hung up.

Then I went upstairs without excusing myself, going over and over the phone call in my mind, trying to extract something new from it, some intelligence that would help me grasp what had been said. I tried to conjure Pearson up, to see him as he had been in the trampoline, or at the zoo, to shore up these images against the finality of Bunker's words but I could see him only as I had seen him for the last time, solitary and furious, and at this sharp, unwanted picture I found myself praying without thinking and praying again, thinking hard, praying that it had been an accident.

I thought, even as I do now, that it was an accident, but at the same time I was chilled because of the way Pat and I had seen him last, caught in his loneliness, our helplessness. He had come to us for help and we had failed him, and then, failing him, had tried to jolly him along. I remember thinking that if it had not been for our nervous little attempts to be funny, to pretend he was like us and try to *make* him like us, to fit him into some framework we could understand, if it had not been for our failure of understanding he might not have gone to the Sound at all, or spent the week alone, and he might never have taken the particular chance he did.

Yet even then, when it was almost too much to handle, I knew that given it to do all over again, with everything known at the start, we would probably have done no better, because we were only *people*, no better than people will ever be.

And this is only one failure.

At the time the knowledge was almost too much for me. I was conscious then of the rush of time, of this particular loss and all the other losses, of moments missed and friends denied, of the baptism in the parking lot, of misunderstandings and more, of wars and all of Pearson's poor, sick millions, of the ways in which God Himself is denied each day and I could not fight back the sense of chaos, of failure, of simple insufficiency that came over me then.

When I was able to control my voice I called the local parish and asked for a Mass for him. It was the only thing I could think of that might help. I remember brooding on that particular loss, on all the failures, and thinking that there must be something more I could do.

Bunker and I met in early autumn, about a month ago, when his ship came to New York as he had said it would, and we met in the lobby of a downtown hotel.

He was there first, already sitting with his back to me when I came in, watching for me at the wrong door. When I called his name he jerked to attention and stood up, tall and flawless in his blues, with the gold j.g.'s stripes on the sleeves. Against the stiff white of his shirt, his face was still tanned from the summer.

"Denny," he said, and stood away from me with an almost professional reserve, greeting me with an automatic grace.

218

He seemed somehow unfamiliar, invulnerable in his uniform.

I said "Hi," and then fell back because he looked so solid, so adult that I was uneasy with him, inept and hesitant.

We should have gone on into the bar, as we had planned, but we didn't seem to be able to get going and instead we stood awkwardly in that slightly run-down lobby, almost choked by a number of things we would never say.

"Dad wanted me to give you this," he said finally, handing me a book. It was one of Pearson's.

I said "Oh. Thanks," and for a minute was alone in memory. Then, because Bunker shifted slightly, polite but diffident, I pulled myself back and said, "How've you been?"

"Fine. I've been fine. How about you?" He tried to smile, to make the meeting easier.

"I'm OK. I've been working up here, but I think I'll be going back to Washington soon."

"New job?"

I looked at my hands. "Not exactly." I couldn't explain that I had come to a time of change, when a few things had to be decided. I couldn't tell him that I had known, almost from the day of his phone call about Pearson, that the time had come for me to begin, to start moving. I had been preoccupied, mulling over the possibilities, but there was no way to tell Bunker, that day.

He smiled politely. "Oh. Well—"

There was a long pause while I watched a covey of old ladies come through the lobby. They poked each other and whispered, obviously impressed by the fine-looking young officer in his blues. I saw, and was warmed by a strong pride that went back to childhood, to a series of hopes and images that were too complex to sort.

When he saw that I wasn't going to say anything Bunker said, "You know Mom and Dad are in Ohio now."

"No, I didn't know."

"Their folks were from Ohio. Dad's retired," he said with an unconscious look at his sleeve. "He was passed over."

I looked at him quickly.

"They've gone into the class below him for Admirals." He seemed to think I needed it explained. "It was time," Bunker said, apparently seeing something in his father that I would not have wanted to be detached enough to see, and I remember being surprised at how far from the war I had come. He lifted his chin in a flash of pride and I knew he would never let it happen to him.

"If you say so," I said.

"I'm going to New London," he said, and waited for me to rejoice.

"Subs?" I said.

"Subs."

There was a silence, simply because it was appropriate. He lifted his head suddenly. "Of course it's nothing like the old R-boats, or S-boats. Everything's changed."

"I know," I said, watching him recede.

Then, unexpectedly, he came back. "Hey, Denny."

"Yes?"

"That business the last time I saw you." He looked at me uncertainly. "You remember?"

I said, "I remember."

"I—uh—" He couldn't seem to find any way to go on. "I wanted you to know—" He flushed and stammered. "Let's forget it," he said finally. "OK?"

"Sure," I said, and I was grateful, even though I knew neither of us ever could. "OK."

"Don't—uh—don't worry about me," he said, frankly uncomfortable, and I could almost see him strain to hide the resentment he would always feel for me, for the way I had touched him when I made the Sign of the Cross over him that night in the parking lot.

I put up one hand, wanting to tell him I was sorry for breaking into his privacy, for assailing his pride, but there was no way to separate that from the baptism, and I found I was not sorry for the fact of the baptism, only the intrusion, so that I could not apologize no matter how much I wanted to mend things between us. Instead I said, "If there's anything I can do—"

He tightened his mouth. "Just don't worry."

"I won't," I said, wishing it would be true, and our eyes met in a stiff, curious species of reconciliation that changed nothing but made possible what happened next.

For a second we stood without moving and then all at once we were both grinning, in that blind, irrational love that has nothing to do with romance and endures even now despite all the misunderstanding, despite all that has happened to us.

Then Bunker said, "Well," shifting from foot to foot and looking like himself. He bit his lip and looked over his shoulder without meaning to, apparently already late for something he wanted to do.

And I said, "It was great seeing you," because I knew he

wanted to go and couldn't think of any way to say goodbye.

"You too," he said.

"Goodbye, Ben."

"Goodbye." He took my hand briefly, flushing brilliantly, and then he turned and was gone.

I stayed where I was, holding the book, for some time. Then I looked down, at Pearson's book, turning it over in my hands. It was one of a trilogy—*The Fellowship of the Ring* —a strange book for him to have had. Perhaps it was not so strange; it is about a quest. I bent over it, riffling through the pages to see if he had left something—some note, something underscored, something more than the name on the flyleaf, some bit of himself for me to keep—and when I had satisfied myself that it was unmarked I found it didn't really matter because books are to some extent the people who have owned them and it was enough for me to have this small part of Pearson, this reminder.

As I stood holding the book memory flooded in with the suddenness of a gift, and by the time I put the book under my arm and started for the door I was surrounded, fortified by Pearson, by quick pictures of him in Providence, at the zoo, on all the hundred times I had seen him, so that hope leaped in me as I came into the bright street and I had the idea that I could turn the next corner or go just one more block, or wander through the station or gallery and bump into him. I hurried along, warmed by the idea, and I found myself joyful without being sure exactly why, grateful for the thin, fine sunlight, for the possibilities, for streets that seemed to shimmer, either from the sunlight or from my quick, unrealized tears. For the first time I saw this completeness of memory, this sense of presence, as more than a sentimental weapon against sorrow. As I went down first one block and then the next, half-expecting to see Pearson, I understood that the gift is something more: the presence is a fact and the memory is a reminder; Pearson is present, as all the others are present, in God, and even though we can't hope to see them again in any of the old settings, we can and will see them in God, because they exist as surely as God exists, and we have only to find our way to Him. I was almost running now, thinking, *Lord, thank you*, wanting to do something more.

I talked to Pat last week for the last time, and I think my mother was impressed that he would call me long distance and talk for half an hour, all the way from New York. Most of it was light; some of it was almost funny, as our talk can be, but I found myself slowing down at the end, wishing we could say something to each other that mattered, wishing I could tell him what I was going to do.

Instead we talked on about Pat's plans for the winter and he said, "I was thinking about coming to Washington over Christmas. There's this girl I want you to meet."

I said, "Gee, Pat—I don't think I'll be here."

"Coming back to the Big City?"

"No more Bigville," I said. "I've figured out what I want to do."

"Good for you." His voice was warm. "So tell Dad."

"I don't know, Pat. It's just something—something I have to do."

"No kidding?"

"Yeah, it's—" I tried to go on and couldn't. We hung on in silence for a minute.

"I know," Pat said, trying to kid me into going on. "You're writing an opera."

"Not exactly."

I could almost see him grinning. "Or marching for peace."

"Sure, Pat," I said, somehow relieved that we were still talking lightly, because it seemed to be the only way we could talk. "I'm going up to Groton and lash myself to the next sub they launch."

"Well, great," he said. "I'll plan to come."

"Please do. Bring lots of champagne."

"We'll crack it over your hull. I christen thee— Say, what are we going to christen thee?"

"Wait a minute," I said. "We'll have to think of something good."

"I'll send you a list of names and you can take your pick."

I found myself mumbling, "That might be a good idea."

"Names like liberté, egalité, fraternité? Maybe Andromache," he said helpfully.

I took a deep breath, made brave by the telephone. "Saints' names," I said, hinting hard.

"For a ship?"

I pushed against my own lungs, wanting to tell him, to tell somebody, and finally I was able to begin. "For me. Pat, I—"

"Wait a minute, huh?" He put his hand over the mouthpiece for a minute, and I could hear him mumbling to somebody else. "Norty's here," he said, when he'd finished. "He wants me to go out to Paramus to look at a house."

"A house?"

"For his bride." Pat tried to pass it off. "He's getting married again. Girl he met in California. Funny damn thing," he said. "I tried to round up some people for a party for him—everybody's *gone* somewhere. Où sont les—"

"I know, I know," I said, cutting him off because it was all past.

He gave a bewildered little laugh. "Anyway, I wanted to talk, so I called you."

"I'm glad you did."

"You were going to tell me something," he said, not quite remembering what it was we had been talking about.

"Not really."

"Oh. Well." I could hear Norty in the background, hurrying him. "Look, I'd better sign off. Norty's badgering me to get going. See you soon?"

I said, "Maybe," knowing he wouldn't. "Thanks for calling, Pat. You're a dear."

"See you soon, sweetie."

"Bye."

And so I couldn't even tell Pat, and I know I will have trouble telling my mother when I start getting ready to leave.

But I have made my decision, and my life as I have known it ends within a few days.

I may have known the facts, intellectually, like some fact of numbers, and instinctively, in my sense of order, my desire to keep right with God, but I do not think any of it became clear or real to me until after Pearson's death, until I stood, holding his book, and in the sudden, almost overwhelming completeness of memory, began to see. This came to me in its own time, in a time of loss and failure, and while I cannot see the pattern clearly I know that out of that loss and failure came a certain understanding of all our failures, even to our failure to come to any adequate comprehension of God. I think this last is because we are people, and those of us who are not saints can't seem even to begin to cope with ultimates. We handle what little parts of the thing we can as best we can and depend on each other, living in our own way, day by day.

It is in this meshing and interlocking of lives that our first understanding comes, as I have begun to learn through so many—Daddy, Bunker, Pearson, Katherine and even Pat —all those whose lives are bound up with mine. This understanding comes, even as memory and some sense of the continuing presence of others as a gift, and I think now that it comes out of the fact that people will depend on each other as long as there are people. It is in the network of lives, touching, growing, changing, that we first know love, and it is in the growth of love that we begin to comprehend God.

I saw some of this as I stood holding Pearson's book and it came to me that I must be able to get closer—there must be something more I could do. Now I think I have found a place to begin. This is something I want—no, more, *have* to do. One day next month, if all goes well, I will be received as a postulant in the order of nuns that taught me through high school and college. I will join them and if I am right and it is right, if I make it through the years of candidature and the novitiate, that will be my life.

Denny McLeod—1958
K.R.—1963